Cover Her Face

P. D. JAMES

SPHERE BOOKS LIMITED
30/32 Gray's Inn Road, London WC1X 8JL

First published in Great Britain by
Faber & Faber Ltd 1962
Copyright © P. D. James 1962
Published in Sphere Books 1974,
Reprinted 1976, 1977, 1978, 1979 (twice), 1980, 1981

Set in Intertype Baskerville

Printed in Canada

CHAPTER ONE

1

EXACTLY three months before the killing at Martingale
Mrs. Maxie gave a dinner party. Years later, when the
trial was a half-forgotten scandal and the headlines were
yellowing on the newspaper lining of cupboard drawers,
Eleanor Maxie looked back on that spring evening as the
opening scene of tragedy. Memory, selective and perverse,
invested what had been a perfectly ordinary dinner party
with an aura of foreboding and unease. It became, in retrospect, a ritual gathering under one roof of victim and
suspects, a staged preliminary to murder. In fact not all
the suspects had been present. Felix Hearne, for one, was
not at Martingale that week-end. Yet, in her memory, he
too sat at Mrs. Maxie's table, watching with amused, sardonic eyes the opening antics of the players.

At the time, of course, the party was both ordinary and
rather dull. Three of the guests, Dr. Epps, the vicar and
Miss Liddell, Warden of St. Mary's Refuge for Girls, had
dined together too often to expect either novelty or stimu-
lation from each other's company. Catherine Bowers was
unusually silent and Stephen Maxie and his sister, Deborah
Riscoe, were obviously concealing with difficulty their irritation that Stephen's first free week-end from the hospital
for over a month should have coincided with a dinner
party. Mrs. Maxie had just employed one of Miss Liddell's
unmarried mothers as house-parlourmaid and the girl was
waiting at table for the first time. But the air of constraint
which burdened the meal could hardly have been caused
by the occasional presence of Sally Jupp who placed the
dishes in front of Mrs. Maxie and removed the plates with
a dextrous efficiency which Miss Liddell noted with complacent approval.

It is probable that at least one of the guests was wholly
happy. Bernard Hinks, the vicar of Chadfleet, was a bache-

lor, and any change from the nourishing but unpalatable meals produced by his housekeeping sister – who was never herself tempted away from the vicarage to dine – was a relief which left small room for the niceties of social intercourse. He was a gentle, sweet-faced man who looked older than his fifty-four years and who had a reputation for vagueness and timidity except on points of doctrine. Theology was his main, almost his sole, intellectual interest and if his parishioners could not always understand his sermons they were happy enough to accept this as sure evidence of their vicar's erudition. It was, however, accepted in the village that you could get both advice and help from the vicarage and that, if the former were sometimes a little muddled, the latter could generally be relied upon.

To Dr. Charles Epps the dinner meant a first-class meal, a couple of charming women to talk to and a restful interlude from the trivialities of a country practice. He was a widower who had lived in Chadfleet for thirty years and knew most of his patients well enough to predict with accuracy whether they would live or die. He believed that there was little any doctor could do to influence the decision, that there was wisdom in knowing when to die with the least inconvenience to others and distress to oneself and that much medical progress only prolonged life for a few uncomfortable months to the greater glory of the patient's doctor. For all that, he had less stupidity and more skill than Stephen Maxie gave him credit for and few of his patients faced the inevitable before their time. He had attended Mrs. Maxie at the births of both her children and was doctor and friend to the husband in so far as Simon Maxie's bemused brain could any longer know or appreciate friendship. Now he sat at the Maxie table and forked up chicken *soufflé* with the air of a man who had earned his dinner and has no intention of being infected by other people's moods.

'So you've taken Sally Jupp and her baby, Eleanor?' Dr. Epps was never inhibited from stating the obvious. 'Nice young things both of them. Rather jolly for you to have a baby about the house again.'

'Let us hope Martha agrees with you,' said Mrs. Maxie dryly. 'She needs help desperately, of course, but she's

6

very conservative. She may feel the situation more than she says.'

'She'll get over it. Moral scruples soon give way when it's a case of another pair of hands at the kitchen sink.' Dr. Epps dismissed Martha Bultitaft's conscience with a wave of his podgy arm. 'She'll be eating out of the baby's hand before long, anyway. Jimmy's an appealing child whoever his father was.'

At this point Miss Liddell felt that the voice of experience should be heard.

'I don't think, Doctor, that we should talk about the problem of these children too lightly. Naturally we must show Christian charity' – here Miss Liddell gave a half bow in the direction of the vicar as if acknowledging the presence of another expert and apologizing for the intrusion into his field – 'but I can't help feeling that society as a whole is getting too soft with these girls. The moral standards of the country will continue to fall if these children are to receive more consideration than those born in wedlock. And it's happening already! There's many a poor, respectable mother who doesn't get half the fussing and attention which is lavished on some of these girls.'

She looked around the table, flushed and began eating again vigorously. Well, what if they did all look surprised? It had needed saying. It was her place to say it. She glanced at the vicar as if enlisting his support but Mr. Hinks, after his first puzzled glance at her, was concentrating on his dinner. Miss Liddell, baulked of an ally, thought irritably that the dear vicar was just a little greedy over his food! Suddenly she heard Stephen Maxie speaking.

'These children are no different, surely, than any others except that we owe them more. I can't see that their mothers are so remarkable either. After all, how many people accept in practice the moral code which they despise these girls for breaking?'

'A great many, Dr. Maxie, I assure you.' Miss Liddell, by nature of her job, was unaccustomed to opposition from the young. Stephen Maxie might be a rising young surgeon but that didn't make him an expert on delinquent girls. 'I should be horrified if I thought that some of the

7

behaviour I have to hear about in my work was really representative of modern youth.'

'Well, as a representative of modern youth, you can take it from me that it's not so rare that we can afford to despise the ones who've been found out. This girl we have seems perfectly normal and respectable to me.'

'She has a quiet and refined manner. She is quite well-educated too. A grammar-school girl! I should never have dreamed of recommending her to your mother if she weren't a most superior type of girl for St. Mary's. Actually, she's an orphan, brought up by an aunt. But I hope you won't let that play on your pity. Sally's job is to work hard and make the most of this opportunity. The past is over and is best forgotten.'

'It must be difficult to forget the past when one has such a tangible memento of it,' said Deborah Riscoe.

Dr. Epps, irked by a conversation which was provoking bad temper and, probably, worse digestion, hastened to contribute his placebo. Unfortunately, the result was to prolong the dissension.

'She's a good mother and a pretty girl. Probably she'll meet some chap and get married yet. Best thing too. I can't say I like this unmarried-mother-with-child relationship. They get too wrapped up in each other and sometimes end up in a mess psychologically. I sometimes think — terrible heresy I know, Miss Liddell — that the best thing would be to get these babies adopted into a good home from the start.'

'The child is the mother's responsibility,' pronounced Miss Liddell. 'It is her duty to keep it and care for it.'

'For sixteen years and without the help of the father?'

'Naturally we get an affiliation order, Dr. Maxie, whenever that is possible. Unfortunately Sally has been very obstinate and won't tell us the name of the father so we are unable to help.'

'A few shillings don't go very far these days.' Stephen Maxie seemed perversely determined to keep the subject alive. 'And I suppose Sally doesn't even get the government children's allowance.'

'This is a Christian country, my dear brother, and the wages of sin are supposed to be death, not eight bob of the taxpayers' money.'

Deborah had spoken under her breath but Miss Liddell had heard and felt that she had been intended to hear. Mrs. Maxie apparently felt that the time had come to intervene. At least two of her guests thought that she might well have done so earlier. It was unlike Mrs. Maxie to let anything get out of hand. 'As I want to ring for Sally,' she said, 'perhaps it would be as well if we changed the subject. I'm going to make myself thoroughly unpopular by asking about the church fête. I know it looks as if I've got you here on false pretences but we really ought to be thinking about the possible dates.' This was a subject on which all her guests could be safely voluble. By the time Sally came in the conversation was as dull, amicable and unembarrassing as even Catherine Bowers could wish.

Miss Liddell watched Sally Jupp as she moved about the table. It was as if the conversation at dinner had stimulated her to see the girl clearly for the first time. Sally was very thin. The heavy, red-gold hair piled under her cap seemed too heavy a weight for so slender a neck. Her childish arms were long, the elbows jutting under the reddened skin. Her wide mouth was disciplined now, her green eyes fixed demurely on her task. Suddenly Miss Liddell was visited by an irrational spasm of affection. Sally was really doing very nicely, very nicely indeed! She looked up to catch the girl's eye and to give her a smile of approval and encouragement. Suddenly their eyes met. For a full two seconds they looked at each other. Then Miss Liddell flushed and dropped her eyes. Surely she must have been mistaken! Surely Sally would never dare to look at her like that! Confused and horrified she tried to analyse the extraordinary effect of that brief contact. Even before her own features had assumed their proprietorial mask of commendation she had read in the girl's eyes, not the submissive gratitude which had characterized the Sally Jupp of St. Mary's Refuge, but amused contempt, a hint of conspiracy and a dislike which was almost frightening in its intensity. Then the green eyes had dropped again and Sally the enigma became once more Sally the submissive, the subdued, Miss Liddell's favourite and most favoured delinquent. But the moment left its legacy. Miss Liddell was suddenly sick with apprehension. She had recommended Sally without reserve. It

9

was all, on the face of it, so very satisfactory. The girl was a most superior type. Too good for the job at Martingale really. The decision had been taken. It was too late to doubt its wisdom now. The worst that could happen would be Sally's ignominious return to St. Mary's. Miss Liddell was aware for the first time that the introduction of her favourite to Martingale might produce complications. She could not be expected to foresee the magnitude of those complications nor that they would end in violent death.

Catherine Bowers, who was staying at Martingale for the week-end, had said little during dinner. Being a naturally honest person she was a little horrified to find that her sympathies were with Miss Liddell. Of course, it was very generous and gallant of Stephen to champion Sally and her kind so vigorously, but Catherine felt as irritated as she did when her non-nursing friends talked about the nobility of her profession. It was all right to have romantic ideas but they were small compensation to those who worked among the bedpans or the delinquents. She was tempted to say as much, but the presence of Deborah across the table kept her silent. The dinner, like all unsuccessful occasions, seemed to last three times its normal length. Catherine thought that never had a family lingered so long over their coffee, never had the men been so dilatory in putting in their appearance. But it was over at last. Miss Liddell had gone back to St. Mary's, hinting that she felt happier if Miss Pollack were not left too long in sole charge. Mr. Hinks murmured about the last touches for tomorrow's sermon and faded like a thin ghost into the spring air. The Maxies and Dr. Epps sat happily enjoying the wood fire in the drawing-room and talking about music. It was not the subject which Catherine would have chosen. Even the television would have been preferable, but the only set at Martingale was in Martha's sitting-room. If there had to be talk Catherine hoped that it would be confined to medicine. Dr. Epps might naturally say, 'Of course you're a nurse, Miss Bowers, how nice for Stephen to have someone who shares his interests.' Then the three of them would chat away while Deborah sat for a change in ineffectual silence and was made to realize that men do get tired of pretty, useless women, however well dressed, and that what Stephen needed was someone who understood his job, someone who could talk to his friends in a sensible and knowledgeable way. It was a pleasant dream and, like most dreams, it bore no relation to reality. Catherine sat holding her hands to the thin flames of the wood fire and tried to look at ease while the others talked about a composer called, unaccountably, Peter Warlock, of whom she had never heard except in some vague and forgotten historical sense. Certainly Deborah claimed not to understand him but she managed, as usual, to make her ignorance amusing. Her efforts to draw Catherine into the conversation by inquiring about Mrs. Bowers was evidence to Catherine of condescension, not of good manners. It was a relief when the new maid came in with a message for Dr. Epps. One of his patients on an outlying farm had begun her labour. The doctor heaved himself reluctantly out of his chair, shook himself like a shaggy dog and made his apologies. Catherine tried for the last time. 'Interesting case, Doctor?' she asked brightly. 'Lord no, Miss Bowers.' Dr. Epps was looking around vaguely in search of his bag. 'Got three already. Pleasant little woman though, and she likes to have me there. God knows why! She could deliver herself without turning a hair. Well, good-bye, Eleanor, and thank you for an excellent dinner. I meant to go up to Simon before I left but I'll be in tomorrow if I may. You'll be needing a new prescription for the Sommeil I expect. I'll bring it with me.' He nodded amiably to the company and shuffled out with Mrs. Maxie into the hall. Soon they could hear his car roaring away down the drive. He was an enthusiastic driver and loved small fast cars from which he could only extricate himself with difficulty, and in which he looked like a wicked old bear out on a spree.

'Well,' said Deborah, when the sound of the exhaust had died down, 'that's that. Now what about going down to the stables to see Bocock about the horses? That is, of Catherine would like a walk.' Catherine was very anxious for a walk but not with Deborah. Really, she thought, it was extraordinary how Deborah couldn't or wouldn't see that she and Stephen wanted to be alone together. But if Stephen didn't make it plain she could hardly do so. The sooner he was married and away from all his female relations the better it would be for him. 'They suck his blood,'

11

thought Catherine, who had met that type in her excursions into modern fiction. Deborah, happily unconscious of these vampire tendencies, led the way through the open window and across the lawn.

The stables which had once been Maxie stables and were now the property of Mr. Samuel Bocock were only two hundred yards from the house and the other side of the home meadow. Old Bocock was there, polishing harness by the light of a hurricane lamp and whistling through his teeth. He was a small brown man with a gnome-like face, slanting of eye and wide of mouth, whose pleasure at seeing Stephen was apparent. They all went to have a look at the three horses with which Bocock was attempting to establish his little business. 'Really,' thought Catherine, 'it was ridiculous the fuss that Deborah made of them, nuzzling up to their faces with soft endearments as if they were human. Frustrated maternal instinct,' she thought disagreeably. 'Do her good to expend some of that energy on the children's ward. Not that she would be much use.' She herself wished that they could go back to the house. The stable was scrupulously clean but there is no disguising the strong smell of horses after exercise and, for some reason, Catherine found it disturbing. At one time, Stephen's lean brown hand lay close to hers on the animal's neck. The urge to touch that hand, to stroke it, even to raise it to her lips was momentarily so strong that she had to close her eyes. And then, in the darkness, came other remembered pictures, shamefully pleasant, of that same hand half-circled around her breast, even browner against her whiteness, and moving slowly and lovingly, the harbinger of delight. She half-staggered out into the spring twilight and heard behind her the slow, hesitant speech of Bocock and the eager Maxie voices replying together. In that moment she knew again one of those devastating moments of panic which had descended upon her at intervals since she had loved Stephen. They came unheralded and all her common sense and will power were helpless against them. They were moments when everything seemed unreal and she could almost physically feel the sand shifting beneath her hopes. All her misery and uncertainty focused itself on Deborah. It was Deborah who was the

12

enemy. Deborah who had been married, who had at least had her chance of happiness. Deborah who was pretty and selfish and useless. Listening to the voices behind her in the growing darkness Catherine felt sick with hate.

By the time they had returned to Martingale she had pulled herself together again and the black pall had lifted. She was restored to her normal condition of confidence and assurance. She went early to bed and, in the conviction of her present mood, she could almost believe that he might come to her. She told herself that it would be impossible in his father's house, an act of folly on his part, an intolerable abuse of hospitality on hers. But she waited in the darkness. After a while she heard footsteps on the stairs – his footsteps and Deborah's. Brother and sister were laughing softly together. They did not even pause as they passed her door.

2

Upstairs in the low white-painted bedroom which had been his since childhood Stephen stretched himself on his bed.

'I'm tired,' he said.

'Me too.' Deborah yawned and sat down on the bed beside him. 'It was a rather grim dinner-party. I wish Mummy wouldn't do it.'

'They're all such hypocrites.'

'They can't help it. They were brought up that way. Besides, I don't think that Eppy and Mr. Hinks have much wrong with them.'

'I suppose I made rather a fool of myself,' said Stephen.

'Well, you were rather vehement. Rather like Sir Galahad plunging to the defence of the wronged maiden, except that she was probably more sinning than sinned against.'

'You don't like her, do you?' asked Stephen.

'My sweet, I haven't thought about it. She just works here. I know that sounds very reactionary to your enlightened notions but it isn't meant to be. It's just that I'm

13

not interested in her one way or the other, nor she, I imagine, in me.'

'I'm sorry for her.' There was a trace of truculence in Stephen's voice.

'That was pretty obvious at dinner,' said Deborah dryly.

'It was their blasted complacency that got me down. And that Liddell woman. It's ridiculous to put a spinster in charge of a Home like St. Mary's.'

'I don't see why. She may be a little limited but she's kind and conscientious. Besides, I should have thought St. Mary's already suffered from a surfeit of sexual experience.'

'Oh, for heaven's sake don't be facetious, Deborah!'

'Well, what do you expect me to be? We only see each other once a fortnight. It's a bit hard to be faced with one of Mummy's duty dinner-parties and have to watch Catherine and Miss Liddell sniggering together because they thought you'd lost your head over a pretty maid. That's the kind of vulgarity Liddell would particularly relish. The whole conversation will be over the village by tomorrow.'

'If they thought that they must be mad. I've hardly seen the girl. I don't think I've spoken to her yet. The idea is ridiculous!'

'That's what I meant. For heaven's sake, darling, keep your crusading instincts under control while you're at home. I should have thought that you could have sublimated your social conscience at the hospital without bringing it home. It's uncomfortable to live with, especially for those of us who haven't got one.'

'I'm a bit on edge today,' said Stephen. 'I'm not sure I know what to do.'

It was typical of Deborah to know at once what he meant.

'She is rather dreary, isn't she? Why don't you close the whole affair gracefully? I'm assuming that there is an affair to close.'

'You know damn well that there is – or was. But how?'

'I've never found it particularly difficult. The art lies in making the other person believe that he has done the chucking. After a few weeks I practically believe it myself.'

'And if they won't play?'

14

'Men have died and worms have eaten them, but not for love.'

Stephen would have liked to have asked when and if Felix Hearne would be persuaded that he had done the chucking. He reflected that in this, as in other matters, Deborah had a ruthlessness that he lacked.

'I suppose I'm a coward about these things,' he said. 'I never find it easy to shake people off, even party bores.'

'No,' replied his sister. 'That's your trouble. Too weak and too susceptible. You ought to get married. Mummy would like it really. Someone with money if you can find her. Not stinking, of course, just beautifully rich.'

'No doubt. But who?'

'Who indeed?'

Suddenly Deborah seemed to lose interest in the subject. She swung herself up from the bed and went to lean against the window-ledge. Stephen watched her profile, so like his own yet so mysteriously different, outlined against the blackness of the night. The veins and arteries of the dying day were stretched across the horizon. From the garden below he could smell the whole rich infinitely sweet distillation of an English spring night. Lying there in the cool darkness he shut his eyes and gave himself up to the peace of Martingale. At moments like this he understood perfectly why his mother and Deborah schemed and planned to preserve his inheritance. He was the first Maxie to study medicine. He had done what he wanted and the family had accepted it. He might have chosen something even less lucrative although it was difficult to imagine what. In time, if he survived the grind, the hazards, the rat race of competition, he might become a consultant. He might even become sufficiently successful to support Martingale himself. In the meantime they would struggle on as best they could, making little housekeeping economies that would never intrude on his own comfort, cutting down the donations to charity, doing more of the gardening to save old Purvis's three shillings an hour, employing untrained girls to help Martha. None of it would inconvenience him very much, and it was all to ensure that he, Stephen Maxie, succeeded his father as Simon Maxie had succeeded his. If only he could have enjoyed Martingale

15

for its beauty and its peace without being chained to it by this band of responsibility and guilt!

There was the sound of slow careful footsteps on the stairs and then a knock on the door. It was Martha with the nightly hot drinks. Back in his childhood old Nannie had decided that a hot drink last thing at night would help to banish the terrifying and inexplicable nightmares from which, for a brief period, he and Deborah had suffered. The nightmares had yielded in time to the more tangible fears of adolescence, but the hot drinks had become a family habit. Martha, like her sister before her, was convinced that they were the only effective talisman against the real or imagined dangers of the night. Now she set down her small tray cautiously. There was the blue Wedgwood mug that Deborah used and the old George V coronation mug which Grandfather Maxie had bought for Stephen. 'I've brought your Ovaltine too, Miss Deborah,' Martha said. 'I thought I should find you here.' She spoke in a low voice as if they shared a conspiracy. Stephen wondered whether she guessed that they had been discussing Catherine. This was rather like the old comfortable Nannie bringing in the night drinks and ready to stay and talk. But yet not really the same. The devotion of Martha was more voluble, more self-conscious and less acceptable. It was a counterfeit of an emotion that had been as simple and necessary to him as the air he breathed. Remembering this he thought also that Martha needed her occasional sop.

'That was a lovely dinner, Martha,' he said.

Deborah had turned from the window and was wrapping her thin, red-nailed hands around the steaming mug.

'It's a pity the conversation wasn't worthy of the food. We had a lecture from Miss Liddell on the social consequences of illegitimacy. What do you think of Sally, Martha?'

Stephen knew that it was an unwise question. It was unlike Deborah to ask it.

'She seems quiet enough,' Martha conceded, 'but, of course, it is early days yet. Miss Liddell spoke very highly of her.'

'According to Miss Liddell,' said Deborah, 'Sally is a

16

model of all the virtues except one, and even that was a slip on the part of nature who couldn't recognize a high-school girl in the dark.'

Stephen was shocked by the sudden bitterness in his sister's voice.

'I don't know that all this education is a good thing for a maid, Miss Deborah.' Martha managed to convey that she had managed perfectly well without it. 'I only hope that she knows how lucky she is. Madam has even lent her our cot, the one you both slept in.'

'Well, we aren't sleeping in it now.' Stephen tried to keep the irritation out of his voice. Surely there had been enough talk about Sally Jupp! But Martha was not to be cautioned. It was as if she personally and not merely the family cradle had been desecrated. 'We've always looked after that cot, Dr. Stephen. It was to be kept for the grandchildren.'

'Damn!' said Deborah. She wiped the spilt drink from her fingers and replaced the mug on the tray. 'You shouldn't count your grandchildren before they're hatched. You can count me as a non-starter and Stephen isn't even engaged – nor thinking of it. He'll probably eventually settle for a buxom and efficient nurse who'll prefer to buy a new hygienic cot of her own from Oxford Street. Thank you for the drink, Martha dear.' Despite the smile, it was a dismissal.

The last 'good nights' were said and the same careful footsteps descended the stairs. When they had died away Stephen said, 'Poor old Martha. We do rather take her for granted and this maid-of-all-work job is getting too much for her. I suppose we ought to be thinking of pensioning her off.'

'On what?' Deborah stood again at the window.

'At least there's some help for her now,' Stephen temporized.

'Provided Sally isn't more trouble than she is worth. Miss Liddell made out that the baby is extraordinarily good. But any baby's considered that who doesn't bawl for two nights out of three. And then there's the washing. Sally can hardly be much help to Martha if she has to spend half the morning rinsing out nappies.'

'Presumably other mothers wash nappies,' said Stephen,

17

'and still find time for other work. I like this girl and I think she can be a help to Martha if only she's given a fair chance.'

'At least she had a very vigorous champion in you, Stephen. It's a pity you'll almost certainly be safely away at hospital when the trouble starts.'

'What trouble, for God's sake? What's the matter with you all? Why on earth should you assume that the girl's going to make trouble?'

Deborah walked over to the door. 'Because,' she said, 'she's making trouble already, isn't she? Good night.'

CHAPTER TWO

1

DESPITE this inauspicious beginning Sally Jupp's first weeks at Martingale were a success. Whether she herself shared this view was not known. No one asked for her opinion. She had been pronounced by the whole village to be a very lucky girl. If, as so often happens with the recipients of favours, she was less grateful than she ought to be, she managed to conceal her feelings behind a front of meekness, respectfulness and willingness to learn, which most people were happy enough to take at its face value. It did not deceive Martha Bultitaft and it is probable that it would not have deceived the Maxies if they had bothered to think about it. But they were too preoccupied with their individual concerns and too relieved at the sudden lightening of the domestic load to meet trouble halfway.

Martha had to admit that the baby was at first very little trouble. She put this down to Miss Liddell's excellent training since it was beyond her comprehension that bad girls could be good mothers. James was a placid child who, for his first two months at Martingale, was content to be fed at his accustomed times without advertising his hunger too loudly and who slept between his feeds in milky contentment. This could not last indefinitely. With the advent of what Sally called 'mixed feeding' Martha added several substantial grievances to her list. It seemed that the kitchen was never to be free of Sally and her demands. Jimmy was fast entering that stage of childhood in which meals became less a pleasant necessity than an opportunity for the exercise of power. Carefully pillowed in his high chair he would arch his sturdy back in an orgasm of resistance, bubbling milk and cereal through his pursed lips in ecstatic rejection before suddenly capitulating into charming and submissive innocence. Sally screamed with laugh-

19

ter at him, caught him to her in a whirl of endearments, loved and fondled him in contemptuous disregard of Martha's muttered disapproval. Sitting there with his tight curled mop of hair, his high beaked little nose almost hidden between plump cheeks as red and hard as apples, he seemed to dominate Martha's kitchen like a throned and imperious miniature Caesar. Sally was beginning to spend more time with her child and Martha would often see her during the mornings, her bright head bent over the pram where the sudden emergence of a chubby leg or arm showed that Jimmy's long periods of sleep were a thing of the past. No doubt his demands would increase. So far Sally had managed to keep up with the work allotted to her and to reconcile the demands of her son with those of Martha. If the strain was beginning to show, only Stephen on his fortnightly visits home noticed it with any compunction. Mrs. Maxie inquired of Sally at intervals whether she was finding the work too much and was glad to be satisfied with the reply she received. Deborah did not notice, or if she did, said nothing. It was, in any case, difficult to know whether Sally was overtired. Her naturally pale face under its shock of hair and her slim brittle-looking arms gave her an air of fragility which Martha, for one, thought highly deceiving. 'Tough as a nut and cunning as a wagon-load of monkeys' was Martha's opinion.

Spring ripened slowly into summer. The beech trees burst their spearheads of bright green and spread a chequered pattern of shade over the drive. The vicar celebrated Easter to his own joy and with no more than the usual recriminations and unpleasantness among his flock over the church decorations. Miss Pollack, at St. Mary's Refuge, endured a spell of sleeplessness for which Dr. Epps prescribed special tablets, and two of the Home's inmates settled for marriage with the unprepossessing but apparently repentant fathers of their babies. Miss Liddell admitted two more peccant mothers in their place. Sam Bocock advertised his stables in Chadfleet New Town and was surprised at the number of youths and girls who, in new, ill-fitting judhpurs and bright yellow gloves, were prepared to pay 7s. 6d. an hour to amble through the village under his tutelage. Simon Maxie lay in his narrow bed and was neither better nor worse. The evenings lengthened and the roses came. The garden at Martingale was heavy with their scent. As Deborah cut them for the house she had a feeling that the garden and Martingale, itself, were waiting for something. The house was always at its most beautiful in summer, but this year she sensed an atmosphere of expectancy, almost of foreboding, which was alien to its usual cool serenity. Carrying the roses into the house, Deborah shook herself out of this morbid fancy with the wry reflection that the most ominous event now hanging over Martingale was the annual church fête. When the words 'waiting for a death' came suddenly into her mind she told herself firmly that her father was no worse, might even be considered a little better, and that the house could not possibly know. She recognized that her love for Martingale was not entirely rational. Sometimes she tried to discipline that love by talking of the time 'when we have to sell' as if the very sound of the words could act both as a warning and a talisman.

St. Cedd's church fête had taken place in the grounds of Martingale every July since the days of Stephen's great-grandfather. It was organized by the fête committee, which consisted of the vicar, Mrs. Maxie, Dr. Epps and Miss Liddell. Their administrative duties were never arduous since the fête, like the church it helped to support, continued virtually unchanging from year to year, a symbol of immutability in the midst of chaos. But the committee took their responsibilities seriously and met frequently at Martingale during June and early July to drink tea in the garden and to pass resolutions which they passed the year before in identical words and in the same agreeable surroundings. The only member of the committee who occasionally felt genuinely uneasy about the fête was the vicar. In his gentle way he preferred to see the best in everyone and to impute worthy motives wherever possible. He included himself in this dispensation, having discovered early in his ministry that charity is a policy as well as a virtue. But once a year Mr. Hinks faced certain unpalatable facts about his church. He worried about its exclusiveness, its negative impact on the seething fringe of Chadfleet New Town, the suspicion that it was more of a social than a spiritual force in the village life.

Once he had suggested that the fête should close as well as open with a prayer and a hymn, but the only committee member to support this startling innovation was Mrs. Maxie, whose chief quarrel with the fête was that it never seemed to end.

This year Mrs. Maxie felt that she was going to be glad of Sally's willing help. There were plenty of workers for the actual fête, even if some of them were out to extract the maximum of personal enjoyment with the minimum of work, but the responsibilities did not end with the successful organization of the day. Most of the committee would expect to be asked to dinner at Martingale and Catherine Bowers had written to say that the Saturday of the fête was one of her off-duty days and would it be too much of an imposition if she invited herself for what she described as 'one of your perfect week-ends away from the noise and grime of this dreadful city'. This letter was not the first of its kind. Catherine was always so much more anxious to see the children than the children were to see Catherine. In some circumstances that would be just as well. It would be an unsuitable match for Stephen in every way, much as poor Katie would like to see her only child eligibly married off. She herself had married, as they said, beneath her. Christian Bowers had been an artist with more talent than money and no pretensions to anything except genius. Mrs. Maxie had met him once and had disliked him but, unlike his wife, she did believe him to be an artist. She had bought one of his early canvases for Martingale, a reclining nude which now hung in her bedroom and gave her a satisfied joy which no amount of intermittent hospitality to his daughter could adequately repay. To Mrs. Maxie it was an object-lesson in the folly of an unwise marriage. But because the pleasure it gave her was still fresh and real, and because she had once been at school with Katie Bowers and placed some importance on the obligations of old and sentimental associations, she felt that Catherine should be welcome at Martingale as her own guest, if not as her children's.

There were other things that were slightly worrying. Mrs. Maxie did not believe in taking too much notice of what other people sometimes describe as 'atmosphere'. She retained her serenity by coping with shattering common sense with those difficulties which were too obvious to ignore and by ignoring the others.

But things were happening at Martingale which were difficult to overlook. Some of them were to be expected, of course. Mrs. Maxie, for all her insensitivity, could not but realize that Martha and Sally were hardly compatible kitchen mates, and that Martha would be bound to find the situation difficult for a time. What she had not expected was that it should become progressively more difficult as the weeks wore on. After a succession of untrained and uneducated housemaids, who had come to Martingale because domesticity offered their only chance of employment, Sally seemed a paragon of intelligence, capability and refinement. Orders could be given in the confident assurance that they would be carried out where, before, even constant and painstaking reiteration had only resulted in the eventual realization that it was easier to do the job oneself.

An almost pre-war feeling of leisure would have returned to Martingale if it had not been for the heavier nursing which Simon Maxie now needed. Dr. Epps was already warning that they could not go on for long. Soon now it would be necessary to install a resident nurse or to move the patient to hospital. Mrs. Maxie rejected both alternatives. The former would be expensive, inconvenient and possibly indefinitely prolonged. The latter would mean that Simon Maxie would die in the hands of strangers instead of in his own house. The family could not afford a nursing home or a private ward. It would mean a bed in the local hospital for chronic cases, barrack-like, over-crowded and understaffed. Before this final stage of his illness had fallen upon him, Simon Maxie had whispered to her, 'You won't let them take me away, Eleanor?' and she had replied, 'Of course I won't.' He had fallen asleep then, secure in a promise which both of them knew was no light assurance. It was a pity that Martha had apparently so short a memory for the overwork which had preceded Sally's arrival. The new régime had given her time and energy to criticize what she had at first found surprisingly easy to accept. But so far she had not come into the open. There had been the veiled innuendoes but no definite complaint. Undoubtedly tension must be building up in the kitchen, thought Mrs. Maxie, and after the fête it would probably have to be coped with. But she was in no hurry; the fête was only a week away and the chief consideration was to get it successfully over.

2

On the Thursday preceding the fête Deborah spent the morning shopping in London, lunched with Felix Hearne at his club and went with him to see a Hitchcock revival at a Baker Street cinema in the afternoon. This agreeable programme was completed with afternoon tea at a Mayfair restaurant which holds unfashionable views on what constitutes an adequate afternoon meal. Replete with cucumber sandwiches and home-made chocolate éclairs Deborah reflected that the afternoon had really been very successful, even if a little low-brow for Felix's taste. But he had borne up under it well. There were advantages in not being lovers. If they had been having a love affair it would have seemed necessary to spend the afternoon together in his Greenwich house since the opportunity offered and an irregular union imposes conventions as rigid and compelling as those of marriage. And while the love-making would no doubt have been pleasant enough the easy undemanding companionship which they had enjoyed was more to her taste.

She did not want to fall in love again. Months of annihilating misery and despair had cured her of that particular folly. She had married young and Edward Riscoe had died of poliomyelitis less than a year later. But a marriage based on companionship, compatible tastes and the satisfactory exchange of sexual pleasure seemed to her a reasonable basis for life and one which could be achieved without too much disturbing emotion. Felix, she suspected, was enough in love with her to be interesting without being boring and she was only spasmodically tempted to consider seriously the expected offer of marriage. It was, nevertheless, beginning to be slightly odd that the offer was not made. It was not, she knew, that he disliked women. Certainly most of their friends considered him to be a natural bachelor, eccentric, slightly pedantic and perennially amusing. They might have been unkinder, but there was the inescapable fact of his war record to be explained away. A man cannot be either effeminate or a fool who holds both French and British decorations for his part in the Resistance Movement. He was one of those whose physical courage, that most respected and most glamorous of virtues, had been tried in the punishment cells of the Gestapo and could never again be challenged. It was less fashionable now to think of those things but they were not yet quite forgotten. What those months in France had done to Felix Hearne was anybody's guess, but he was allowed his eccentricities and presumably he enjoyed them. Deborah liked him because he was intelligent and amusing and the most diverting gossip she knew. He had a woman's interest in the small change of life and an intuitive concern for the minutiae of human relationships. Nothing was too trivial for him and he sat now listening with every appearance of amused sympathy to Deborah's report on Martingale.

'So you see, it's bliss to have some free time again, but I really can't see it lasting. Martha will have her out in time. And I don't really blame her. She doesn't like Sally and neither do I.'

'Why? Is she chasing Stephen?'

'Don't be vulgar, Felix. You might give me the benefit of a more subtle reason than that. Actually, though, she does seem to have impressed him and I think it's deliberate. She asks his advice about the baby whenever he's at home, although I have tried to point out that he's supposed to be a surgeon not a paediatrician. And poor old Martha can't breathe a word of criticism without his rushing to Sally's defence. You'll see for yourself when you come on Saturday.'

'Who else will be there apart from this intriguing Sally Jupp?'

'Stephen, of course. And Catherine Bowers. You met her the last time you were at Martingale.'

'So I did. Rather poached-egg eyes but an agreeable figure and more intelligence than you or Stephen were willing to allow her.'

'If she impressed you so much,' retorted Deborah easily, 'you can demonstrate your admiration this weekend and give Stephen a respite. He was rather taken with her once and now she sticks to him like a limpet and it bores him horribly.'

'How incredibly ruthless pretty women are to plain ones! And by "rather taken with her" I suppose you mean that Stephen seduced her. Well, that usually does lead to complications and he must find his own way out as better men have done before him. But I shall come. I love Martingale and I appreciate good cooking. Besides, I have a feeling that the week-end will be interesting. A house full of people all disliking each other is bound to be explosive.'

'Oh, it isn't as bad as that!'

'Very nearly. Stephen dislikes me. He has never bothered to hide it. You dislike Catherine Bowers. She dislikes you and will probably extend the emotion to me. Martha and you dislike Sally Jupp and she, poor girl, probably loathes you all. And that pathetic creature, Miss Liddell, will be there, and your mother dislikes her. It will be a perfect orgy of suppressed emotion.'

'You needn't come. In fact, I think it would be better if you didn't.'

'But, Deborah, your mother has already asked me and I've accepted. I wrote to her last week in my nice formal way, and I shall now make a note in my little black book to settle it beyond doubt.' He bent his sleek fair head over his engagement diary. His face, with the pale skin which made the hair-line almost indistinguishable, was turned away from her. She noticed how sparse were the eyebrows against the pallid forehead and the intricate folds and crinkles around his eyes. Deborah thought that he must once have had beautiful hands before the Gestapo played about with them. The nails had never fully grown again. She tried to picture those hands moving about the intricacies of a gun, curled into the cords of a parachute, clenched in defiance or endurance. But it was no good. There seemed no point of contact between that Felix who had apparently once known a cause worth suffering for and the facile, sophisticated, sardonic Felix Hearne of Hearne and Illingworth, publishers, just as there was none between the girl who had married Edward Riscoe and the woman she was today. Suddenly Deborah felt again

the familiar *malaise* of nostalgia and regret. In this mood
she watched Felix writing under Saturday's date in his
cramped meticulous hand as if he were making a date
with death.

3

After tea Deborah decided to visit Stephen, partly to
avoid the rush-hour crowds but chiefly because she seldom
came up to London without calling at St. Luke's Hospital.
She invited Felix to accompany her but he excused himself on the grounds that the smell of disinfectant made
him sick, and sent her off in a taxi with formal expres-
sions of thanks for her company. He was punctilious about
these matters. Deborah fought against the unflattering
suspicion that he had tired of her conversation and was
relieved to see her borne away in comfort and with speed,
and concentrated on the pleasure of seeing Stephen. It
was all the more disconcerting to find that he was not in
the hospital. It was unusual too. Colley, the hall porter,
explained that Mr. Maxie had had a telephone call and
had gone out to meet someone saying that he wouldn't be
long. Mr. Donwell was on duty for him. But Mr. Maxie
would certainly not be long now. He had been gone
nearly an hour. Perhaps Mrs. Riscoe would like to go up
to the residents' sitting-room? Deborah stayed for a few
minutes' chat with Colley whom she liked and then took
the lift to the fourth floor. Mr. Donwell, a shy and spotty
young registrar, mumbled a greeting and made a speedy
escape to the wards leaving Deborah in sole possession of
four grubby armchairs, an untidy heap of medical period-
icals and the half-cleared remnants of the residents' tea.
It appeared that they had had Swiss roll again and, as
usual, someone had used his saucer as an ash-tray. Deborah began to pile up the plates, but, realizing that this
was a somewhat pointless activity since she did not know
what to do with them, she took up one of the papers and
moved to the window where she could divide her interest
between waiting for Stephen and scanning the more intriguing or comprehensible of the medical articles. The
window gave a view of the main hospital entrance farther
along the street. In the distance she could discern the

27

shining curve of the river and the towers of Westminster. The ceaseless rumbling of traffic was muted, an unobtrusive background to the occasional noises of the hospital, the clang of the lift gates, the ringing of telephone bells, the passing of brisk feet along the corridor. An old woman was being helped into an ambulance at the front door. From a height of four floors the figures below seemed curiously foreshortened. The ambulance door was shut without a sound and it slid away noiselessly. Suddenly she saw them. It was Stephen she noticed first, but the flaming red-gold head almost level with his shoulder was unmistakable. They paused at the corner of the building. They seemed to be talking. The black head was bent towards the gold. After a moment she saw him shake hands and then Sally turned in a flash of sunlight and walked swiftly away without a backward glance. Deborah missed nothing. Sally was wearing her grey suit. It was mass-produced and bought off the peg, but it fitted well and was a foil for the shining cascade of hair, released now from the restraint of cap and pins.

She was clever, thought Deborah. Clever to know that you had to dress simply if you wanted to wear your hair loose like that. Clever to avoid the greens for which most redheads had a predilection. Clever to have said 'goodbye' outside the hospital and to have resisted the certain invitation to a hospital supper with its inevitable openings for embarrassment or regret. Afterwards Deborah was surprised that she should have noticed so keenly what Sally was wearing. It was as if she saw her for the first time through Stephen's eyes, and seeing her was afraid. It seemed a long time before she heard the drone of the lift and his quick footsteps along the corridor. Then he was by her side. She did not move away from the window so that he should know at once she had seen. She felt that she could not bear it if he did not tell her and it was easier that way. She did not know what she expected but when he spoke it was a surprise.

'Have you seen these before?' he asked.

In his outstretched palm was a rough bag made from a man's handkerchief tied together at the corners. He lifted one of the knots, gave a little jerk, and spilled out three or four of the tiny tablets. Their grey-brown colour was unmistakable.

'Aren't they some of Father's tablets?' It seemed as if he were accusing her of something. 'Where did you get them?'

'Sally found them and brought them up to me. I expect you saw us from the window.'

'What did she do with the baby?' The silly irrelevant question was out before she had time to think.

'The baby? Oh, Jimmy, I don't know. Sally left him with someone in the village I suppose or with Mother or Martha. She came up to bring me these and 'phoned from Liverpool Street to ask me to meet her. She found them in Father's bed.'

'But how, in his bed?'

'Between the mattress cover and the mattress. Down the side. His draw-sheet was rucked and she was smoothing it and pulling the mackintosh tight when she noticed a little bulge in the corner of the mattress underneath the fitted cover. She found this. Father must have been saving them over several weeks, perhaps months. I can guess why.'

'Does he know she found them?'

'Sally doesn't think so. He was lying on his side with his face away from her as she attended to the draw-sheet. She just put the handkerchief and the tablets in her pocket and went on as if nothing had happened. Of course they may have been there for a long time – he's been on Sommeil for eighteen months or more – and he may have forgotten about them. He may have lost the power to get at them and use them. We can't tell what goes on in his mind. The trouble is that we haven't bothered even to try. Except Sally.'

'But Stephen, that isn't true. We do try. We sit with him and nurse him and try to make him feel that we're there. But he just lies, not moving, not speaking, not even seeming to notice people any more. He isn't really Father. There isn't any contact between us. I have tried, I swear I have, but it isn't any use. He can't really have meant to take those tablets. I can't think how he even managed to collect them, to plan it all.'

'When it's your turn to give him his tablets, do you watch him while he swallows them?'

29

'No, not really. You know how he used to hate us to help him too much. Now I don't think he minds, but we still give him the tablets and then pour out the water and hold it up to his lips if he seems to want it. He must have secreted these away months ago. I can't believe he could manage it now, not without Martha knowing. She does most of the lifting and the heavier nursing.'

'Well, apparently he managed to deceive Martha. But, by God, Deborah, I ought to have guessed, ought to have known. I call myself a doctor. This is the kind of thing which makes me feel like a specialized carpenter, good enough to carve patients up as long as I'm not expected to bother with them as people. At least Sally treated him as a human being.'

Deborah was momentarily tempted to point out that she, her mother and Martha were at least managing to keep Simon Maxie comfortable, clean and fed at no small cost and that it was difficult to see where Sally had done more. But if Stephen wanted to indulge in remorse there was little to be gained by stopping him. He usually felt better afterwards, even if other people felt worse. She watched in silence as he rummaged about in the drawer of the desk, found a small bottle which had apparently once held aspirin, carefully counted the tablets – there were ten of them – into the bottle and labelled it with the name of the drug and the dose. They were the almost automatic actions of a man trained to keep medicines properly labelled. Deborah's mind was busy with questions she dared not ask. 'Why did Sally come to you? Why not Mother? Did she really find those tablets or was it just a convenient ruse to see you alone? But she must have found them. No one could make up a story like that. Poor Father. What has Sally been saying? Why should I mind so much about this, about Sally? I hate her because she has a child and I haven't. Now I've said it, but admitting it doesn't make it any easier. That handkerchief bag. It must have taken him hours to tie it together. It looked like something made by a child. Poor Father. He was so tall when I was a child. Was I really rather afraid of him? Oh God, please help me to feel pity. I want to be sorry for him. What is Sally thinking now? What did Stephen say to her?'

30

He turned back from the desk and held out the bottle.

'I think you had better take this home. Put it in the medicine cupboard in his room. Don't say anything to Mother yet or to Dr. Epps. I think it would be wiser if we stopped the tablets for Father. I'll get you a prescription made up in the dispensary before you leave, the same kind of drug only in solution. Give him a tablespoonful at night in water. I should see to it yourself. Just tell Martha that I have stopped the tablets. When does Dr. Epps see him again?'

'He's coming in to see Mother with Miss Liddell after dinner. I suppose he may go up then. But I don't expect he'll ask about the tablets. They've been going on for so long now. We just say when the bottle is getting empty and he gives us a fresh prescription.'

'Do you know how many tablets there are in the house now?'

'There's a new bottle with the seal unbroken. We were to start it tonight.'

'Then leave it in the cupboard and give him the medicine. I shall be able to talk to Eppy about it when I see him on Saturday. I'll get down late tomorrow night. You had better come with me to the dispensary now and it would be wiser to get home straight away. I'll telephone Martha and ask her to keep you some dinner.'

'Yes, Stephen.' Deborah did not regret the loss of her meal. All the pleasure of the day had evaporated. It was time to be going home.

'And I would rather you said nothing to Sally about this.'

'I hadn't the slightest intention of doing so. I only hope she's capable of a similar discretion. We don't want this story all over the village.'

'That's an unfair thing to say, Deborah, and you don't even believe it. You couldn't have anyone safer than Sally. She was very sensible about it. And rather sweet.'

'I'm sure she was.'

'She was naturally worried about it. She's very devoted to Father.'

'She seems to be extending her devotion to you.'

'What on earth do you mean?'

31

'I was wondering why she didn't tell Mother about the tablets. Or me.'

'You haven't done much to encourage her to confide in you, have you?'

'What on earth do you expect me to do? Hold her hand? I'm not particularly interested in her as long as she does her work efficiently. I don't like her and I don't expect her to like me.'

'It's not true that you don't like her,' said Stephen. 'You hate her.'

'Did she complain of the way she's been treated?'

'Of course she didn't. Do be sensible, Deb. This isn't like you.'

'Isn't it?' thought Deborah. 'How do you know what's like me?' But she recognized in Stephen's last words a plea for peace and she held out her hand to him, saying, 'I'm sorry. I don't know what's wrong with me lately. I'm sure Sally did what she thought best. It isn't worth quarrelling about anyway. Do you want me to wait up for you tomorrow night? Felix won't be able to get down until Saturday morning, but Catherine is expected for dinner.'

'Don't bother. I may have to get the last bus. But I'll ride with you before breakfast if you like to call me.'

The significance of this formal offer in place of the previously happily established routine did not escape Deborah. The chasm between them had only been precariously bridged. She felt that Stephen, too, was uneasily aware of the cracking ice beneath their feet. Never since the death of Edward Riscoe had she felt so alienated from Stephen; never since then had she been so in need of him.

4

It was nearly half past seven before Martha heard the sound she had been listening for, the squeak of pram wheels on the drive. Jimmy was whining softly and was obviously only persuaded from open bawling by the soothing motion of the pram and the soft reassurances of his mother. Soon Sally's head was seen to pass the kitchen window, the pram was wheeled into the scullery and, almost immediately, mother and child appeared through

32

the kitchen door. There was an air of suppressed emotion about the girl. She seemed at once nervous and yet pleased with herself. Martha did not think that an afternoon wheeling Jimmy in the forest could altogether account for that look of secretive and triumphant pleasure.

'You're late,' she said. 'I should think the child is starving, poor mite.'

'Well, he won't have to wait much longer, will you my pet? I suppose there isn't any milk boiled?'

'I'm not here to wait on you, Sally, please remember. If you want milk you must boil it yourself. You know well enough what time the child should be fed.'

They did not speak again while Sally boiled the milk and tried, rather ineffectually, to cool it quickly whilst holding Jimmy on one arm. It was not until Sally was ready to take her child upstairs that Martha spoke.

'Sally,' she said, 'did you take anything from the master's bed when you made it this morning? Anything belonging to him? I want the truth now!'

'It's obvious from your tone that you know I did. Do you mean that you know that he had those tablets hidden? And you said nothing about them?'

'Of course I knew. I've looked after him now for five years haven't I? Who else would know what he does, what he's feeling? I suppose you thought he'd take them. Well, that needn't worry you. What business is it of yours anyway? If you had to lie there, year after year, perhaps you might like to know that you had something, a few little tablets maybe, that would end all the pain and the tiredness. Something that nobody else knew about, until a silly little bitch, no better than she should be, came ferreting them out. Very clever, weren't you? But he wouldn't have taken them! He's a gentleman. You wouldn't understand that either. But you can give me back those tablets. And if you mention a word of this to anyone or lay a hand on anything else belonging to the master, I'll have you out. You and that brat. I'll find a way, never fear!'

She held out her hand towards Sally. Never once had she raised her voice but her calm authority was more frightening than anger and the girl's voice was tinged with hysteria as she replied.

33

'I'm afraid you're unlucky. I haven't got the tablets. I took them to Stephen this afternoon. Yes, Stephen! And now I've heard your silly twaddle I'm glad I did. I'd like to see Stephen's face if I told him that you knew all the time! Dear, faithful old Martha! So devoted to the family! You don't care a damn for any of them, you old hypocrite, except for your precious master! Pity you can't see yourself! Washing him, stroking his face, cooing to him as if he were your baby. I could laugh sometimes if it weren't so pitiful. It's indecent! Lucky for him he's half gaga! Being mauled about by you would make any normal man sick!'

She swung the child on to her hip and Martha heard the door close behind her.

Martha lurched over to the sink and clutched it with shaking hands. She was seized with a physical revulsion that made her retch but her body found no relief in sickness. She put her hand to her forehead in a stock gesture of despair. Looking at her fingers she saw that they were wet with perspiration. As she fought for control the echo of that high, childish voice beat into her brain. 'Being mauled about by you would make any normal man sick . . . being mauled about by you . . . mauled about.' When her body stopped its shaking, nausea gave way to hate. Her mind solaced its misery with the sweet images of revenge. She indulged in phantasies of Sally disgraced, Sally and her child banished from Martingale, Sally found out for what she was, lying, wicked and evil. And, since all things are possible, Sally dead.

CHAPTER THREE

1

THE fickle summer weather which, for the last few weeks, had provided a sample of every climatic condition known to the country with the sole exception of snow, now settled into the warm grey normality for the time of the year. There was a chance that the fête would be held in dry weather if not in sun. Deborah, pulling on her jodhpurs for her morning ride with Stephen, could see the red and white marquee from her window, and scattered around the lawn, the skeletons of a dozen half-erected stalls awaiting their final embellishment of crêpe paper and Union Jacks. Away in the home field a course had already been ringed for the children's sports and the dancing display. An ancient car surmounted by a loudspeaker was parked under one of the elms at the end of the lawn and several lengths of wire coiled on the paths and slung between the trees bore witness to the efforts of the local wireless enthusiasts to provide a loudspeaker system for the music and the announcements. Deborah, after a good night's rest, was able to survey these preparations with stoicism. She knew from experience that a very different sight would meet her eyes by the time the fête was over. However careful people were – and many of them only began to enjoy themselves when they were surrounded by a familiar litter of cigarette packets and fruit peelings – it was at least a week's work before the garden lost its look of ravaged beauty. Already the rows of bunting stretched from side to side of the green walks gave the spinney an air of incongruous frivolity and the rooks seemed shocked into noisier than usual recriminations.

In Catherine's favourite day-dream of the Martingale fête she spent the afternoon helping Stephen with the horses, the centre of an interested, deferential and specu-lating group of the Chadfleet villagers. Catherine had

35

picturesque if outdated notions of the place and importance of the Maxies in their community. This happy imagining faded in face of Mrs. Maxie's determination that both her guests should help where they were most needed. For Catherine this was plainly to be with Deborah on the white elephant stall. When the first disappointment had subsided it was surprising how pleasant the experience proved. The morning was spent in sorting, examining and pricing the miscellaneous hoard that had still to be dealt with. Deborah had an amazing knowledge, born of long experience, of the source of most of her wares, what each article was worth and who was likely to buy it. Sir Reynold Price had contributed a large shaggy coat with a detachable waterproof lining which was immediately placed on one side for the private consideration of Dr. Epps. It was just the thing he needed for winter visiting in his open car and, after all, no one noticed what you wore when you were driving. There was an old felt hat which belonged to the doctor himself and which his daily help tried to get rid of every year only to have it bought back by its irate owner. It was marked sixpence and prominently displayed. There were hand-knitted jumpers of startling style and hue, small objects in brass and china from the village mantelpieces, bundles of books and magazines and a fascinating collection of prints in heavy frames, appropriately named in spidery copper-plate. There were 'The First Love Letter', 'Daddy's Darling', an ornate twin pair called 'The Quarrel' and 'Reconciliation' and several showing soldiers either kissing their wives farewell or enjoying the chaster pleasures of reunion. Deborah prophesied that the customers would love them and declared that the frames alone were worth half a crown.

By one o'clock the preparations were complete and the household had time for a hurried luncheon waited on by Sally. Catherine remembered that there had been some trouble that morning with Martha because the girl had overslept. Apparently she had had to rush to make up the lost time for she looked flushed and was, Catherine thought, concealing some excitement behind an outward air of docile efficiency. But the meal passed happily enough since the company was at present united in a common

36

preoccupation and a shared activity. By two o'clock the bishop and his wife had arrived, the committee came out of the drawing-room windows to arrange themselves a little self-consciously on the circle of waiting chairs and the fête was formally opened. Although the bishop was old and retired he was not senile and his short speech was a model of simplicity and grace. As the lovely old voice came to her across the lawn, Catherine thought of the church for the first time with interest and affection. Here was the Norman font where she and Stephen would stand at the christening of their children. In these aisles were commemorated his ancestors. Here the kneeling figures of a sixteenth-century Stephen Maxie and Deborah, his wife, faced each other for ever petrified in stone, their thin hands curved in prayer. Here were the secular and ornate busts of the eighteenth-century Maxies and the plain tablets which told briefly of sons killed in Gallipoli and on the Marne. Catherine had often thought that it was as well the family obsequies had become progressively less extravagant since the Church of St. Cedd with St. Mary the Virgin, Chadfleet, was already less a public place of worship than a private repository for Maxie bones. But today, in a mood of confidence and exultation, she could think of all the family, dead and alive, without criticism and even a baroque reredos would have seemed no more than their due.

Deborah took her place with Catherine behind their stall and the customers began to approach and search warily for bargains. It was certainly one of the most popular attractions and business was brisk. Dr. Epps came early for his hat and was easily persuaded to buy Sir Reynold's coat for £1. The clothes and shoes were snapped up, usually by the very people Deborah had foretold would want them, and Catherine was kept busy handing out change and replenishing the stall from the large box of reinforcements which they kept under the counter. At the gate of the drive little groups of people continued to come in throughout the afternoon, the children's faces stretched into fixed unnatural smiles for the benefit of a photographer who had promised a prize for the 'Happiest Looking Child' to enter the garden during the afternoon. The loudspeaker exceeded everyone's wildest hopes and poured forth a medley of Sousa marches and Strauss waltzes, announcements about teas and competitions, and occasional admonitions to use the rubbish baskets and keep the garden tidy. Miss Liddell and Miss Pollack, helped by the plainest, oldest and most reliable of their delinquent girls, bustled from St. Mary's to the fête and back again at the call of a conscience or duty. Their stall was by far the most expensive and the hand-made underclothes display suffered from an unhappy compromise between prettiness and respectability. The vicar, his soft white hair damped by exertion, beamed happily upon his flock, who were for once at peace with the world and each other. Sir Reynold arrived late, voluble, patronizing and generous. From the tea lawn came the sound of earnest admonitions as Mrs. Cope and Mrs. Nelson, with the help of the boys' class from the Sunday school, busied themselves with bridge tables, chairs from the village hall, and assorted table-cloths which would all have to find their eventual way back to their owners. Felix Hearne seemed to be enjoying himself as a free-lance. He did appear once or twice to help Deborah or Catherine but announced that he was having a much better time with Miss Liddell and Miss Pollack. Once Stephen came to inquire after business. For someone who habitually referred to the fête as 'The Curse of the Maxies', he seemed happy enough. Soon after four o'clock Deborah went into the house to see if her father needed attention and Catherine was left in charge. Deborah returned after half an hour or so and suggested that they might go in search of tea. It was being served in the larger of the two tents and late arrivals, Deborah warned, were usually faced with a weak beverage and the less attractive cakes. Felix Hearne, who had stopped at the stall to chat and pass judgment on the remaining merchandise, was commandeered to take their places and Deborah and Catherine went into the house to wash. One or two people were usually found passing through the hall either because they thought it would be a short cut or because they were strangers to the village and thought their entrance fee included a free tour of the house. Deborah seemed unconcerned. 'There's Bob Gittings, our local P.C.,

38

keeping an eye on things in the drawing-room,' she pointed out. 'And the dining-room's locked. This always happens. No one's ever taken anything yet. We'll go in the south door now and use the small bathroom. It'll be quicker.' All the same it was disconcerting for them both when a man brushed past them on the back stairs with a hasty apology. They stopped and Deborah called after him. 'Were you looking for someone? This is a private house.' He turned and looked back at them, a nervous, lean man with greying hair swept back from a high forehead and a thin mouth which he drew back into a propitiatory smile. 'Oh, I'm sorry. I didn't realize. Please excuse me. I was looking for the toilet.' It was not an attractive voice. 'If you mean the lavatory,' said Deborah shortly, 'there's one in the garden. It seemed adequately sign-posted to me.' He flushed and mumbled some reply and then was gone. Deborah shrugged her shoulders. 'What a scared rabbit! I don't suppose he was doing any harm. But I wish they'd keep out of the house.' Catherine made a mental resolve that when she was mistress of Martingale arrangements would be made to see that they did.

The tea-tent was certainly crowded and the confused clatter of crockery, the babble of voices and the hissing of the tea-urn were heard against a background of the broadcast music which came muted through the canvas. The tables had been decorated by the Sunday school children as part of their competition for the best arrangements of wild flowers. Each table bore its labelled jam jar and the harvest of poppy, campion, sorrel and dog-rose, revived from the hours of clutching in hot hands, had a delicate and unselfconscious beauty, although the scent of the flowers was lost in the strong smell of trampled grass, hot canvas and food. The concentration of noise was so great that a sudden break in the clatter of voices seemed to Catherine as if a total silence had fallen. Only afterwards did she realize that not everybody had stopped talking, that not every head was turned to where Sally had come into the tent by the opposite entrance, Sally in a white dress with a low boat-shaped neckline and a skirt of swirling pleats, identical with the one Deborah was wearing, Sally with a green cummerbund which was a replica of

39

the one round Deborah's waist, and with green ear-rings gleaming on each side of flushed cheeks. Catherine felt her own cheeks redden and could not help her quick inquiring glance at Deborah. She was not the only one. Faces were turning towards them from more and more of the tables. From the far end of the tent where some of Miss Liddell's girls were enjoying an early tea under Miss Pollack's supervision, there was a quickly suppressed giggling. Someone said softly, but not softly enough, 'Good old Sal.' Only Deborah appeared unconcerned. Without a second glance at Sally she walked up to the counter of trestle tables and asked equally for tea for two, a plate of bread and butter and one of cakes. Mrs. Pardy splashed tea from the urn into the cups with embarrassed haste, and Catherine followed Deborah to one of the vacant tables, clutching the plate of cakes and unhappily aware that she was the one who looked a fool.

'How dare she?' she muttered, bending her hot face over the cup. 'It's a deliberate insult.' Deborah gave a slight shrug of her shoulders. 'Oh, I don't know. What does it matter? Presumably the poor little devil is getting a kick out of her gesture and it isn't hurting me.'

'Where did she get the dress from?'

'The same place as I did, I imagine. The name's inside. It isn't a model or anything like that. Anyone could buy it who took the trouble to find it. Sally must have thought it worth the trouble.'

'She couldn't have known you were going to wear it today.'

'Any other occasion would have done as well, I expect. Must you go on about it?'

'I can't think why you take it so calmly. I wouldn't.'

'What do you expect me to do? Go and tear it off her? There's a limit to the free entertainment the village can expect.'

'I wonder what Stephen will say,' said Catherine. Deborah looked surprised. 'I doubt whether he will even notice, except to think how well it suits her. It's more her dress than mine. Are those cakes all right for you or would you rather forage for sandwiches?' Catherine, baulked of further discussion, went on with her tea.

40

The afternoon wore on. After the scene in the tea-tent the fun had gone out of the fête for Catherine and the rest of the jumble sale was little more than a laborious chore. They were sold out before five as Deborah had predicted, and Catherine was free to offer her help with the pony rides. She arrived in the home field to see Stephen lift Jimmy, screaming with delight, into the saddle in front of his mother. The sun, mellowing now at the ending of the day, shone through the child's hair and turned it into fire. Sally's shining hair swung forward as she leaned down to whisper to Stephen. Catherine heard his answering laugh. It was a moment of time she was never to forget. She turned back to the lawns and tried to recapture some of the confidence and happiness with which she had started the day. But it was of no use. After wandering about in desultory search for something to occupy her mind, she decided to go up to her room and lie down before dinner. She did not see Mrs. Maxie or Martha on her way through the house. Presumably they were busy either with Simon Maxie or with preparations for the cold meal which was to end the day. Through her window she did see that Dr. Epps was still dozing beside his darts and treasure hunt, although the busiest part of the afternoon was over. The winners of the competitions would soon be announced, rewarded and acclaimed and a thin but steady stream of people was already passing out of the grounds to the bus terminus.

Apart from that moment in the home field Catherine had not seen Sally again, and when she had washed and changed and was on the way to the dining-room she met Martha on the stairs and heard from her that Sally and Jimmy were not yet in. The dining-room table had been set with cold meats, salads and bowls of fresh fruit, and all the party except Stephen were gathered there. Dr. Epps, voluble and cheerful as ever, was busying himself with the cider bottles. Felix Hearne was setting out the glasses. Miss Liddell was helping Deborah to finish laying the table. Her little squeals of dismay when she could not find what she wanted and her ineffectual jabberings at the table napkins were symptomatic of more than normal unease. Mrs. Maxie stood with her back to the others, looking into the glass above the chimneypiece. When she turned, Catherine was shocked by the lines and weariness of her face.

'Isn't Stephen with you?' she asked.

'No. I haven't seen him since he was with the horses. I've been in my room.'

'He probably walked home with Bocock to help with the stabling. Or perhaps he's changing. I don't think we'll wait.'

'Where's Sally?' asked Deborah.

'Not in apparently. Martha tells me that Jimmy is in his cot so she must have come in and gone out again.' Mrs. Maxie spoke calmly. If this was a domestic crisis she evidently regarded it as a comparatively minor one which warranted no further comment in front of her guests. Felix Hearne glanced at her and felt a familiar tinge of anticipation and foreboding which startled him. It seemed so extravagant a reaction for so ordinary an occasion. Looking across to Catherine Bowers he had a feeling that she shared his unease. The whole party was a little jaded. Except for Miss Liddell's inconsequential and maddening chatter they had little to say. There was the sense of anti-climax which follows most long-planned social functions. The affair was over yet too much with them to permit re-laxation. The bright sun of the day had given way to heaviness. There was no breeze now and the heat was greater than ever.

When Sally appeared at the door they turned to face her as if stung by a common urgency. She leaned back against the linen-fold panelling, the white pleats of her dress fanned out against its sombre darkness like a pigeon's wing. In this strange and stormy light her hair burned against the wood. Her face was very pale but she was smiling. Stephen was at her side.

Mrs. Maxie was aware of a curious moment in which each person present seemed separately aware of Sally and in which they yet moved quietly together as if tensed to face a common challenge. In an effort to restore norm-ality she spoke casually. 'I'm glad you're in, Stephen. Sally, you had better change back into your uniform and help Martha.'

42

The girl's self-contained little smile cracked into laughter. It took her a second to gain sufficient control to reply in a voice which was almost obsequious in its derisive respectfulness.

'Would that be appropriate, madam, for the girl your son has asked to marry him?'

3

Simon Maxie had a night which was no worse and no better than any other. It was doubtful whether anyone else beneath his roof was as fortunate. His wife kept her vigil on the day bed in his dressing-room and heard the hours strike while the luminous hand on the clock beside her bed jerked forward towards the inevitable day. She lived through the scene in the drawing-room so many times that there now seemed no second of it which was not remembered with clarity, no nuance of voice or emotion which was lost. She could recall every word of Miss Liddell's hysterical attack, the spate of vicious and half-demented abuse which had provoked Sally's retort.

'Don't talk about what you've done for me. What have you ever cared about me, you sex-starved old hypocrite? Be thankful that I know how to keep my mouth shut. There are some things I could tell the village about you.'

She had gone after that and the party had been left to enjoy their dinner with as much appetite as they could muster or simulate. Miss Liddell had made little effort. Once Mrs. Maxie noticed a tear on her cheek and she was touched with the thought that Miss Liddell was genuinely suffering, had cared to the limit of her capacity for Sally and had honestly taken pleasure in her progress and happiness. Dr. Epps had champed through his meal in an unwonted silence, a sure sign that jaw and mind were together exercised. Stephen had not followed Sally from the room but had taken his seat by his sister. In reply to his mother's quiet 'Is this true, Stephen?' he had replied simply, 'Of course.' He had made no further mention of it and brother and sister had sat through the meal together, eating little but presenting a united front to Miss

Liddell's distress and Felix Hearne's ironic glances. He, thought Mrs. Maxie, was the only member of the party who had enjoyed his dinner. She was not sure that the preliminaries had not sharpened his appetite. She knew that he had never liked Stephen and this engagement, if persisted in, was likely to afford him amusement as well as increasing his chances with Deborah. No one could suppose that Deborah would remain at Martingale once Stephen had married. Mrs. Maxie found that she could remember with uncomfortable vividness Catherine's bent face, flushed unbecomingly with grief or resentment and the calm way in which Felix Hearne had roused her to make at least a decent effort at concealment. He could be very amusing when he cared to exert himself and last night he had exerted himself to the full. Surprisingly, he had succeeded in producing laughter by the end of the meal. Was that really only seven hours ago?

The minutes ticked away sounding unnaturally loud in the quietness. It had rained heavily earlier in the night but had now stopped. At five o'clock she thought she heard her husband stirring and went to him, but he still lay in the rigid stupor which they called sleep. Stephen had changed his sleeping-drug. He had been given medicine instead of the usual tablet but the result appeared much the same. She went back to bed but not to sleep. At six o'clock she got up and put on her dressing-gown, then she filled and plugged in the electric kettle for her morning tea. The day with its problems had come at last.

It was a relief to her when there was a knock on the door and Catherine slipped in, still in her pyjamas and dressing-gown. Mrs. Maxie had a moment of acute fear that Catherine had come to talk, that the affairs of the previous evening would have to be discussed, assessed, deprecated and re-lived. She had spent most of the night making plans that she could not share nor would wish to share with Catherine. But she found herself unaccountably glad to see another human being. She noticed that the girl looked pale. Obviously someone else had enjoyed little sleep. Catherine confessed that the rain had kept her awake and that she had woken early with a bad headache. She did not get them very often now but, when she did,

44

they were bad. Had Mrs. Maxie any aspirin? She preferred the soluble kind but any would do. Mrs. Maxie reflected that the headache might be an excuse for a confidential chat on the Sally–Stephen situation but a longer look at the girl's heavy eyes decided her that the pain was genuine enough. Catherine was obviously in no state for planning anything. Mrs. Maxie invited her to help herself to the aspirin from the medicine cupboard and put out an extra cup of tea on the tray. Catherine was not the companion she would have chosen, but at least the girl seemed prepared to drink her tea in silence.

They were sitting together in front of the electric fire when Martha arrived, her bearing and tone demonstrating a nice compromise between indignation and anxiety.

'It's Sally, madam,' she said. 'She's overslept again I suppose. She didn't answer when I called her and when I tried the door, I found that she's bolted it. I can't get in. I'm sure I don't know what she's playing at, madam.' Mrs. Maxie replaced her cup in its saucer and noticed with clinical detachment and a kind of wonder that her hand was not shaking. The imminence of evil took hold of her and she had to pause for a second before she could trust her voice. But when the words came, neither Catherine nor Martha seemed aware of any change in her.

'Have you really knocked hard?' she inquired.

Martha hesitated. Mrs. Maxie knew what that meant. Martha had not chosen to knock very hard. It was suiting her purpose better to let Sally oversleep. Mrs. Maxie, after her broken night, found this pettiness too much to bear.

'You had better try again,' she said shortly. 'Sally had a busy day yesterday as we all did. People don't oversleep without reason.'

Catherine opened her mouth as if to make some comment, thought better of it, and bent her head over her tea. Within two minutes Martha was back and, this time, there was no doubt of it. Anxiety had conquered irritation and there was something very like panic in her voice.

'I can't make her hear me. The baby's awake. He's whimpering in there. I can't make Sally hear!'

Mrs. Maxie had no memory of getting to the door of Sally's room. She was so certain, beyond any possible doubt, that the room must be open that she beat and tugged ineffectually at the door for several seconds before her mind accepted the truth. The door was bolted on the inside. The noise of the knocking had thoroughly woken Jimmy and his early morning whimpering was now rising into a crescendo of wailing fear. Mrs. Maxie could hear the rattling of his cot bars, and could picture him, cocooned in his woollen sleeping-bag, pulling himself up to scream for his mother. She felt the cold sweat starting on her forehead. It was all she could do to prevent herself from beating in mad panic at the unyielding wood. Martha was moaning now and it was Catherine who laid a comforting and restraining hand on Mrs. Maxie's shoulder.

'Don't worry too much. I'll get your son.' 'Why doesn't she say "Stephen"?' thought Mrs. Maxie irrelevantly. 'Stephen is my son.' In a moment he was with them. The knocking must have aroused him for Catherine could not have fetched him so quickly. Stephen spoke calmly.

'We'll have to get in by the window. The ladder in the outhouse will do. I'll get Hearne.' He was gone and the little group of women waited in silence. The moments slowly passed.

'It's bound to take a little time,' said Catherine reassuringly. 'But they won't be long. I'm sure she's all right. She's probably still asleep.'

Deborah gave her a long look. 'With all this noise from Jimmy? My guess is that she won't be there. She's gone.'

'But why should she?' asked Catherine. 'And what about the locked door?'

'Knowing Sally, I presume that she wanted to do it the spectacular way and got out through the window. She seems to have a penchant for making scenes even when she can't be present to enjoy them. Here we are shivering with apprehension while Stephen and Felix lug ladders about, and the whole of the household is disorganized. Very satisfying to her imagination.'

'She wouldn't leave the baby,' said Catherine suddenly. 'No mother would.'

'This one apparently has,' replied Deborah dryly. But her mother noticed that she made no move to leave the party.

Jimmy's yells had now reached a sustained climax

which drowned any sound of the men's activities with the
ladder or their entrance through the window. The next
sound heard from the room was the quick scraping of the
lock. Felix stood in the doorway. At the sight of his face
Martha gave a scream, a high-pitched animal squeal of
terror. Mrs. Maxie felt rather than heard the thud of her
retreating footsteps, but no one followed her. The other
women pushed past Felix's restraining arm and moved
silently as if under some united compulsion to where Sally
lay. The window was open and the pillow of the bed was
blodged with rain. Over the pillow Sally's hair was spread
like a web of gold. Her eyes were closed but she was not
asleep. From the clenched corner of her mouth a thin
trickle of blood had dried like a black slash. On each side
of her neck was a bruise where the killer's hands had
choked the life from her.

CHAPTER FOUR

1

'NICE-LOOKING place, sir,' said Detective-Sergeant Martin as the police car drew up in front of Martingale. 'Bit of a change from our last job.' He spoke with satisfaction for he was a countryman by birth and inclination and was often heard to complain of the proclivity of murderers to commit their crimes in overcrowded cities and unsalubrious tenements. He sniffed the air appreciatively and blessed whatever reasons of policy or prudence had led the local chief constable to call in the Yard. It had been rumoured that the chief constable personally knew the people concerned and, what with that and the still unsolved business on the fringe of the county, had thought it advisable to hand over this spot of trouble without delay. That suited Detective-Sergeant Martin all right. Work was work wherever you did it, but a man was entitled to his preferences.

Detective Chief-Inspector Adam Dalgleish did not reply but swung himself out of the car and stood back for a moment to look at the house. It was a typical Elizabethan manor house, simple but strongly formalized in design. The large, two-storeyed bays with their mullioned and transomed windows stood symmetrically on each side of the square central porch. Above the dripstone was a heavy carved coat of arms. The roof sloped to a small open stone balustrade also carved with symbols in relief and the six great Tudor chimneys stood up boldly against a summer sky. To the west curved the wall of a room which Dalgleish guessed had been added at a later date – probably during the last century. The french windows were of plate glass and led into the garden. For a moment he saw a face at one of them, but then it turned away. Someone was watching for his arrival. To the west a grey stone wall ran from the corner of the house in a wide sweep towards the gates and lost itself behind the shrubs and the tall beeches. The trees came very close to the house on this side. Above the wall and half-concealed behind a mosaic of leaves he could just see the top of a ladder placed against an oriel window. That presumably was the dead girl's room. Her mistress could hardly have chosen one more suitably placed for an illicit entry. Two vehicles were parked behind the porch, a police car with a uniformed man sitting impassive at the wheel and a mortuary van. Its driver, stretched back in his seat and with his peaked cap tilted forward, took no notice of Dalgleish's arrival while his mate merely looked up perfunctorily before returning to his Sunday newspaper.

The local superintendent was waiting in the hall. They knew each other slightly as was to be expected with two men both eminent in the same job, but neither had ever wished for a closer acquaintanceship. It was not an easy moment. Manning was finding it necessary to explain exactly why his chief had thought it advisable to call in the Yard. Dalgleish replied suitably. Two reporters were sitting just inside the door with the air of dogs who have been promised a bone if they behave and who have resigned themselves to patience. The house was very quiet and smelt faintly of roses. After the torrid heat of the car the air struck so cold that Dalgleish gave an involuntary shiver.

'The family are together in the drawing-room,' said Manning. 'I've left a sergeant with them. Do you want to see them now?'

'No, I'll see the body first. The living will keep.'

Superintendent Manning led the way up the vast square staircase talking back at them as he went.

'I got a bit of ground covered before I knew they were calling in Central Office. They've probably given you the gist. Victim is the maid here. Unmarried mother aged twenty-two. Strangled. The body was discovered at about 7.15 a.m. this morning by the family. The girl's bedroom door was bolted. Exit, and probably entrance too, was via the window. You'll find evidence of that on the stack pipe and the wall. It looks as if he fell the last five feet or so. She was last seen alive at 10.30 p.m. last night carrying

49

her late-night drink up to bed. She never finished it. The mug's on the bedside table. I thought it was almost certainly an outside job at first. They had a fête here yesterday and anyone could have got into the grounds. Into the house, too, for that matter. But there are one or two odd features.'

'The drink, for example?' asked Dalgleish.

They had reached the landing now and were passing towards the west wing of the house. Manning looked at him curiously.

'Yes. The cocoa. It may have been doped. There's some stuff missing. Mr. Simon Maxie is an invalid. There's a bottle of sleeping dope missing from his medicine cupboard.'

'Any evidence of doping on the body?'

'The police surgeon's with her now. I doubt it though. Looked a straightforward strangling to me. The P.M. will probably have the answer.'

'She could have taken the stuff herself,' said Dalgleish. 'Is there any obvious motive?'

Manning paused.

'There could be. I haven't got any of the details but I've heard gossip.'

'Ah. Gossip.'

'A Miss Liddell came this morning to take away the girl's child. She was here to dinner last night. Quite a meal it must have been by her account. Apparently Stephen Maxie had proposed to Sally Jupp. You could call that a motive for the family, I suppose.'

'In the circumstances I think I could,' said Dalgleish.

The bedroom was white-walled and full of light. After the dimness of the hall and corridors bounded with oak linen-fold panelling, this room struck with the artificial brightness of a stage. The corpse was the most unreal of all, a second-rate actress trying unconvincingly to simulate death. Her eyes were almost closed, but her face held that look of faint surprise which he had often noticed on the faces of the dead. Two small and very white front teeth were clenched against the lower lip, giving a rabbit-look to a face which, in life, must, he felt, have been striking, perhaps even beautiful. An aureole of hair flamed over the pillow in incongruous defiance of death. It felt slightly damp to his hand. Almost he wondered that its brightness had not drained away with the life of her body. He stood very still looking down at her. He was never conscious of pity at moments like this and not even of anger, although that might come later and would have to be resisted. He liked to fix the sight of the murdered body firmly in his mind. This had been a habit since his first big case seven years ago when he had looked down at the battered corpse of a Soho prostitute in silent resolution and had thought, 'This is it. This is my job.'

The photographer had completed his work with the body before the police surgeon began his examination. He was now finishing with shots of the room and the window before packing up his equipment. The print man had likewise finished with Sally and, intent on his private world of whorls and composites, was moving with unobtrusive efficiency from door-knob to lock, from cocoa-beaker to chest of drawers, from bed to window-ledge before heaving himself out on the ladder to work on the stack-pipe and on the ladder itself. Dr. Feltman, the police surgeon, balding, rotund and self-consciously cheerful, as if under a perpetual compulsion to demonstrate his professional imperturbability in the face of death, was replacing his instruments in a black case. Dalgleish had met him before and knew him for a first-class doctor who had never learned to appreciate where his job ended and the detective's began. He waited until Dalgleish had turned away from the body before speaking.

'We're ready to take her away now if that's all right by you. It looks simple enough medically speaking. Manual strangulation by a right-handed person standing in front of her. She died quickly, possibly by vagal inhibition. I'll be able to tell you more after the P.M. There's no sign of sexual interference but that doesn't mean that sex wasn't the motive. I imagine there's nothing like finding a dead body on your hands to take away the urge. When you pull him in you'll get the same old story, "I put my hands round her neck to frighten her and she went limp". He got in by the window by the look of it. You might find fingerprints on that stack-pipe but I doubt whether the ground will be much help. It's a kind of courtyard underneath. No nice soft earth with a couple of handy sole

51

marks. Anyway, it rained pretty hard last night which doesn't help matters. Well, I'll go and get the stretcher party if your man here has finished. Nasty business for a Sunday morning.'

He went and Dalgleish inspected the room. It was large and sparsely furnished, but the overall impression it gave was one of sunlight and comfort. He thought that it had probably previously been the family day nursery. The old-fashioned fireplace on the north wall was surrounded by a heavy meshed fireguard behind which an electric fire had been installed. On each side of the fireplace were deep recesses fitted with bookcases and low cupboards. There were two windows. The smaller oriel window against which the ladder stood was on the west wall and looked over the courtyard to the old stables. The larger window ran almost the whole length of the south wall, giving a panoramic view of the lawns and gardens. Here the glass was old and set with occasional medallions. Only the top mullioned windows could be opened.

The cream-painted single bed was set at right-angles to the smaller window and had a chair on one side and a bedside table with a lamp on the other. The child's cot was in the opposite corner half-hidden by a screen. It was the kind of screen which Dalgleish remembered from his own childhood, composed of dozens of coloured pictures and postcards stuck in a pattern and glazed over. There were a rug before the fireplace and a low nursing chair. Against the wall were a plain wardrobe and a chest of drawers.

There was a curious anonymity about the room. It had the intimate fecund atmosphere of almost any nursery compounded of the faint smell of talcum powder, baby-soap and warmly-aired clothes. But the girl herself had impressed little of her personality on her surroundings. There was none of the feminine clutter which he had half expected. Her few personal belongings were carefully arranged but they were uncommunicative. Primarily it was just a child's nursery with a plain bed for his mother. The few books on the shelves were popular works on baby care. The half-dozen magazines were those devoted to the interests of mothers and housewives rather than to the more romanticized and varied concerns of young working-women. He picked one from the shelf and flicked through it. From its pages dropped an envelope bearing a Venezuelan stamp. It was addressed to:

> D. Pullen, Esq.,
> Rose Cottage, Nessingford-road,
> Little Chadfleet, Essex, England.

On the reverse were three dates scribbled in pencil – Wednesday 18th, Monday 23rd, Monday 30th.

Prowling from the bookshelf to the chest of drawers, Dalgleish pulled out each drawer and systematically turned over its contents with practised fingers. They were in perfect order. The top drawer held only baby clothes. Most of them were hand-knitted, all were well washed and cared for. The second was full of the girl's own underclothes, arranged in neat piles. It was the third and bottom drawer which held the surprise.

'What do you make of this?' he called to Martin.

The sergeant moved to his chief's side with a silent swiftness which was disconcerting in one of his build. He lifted one of the garments in his massive fist.

'Hand-made by the look of it, sir. Must have embroidered it herself, I suppose. There's almost a drawer full. It looks like a trousseau to me.'

'I think that's what it is all right. And not only clothes too. Table-cloths, hand-towels, cushion covers.' He turned them over as he spoke. 'It's rather a pathetic little dowry, Martin. Months of devoted work pressed away in lavender bags and tissue paper. Poor little devil. Do you suppose this was for the delight of Stephen Maxie? I can hardly picture these coy tray-cloths being used at Martingale.'

Martin picked one up and examined it appreciatively.

'She can't have had him in mind when she did this. He only proposed yesterday according to the Super and she must have been working on this for months. My mother used to do this kind of work. You buttonhole round the pattern and then cut out the middle bits. Richelieu or something they call it. Pretty effect it gives – if you like that sort of thing,' he added in deference to his Chief's obvious lack of enthusiasm. He ruminated over the embroidery in nostalgic approval before yielding it up for replacement in the drawer.

Dalgleish moved over to the oriel window. The wide window-ledge was about three feet high. It was scattered now with the bright glass fragments of a collection of miniature animals. A penguin lay wingless on its side and a brittle dachshund had snapped in two. One Siamese cat, startlingly blue of eye, was the sole survivor among the splintered holocaust.

The two largest and middle sections of the window opened outwards with a latch and the stack-pipe, skirting a similar window about six feet below, ran directly to the paved terrace beneath. It would hardly be a difficult descent for anyone reasonably agile. Even the climb up would be possible. He noticed again how safe from un-wanted observation such an entry or exit would be. To his right the great brick wall, half hidden by overhanging beech boughs, curved away towards the drive. Immedi-ately facing the window and about thirty yards away were the old stables with their attractive clock turret. From their open shelter the window could be watched, but from nowhere else. To the left only a small part of the lawn was visible. Someone seemed to have been messing about with it. There was a small patch ringed with cord where the grass had been hacked or cut. Even from the window Dalgleish could see the lifted sods and the rash of brown soil beneath. Superintendent Manning had come up behind him and answered his unspoken question.

'That's Doctor Epps's treasure hunt. He's had it in the same spot for the last twenty years. They had the church fête here yesterday. Most of the bunting's down – the vicar likes to get the place cleared up before Sunday – but it takes a day or two to erase all the evidence.'

Dalgleish remembered that the Super was almost a local man. 'Were you here?' he asked.

'Not this year. I've been on duty almost continuously for the last week. We've still got that killing on the county border to clear up. It won't be long now, but I've been pretty tied up with it. The wife and I used to come over here once a year for the fête but that was before the war. It was different then. I don't think we'd bother now. They still get a fair crowd though. Someone could have met the girl and found out from her where she slept. It's going to mean a lot of work checking on her movements during yesterday afternoon and evening.' His tone implied that he was glad the job was not his.

Dalgleish did not theorize in advance of his facts. But the facts he had garnered so far did not support this comfortable thesis of an unknown casual intruder. There had been no sign of attempted sexual assault, no evidence of theft. He had a very open mind on the question of that bolted door. Admittedly, the Maxie family had all been on the right side of it at 7 a.m. that morning, but they were presumably as capable as anyone else of climbing down stack-pipes or descending ladders.

The body had been taken away, a white-sheeted lumpy shape stiff on the stretcher, destined for the pathologist's knife and the analyst's bottle. Manning had left them to telephone his office. Dalgleish and Martin continued their patient inspection of the house. Next to Sally's room was an old-fashioned bathroom, the deep bath boxed round with mahogany and the whole of one wall covered with an immense airing cupboard, fitted with slatted shelves. The three remaining walls were papered in an elegant floral design faded with age and there was an old but still unworn fitted carpet on the floor. The room offered no possible hiding-place. From the landing outside a flight of drugget-covered stairs curved down to the panelled corridor which led on the one side to the kitchen quarters and on the other to the main hall. Just at the bottom of these stairs was the heavy south door. It was ajar, and Dalgleish and Martin passed out of the coolness of Martingale into the heavy heat of the day. Somewhere the bells of a church were ringing for Sunday matins. The sound came clearly and sweetly across the trees bringing to Martin a memory of boyhood's country Sundays and to Dalgleish a reminder that there was much to be done and little left of the morning.

'We'll have a look at that old stable block and the west wall beneath her window. After that I'm rather interested in the kitchen. And then we'll get on with the questioning. I've a feeling that the person we're after slept under this roof last night.'

In the drawing-room the Maxies with their two guests and Martha Bultitaft waited to be questioned, unobtrusively watched over by a detective-sergeant who had stationed himself in a small chair by the door and who sat in apparently solid indifference, seeming far more at his ease than the owners of the house. His charges had their various reasons for wondering how long they would be kept waiting, but no one liked to reveal anxiety by asking. They had been told that Detective Chief-Inspector Dalgleish from Scotland Yard had arrived and would be with them shortly. How shortly no one was prepared to ask. Felix and Deborah were still in their riding-clothes. The others had dressed hurriedly. All had eaten little and now they sat and waited. Since it would have seemed heartless to read, shocking to play the piano, unwise to talk about the murder and unnatural to talk about anything else, they sat in almost unbroken silence. Felix Hearne and Deborah were together on the sofa but sitting a little apart and occasionally he leaned across to whisper something in her ear. Stephen Maxie had stationed himself at one of the windows and stood with his back to the room. It was a stance which, as Felix Hearne had noticed cynically, enabled him to keep his face hidden and to demonstrate an inarticulate sorrow with the back of his bent head. At least four of the watchers would have liked very much to know whether the sorrow was genuine. Eleanor Maxie sat calmly in a chair apart. She was either numbed by grief or thinking deeply. Her face was very pale but the brief panic which had caught her at Sally's door was over now. Her daughter noticed that she at least had taken trouble in her dressing and was presenting an almost normal appearance to her family and guests. Martha Bultitaft also sat a little apart, ill at ease on the edge of her chair and darting occasional furious looks at the sergeant whom she obviously held responsible for her embarrassment at having to sit with the family and in the drawing-room, too, while there was work to be done. She who had been most upset and terrified at the morning's discovery now seemed to regard the whole thing as a personal insult, and she sat in sullen resentment. Catherine Bowers gave the greatest appearance of ease. She had taken a small notebook from her handbag and was writing in it at intervals as if refreshing her memory about the events of the morning. No one was deceived by this appearance of normality and efficiency, but they all envied her the opportunity of putting up so good a show. All of them sat in essential isolation and thought their own thoughts. Mrs. Maxie kept her eyes on the strong hands folded in her lap but her mind was on her son.

'He will get over it, the young always do. Thank God Simon will never know. It's going to be difficult to manage the nursing without Sally. One oughtn't to think about that I suppose. Poor child. There may be finger-prints on that lock. The police will have thought of that. Unless he wore gloves. We all know about gloves these days. I wonder how many people got through that window to her. I suppose I ought to have thought of it, but how could I? She had the child with her after all. What will they do with Jimmy? A mother murdered and a father he'll never know now. That was one secret she kept. One of many probably. One never knows people. What do I know about Felix? He could be dangerous. So could this chief inspector. Martha ought to be seeing to luncheon. That, is, if anyone wants luncheon. Where will the police feed? Presumably they'll only want to use our rooms today. Nurse will be here at twelve so I'll have to go to Simon then. I suppose I could go now if I asked. Deborah is on edge. We all are. If only we can keep our heads.'

Deborah thought, 'I ought to dislike her less now that she's dead, but I can't. She always did make trouble. She would enjoy watching us like this, sweating on the top line. Perhaps she can. I mustn't get morbid. I wish we could talk about it. We might have kept quiet about Stephen and Sally if Eppy and Miss Liddell hadn't been at dinner. And Catherine of course. There's always Catherine. She's going to enjoy this all right. Felix knows that Sally was doped. Well, if she was, it was in my drinking mug. Let them make what they like of that.'

Felix Hearne thought, 'They can't be much longer. The thing is not to lose my temper. These will be English policemen, extremely polite English policemen asking questions in strict compliance with judges' rules. Fear is the devil to hide. I can imagine Dalgleish's face if I decided to explain. Excuse me, Inspector, if I appear to be terrified of you. The reaction is purely automatic, a trick of the nervous system. I have a dislike of formal questioning, and even more of the carefully staged informal session. I had some experience of it in France. I have recovered completely from the effects, you understand, except for this one slight legacy. I tend to lose my temper. It is only pure bloody funk. I am sure you will understand, Herr Inspector. Your questions are so very reasonable. It is unfortunate that I mistrust reasonable questions. We mustn't get this thing out of proportion of course. This is a minor disability. A comparatively small part of one's life is spent in being questioned by the police. I got off lightly. They even left me some of my fingernails. I'm just trying to explain that I may find it difficult to give you the answers you want.'

Stephen turned round.

'What about a lawyer?' he asked suddenly. 'Oughtn't we to send for Jephson?'

His mother looked up from a silent contemplation of her folded hands. 'Matthew Jephson is motoring somewhere on the Continent. Lionel is in London. We could get him if you feel it to be necessary.'

Her voice held a note of interrogation. Deborah said impulsively, 'Oh, Mummy! *Not* Lionel Jephson. He's the world's most pompous bore. Let's wait until we're arrested before we encourage him to come beetling down. Besides, he's not a criminal lawyer. He only knows about trusts and affidavits and documents. This would shock his respectable soul to the core. He couldn't help.'

'What about you, Hearne?' asked Stephen.

'I'll cope unaided, thank you.'

'We should apologize for mixing you up in this,' said Stephen with stiff formality. 'It's unpleasant for you and may be inconvenient. I don't know when you'll get back to London.' Felix thought that this apology should more appropriately be made to Catherine Bowers. Stephen was apparently determined to ignore the girl. Did the arrogant young fool seriously believe that this death was merely a matter of unpleasantness and inconvenience? He looked across at Mrs. Maxie as he replied.

'I shall be very glad to stay – voluntarily or involuntarily – if I can be of use.'

Catherine was adding her eager assurances to the same effect when the silent sergeant, galvanized into life, sprang to attention in a single movement. The door opened and three plain-clothes policemen came in. Superintendent Manning they already knew. Briefly he introduced his companions as Detective Chief-Inspector Adam Dalgleish and Detective-Sergeant George Martin. Five pairs of eyes swung simultaneously to the taller stranger in fear, appraisal or frank curiosity.

Catherine Bowers thought, 'Tall, dark and handsome. Not what I expected. Quite an interesting face really.'

Stephen Maxie thought, 'Supercilious-looking devil. He's taken his time coming. I suppose the idea is to soften us up. Or else he's been snooping round the house. This is the end of privacy.'

Felix Hearne thought, 'Well, here it comes. Adam Dalgleish, I've heard of him. Ruthless, unorthodox, working always against time. I suppose he has his own private compulsions. At least they've thought us adversaries worthy of the best.'

Eleanor Maxie thought, 'Where have I seen that head before? Of course. That Dürer. In Munich was it? Portrait of an Unknown Man. Why does one always expect police officers to wear bowlers and raincoats?'

Through the exchange of introductions and courtesies Deborah Riscoe stared at him as if she saw him through a web of red-gold hair.

When he spoke it was in a curiously deep voice, relaxed and unemphatic.

'I understand from Superintendent Manning that the small business room next door has been placed at my disposal. I hope it won't be necessary to monopolize either it or you for a very long time. I should like to see you separately please and in this order.'

'See me in my study at nine, nine-five, nine-ten . . .' whispered Felix to Deborah. He was not sure whether he sought relief for himself or her, but there was no answering smile.

Dalgleish let his glance move briefly over the group. 'Mr. Stephen Maxie, Miss Bowers, Mrs. Maxie, Mrs.

Riscoe, Mr. Hearne and Mrs. Bultitaft. Will those who are waiting please stay here. If any of you need to leave this room there is a woman police officer and a constable outside in the hall who can go with you. This surveillance will be relaxed as soon as everyone has been interviewed. Would you come with me please, Mr. Maxie?'

3

Stephen Maxie took the initiative.

'I think I had better begin by letting you know that Miss Jupp and I were engaged to be married. I proposed to her yesterday evening. There's no secret about it. It can't have anything to do with her death and I might not have bothered to mention it except that she broke the news in front of the village's prize gossip, so you'd probably find out fairly soon.'

Dalgleish, who had already found out and was by no means convinced that the proposal was nothing to do with the murder, thanked Mr. Maxie gravely for his frankness and expressed formal condolences on the death of his fiancée. The boy looked up at him with a sudden direct glance.

'I don't feel I've any right to accept condolences. I can't even feel bereaved. I suppose I shall when the shock of this has worn off a little. We were only engaged yesterday and now she's dead. It still isn't believable.'

'Your mother was aware of this engagement?'

'Yes. All the family were except my father.'

'Did Mrs. Maxie approve?'

'Hadn't you better ask her that yourself?'

'Perhaps I had. What were your relations with Miss Jupp before yesterday evening, Dr. Maxie?'

'If you are asking whether we were lovers the answer is "no". I was sorry for her, I admired her and I was attracted by her. I have no idea what she thought about me.'

'Yet she accepted your offer of marriage?'

'Not specifically. She told my mother and her guests that I had proposed so I naturally assumed that she intended to accept me. Otherwise there would have been no point in breaking the news.'

Dalgleish could think of several reasons why the girl should have broken the news, but he was not prepared to discuss them. Instead he invited his witness to give his own account of recent events from the time that the missing Sommeil tablets were first brought into the house.

'So you think she was drugged, Inspector? I told the Superintendent about the tablets when he arrived. They were certainly in my father's medicine chest early this morning. Miss Bowers noticed them when she went to the cupboard for aspirin. They aren't there now. The only Sommeil in the cupboard now is in a sealed packet. The bottle has gone.'

'No doubt we shall find it, Dr. Maxie. The autopsy will discover whether or not Miss Jupp was drugged, and if so, how much of the stuff was taken. There is almost certainly something other than cocoa in that mug by the bed. She may, of course, have put the stuff in it herself.'

'If she didn't, Inspector, who did? The stuff might not even have been meant for Sally. That was my sister's drinking-mug by the bed. We each have our own and they are all different. If the Sommeil was meant for Sally it must have been put in the drink after she had taken it up to her room.'

'If the drinking-mugs are so distinctive it is curious that Miss Jupp should have taken the wrong one. That was an unlikely mistake surely?'

'It may not have been a mistake,' said Stephen shortly.

Dalgleish did not ask him to explain but listened in silence as his witness described the visit of Sally to St. Luke's on the previous Thursday, the events of the church fête, the sudden impulse which had led him to propose marriage and the finding of his fiancée's body. The account he gave was factual, concise and almost unemotional. When he came to describe the scene in Sally's bedroom his voice was almost clinically detached. Either he had greater control than was good for him or he had anticipated this interview and had schooled himself in advance against every betrayal of fear or remorse.

'I went with Felix Hearne to get the ladder. He was dressed but I was still in my dressing-gown. I shed one of my bedroom slippers on the way to the outhouses opposite Sally's window so he reached them first and gripped the ladder. It's always kept there. Hearne had dragged it out by the time I caught up with him and was calling out to know which way to carry it. I pointed towards Sally's window. We carried the ladder between us although it's quite light. One person could manage it, although I'm not sure about a woman. We put it against the wall and Hearne went up first while I steadied it. I followed him at once. The window was open but the curtains were drawn across. As you saw, the bed is at right angles to the window with the head towards it. There's a wide window-ledge where the oriel window juts out and Sally apparently kept a collection of small glass animals there. I noticed that they had been scattered and most were broken. Hearne went over to the door and pulled back the lock. I stood looking at Sally. The bed-clothes were pulled up as far as her chin but I could see at once that she was dead. By this time the rest of the family were around the bed, and when I turned back the clothes we could see what had happened. She was lying on her back — we didn't disturb her — and she looked quite peaceful. But you know what she looked like. You saw her.'

'I know what I saw,' said Dalgleish. 'I'm asking now what you saw.'

The boy looked at him curiously and then closed his eyes for a second before replying. He spoke in a flat expressionless voice as if repeating a lesson learnt by rote. 'There was a trickle of blood at the corner of her mouth. Her eyes were almost closed. There was a fairly distinct thumb impression under the right lower jaw over the cornu of the thyroid and a less clear indication of finger-marks on the left side of the neck lying along the thyroid cartilage. It was an obvious case of manual strangulation with the right hand and from the front. Considerable force must have been used, but I thought that death was possibly due to vagal inhibition and may have been very sudden. There were few of the classic signs of asphyxia. But no doubt you will get the facts from the autopsy.'

'I expect them to be in line with your own views. Did you form any idea of the time of death?'

'There was some rigor mortis in the jaw and neck

muscles. I don't know whether it had spread any farther. I'm describing the signs that I noticed almost subconsciously. You will hardly expect a full post-mortem account in the circumstances.'

Sergeant Martin, his head bent over his notebook, detected unerringly the first note of near hysteria and thought 'Poor devil. The old man can be pretty brutal. He's stood up to it all right so far, though. Too well for a man who has just discovered the body of his girl. If she was his girl.'

'I shall get the full post-mortem report in due course,' said Dalgleish equably. 'I was interested in your assessment of the time of death.'

'It was a fairly warm night despite the rain. I should say not less than five hours nor more than eight.'

'Did you kill Sally Jupp, Doctor?'

'No.'

'Do you know who did?'

'No.'

'What were your movements from the time that you finished dinner on Saturday night until Miss Bowers called you this morning with the news that Sally Jupp's door was bolted?'

'We had our coffee in the drawing-room. At about nine o'clock my mother suggested that we should start counting the money. It was in the safe here in the business room. I thought they might be happier without me and I was feeling restless, so I went out for a walk. I told my mother that I might be late and asked her to leave the south door open for me. I hadn't any particular idea in mind, but as soon as I'd left the house I felt I should like to see Sam Bocock. He lives alone in the cottage at the far end of the home meadow. I walked through the garden and over the meadow to his cottage and stayed there with him until pretty late. I can't exactly remember when I left, but he may be able to help. I think it was just after eleven. I walked back alone, entered the house through the south door, bolted it behind me and went to bed. That's all.'

'Did you go straight home?'

The almost imperceptible hesitation was not lost on Dalgleish.

'Yes.'

'That means you would have been back in the house by when?'

'It's only five minutes' walk from Bocock's cottage, but I didn't hurry. I suppose I was indoors and in bed by eleven-thirty.'

'It's a pity that you can't be precise about the time, Dr. Maxie. It's also, surely, surprising in view of the fact that you have a small clock on your bedside table with a luminous dial.'

'I may have. That doesn't mean that I always take a note of the times I sleep or get up.'

'You spent about two hours with Mr. Bocock. What did you talk about?'

'Horses and music mainly. He has a rather fine record-player. We listened to his new record – Klemperer conducting the *Eroica* to be precise.'

'Are you in the habit of visiting Mr. Bocock and spending the evening with him?'

'Habit? Bocock was groom to my grandfather. He's my friend. Don't you visit your friends when you feel like it, Inspector, or haven't you any?'

It was the first flash of temper. Dalgleish's face showed no emotion, not even satisfaction. He pushed a small square of paper across the table. On it were three minute splinters of glass.

'These were found in the outhouse opposite Miss Jupp's room, where you say that the ladder is normally kept. Do you know what they are?'

Stephen Maxie bent forward and studied this exhibit without apparent interest. 'They're splinters of glass obviously. I can't tell you any more about them. They could be part of a broken watch-glass I suppose.'

'Or part of one of the smashed glass animals from Miss Jupp's room.'

'Presumably.'

'I see you are wearing a small piece of plaster across your right knuckle. What's wrong?'

'I grazed myself slightly when I was coming home last night. I brushed my hand against the bark of a tree. At least, that's the most probable explanation. I can't remember it happening and only noticed the blood when I got to my room. I stuck this plaster on before I went to bed and I'd normally have taken it off by now. The graze wasn't really worth bothering about, but I have to look after my hands.'

'May I see, please?'

Maxie came forward and placed his hand, palm down, on the desk. Dalgleish noted that it did not tremble. He picked at the corner of the plaster and ripped it off. Together they inspected the whitened knuckle underneath. Maxie still showed no sign of anxiety, but scrutinized his hand with the air of a connoisseur condescendingly inspecting an exhibit which was hardly worthy of his attention. He picked up the discarded plaster, folded it neatly and flicked it accurately into the waste-paper basket.

'That looks like a cut to me,' said Dalgleish. 'Or it could, of course, be a scratch from a finger-nail.'

'It could, of course,' agreed his suspect easily. 'But if it were wouldn't you expect to find blood and skin under the nail which did the scratching? I'm sorry I can't remember how it happened.' He looked at it again and added. 'It certainly looks like a small cut but it's ridiculously small. In two days it won't be visible. Are you sure you don't want to photograph it?'

'No thank you,' said Dalgleish. 'We've had something rather more serious to photograph upstairs.'

It gave him considerable satisfaction to watch the effect of his words. While he was in charge of this case none of his suspects need think that they could retreat into private worlds of detachment or cynicism from the horror of what had lain on the bed upstairs. He waited for a moment and then continued remorselessly.

'I want to be perfectly clear about this south door. It leads directly to the flight of stairs which go up to the old nursery. To that extent Miss Jupp slept in a part of the house which can be said to have its own entrance. Almost a self-contained flat in effect. Once the kitchen quarters were closed for the night she could let a visitor in through that door with little risk of discovery. If the door were left unbolted a visitor could gain entrance to her door with reasonable ease. Now you say that the south door was left unbolted for you from nine o'clock when you had finished dinner until shortly after eleven p.m. when you returned from Mr. Bocock's cottage. During that time is it true to say that anyone could have gained access to the house through the south door?'

'Yes. I suppose so.'

'Surely you know definitely whether they could or not, Mr. Maxie?'

'Yes, they could. As you probably saw, the door has two heavy inside bolts and a mortice lock. We haven't used the lock for years. There are keys somewhere, I suppose. My mother might know. We normally keep the door closed during the day and bolt it at night. In the winter it is usually kept bolted all the time and is hardly used. There is another door into the kitchen quarters. We're rather slack about locking up, but we've never had any trouble here. Even if we did lock the doors carefully the house wouldn't be burglar-proof. Anyone could get in through the french windows in the drawing-room. We do lock them, but the glass could easily be broken. It has never seemed worth while worrying too much about security.'

'And, in addition to this ever-open door, there was a convenient ladder in the old stable-block?'

Stephen Maxie gave a slight shrug.

'It has to be kept somewhere. We don't lock up the ladders just in case someone gets the idea of using them to get through the windows.'

'We have no evidence yet that anyone did. I am still interested in that door. Would you be prepared to swear that it was unbolted when you returned from Mr. Bocock's cottage?'

'Of course. Otherwise I couldn't have got in.'

Dalgleish said quickly, 'You realize the importance of determining at what time you finally bolted that door?'

'Of course.'

'I'm going to ask you once more what time you bolted it and I advise you to think very carefully before you reply.'

Stephen Maxie looked him straight in the eye and said almost casually.'

'It was thirty-three minutes past twelve by my watch. I wasn't able to get to sleep and at twelve-thirty I suddenly remembered that I hadn't locked up. So I got out of bed and did so. I didn't see anyone or hear anything and I went straight back to my room. It was no doubt very careless of me, but if there's a law against forgetting to lock up I should like to hear of it.'

'So that at twelve thirty-three you bolted the south door?'

'Yes,' replied Stephen Maxie easily. 'At thirty-three minutes past midnight.'

4

In Catherine Bowers Dalgleish had a witness after every policeman's heart, composed, painstaking and confident. She had walked in with great self-possession, showing no signs of either nervousness or grief. Dalgleish did not like her. He knew that he was prone to these personal antipathies and he had long ago learned both to conceal and evaluate them. But he was right in supposing her to be an accurate observer. She had been quick to watch people's reactions as she had been to note the sequence of events. It was from Catherine Bowers that Dalgleish learned how shocked the Maxies had been at Sally's announcement, how triumphantly the girl had laughed out her news and what an unusual effect her remarks to Miss Liddell had produced on that lady. Miss Bowers was perfectly prepared, too, to discuss her own feelings.

'Naturally it was a terrible shock when Sally gave us her news, but I can quite see how it happened. No one is kinder than Dr. Maxie. He has too much social conscience as I am always telling him and the girl just took advantage of it. I know he couldn't have loved her really. He never mentioned it to me and he would have told me before anyone. If they had really loved each other he could have relied on me to understand and release him.'

'Do you mean that there was an engagement between you?'

Dalgleish had difficulty in keeping the surprise out of his voice. It needed only one more fiancée to make the case fantastic.

'Not exactly an engagement, Inspector. No ring or anything like that. But we have been close friends for so

67

long now that it was rather taken for granted . . . I suppose you might say we had an understanding. But there were no definite plans. Dr. Maxie has a long way to go before he can think of marriage. And there is his father's illness to consider.'

'So that you were not, in fact, engaged to be married to him?'

Faced with this uncompromising question Catherine admitted as much, but with a little self-satisfied smile which conveyed that it could only be a matter of time.

'When you arrived at Martingale for this week-end, did anything strike you as unusual?'

'Well, I was rather late on Friday evening. I didn't arrive until just before dinner. Dr. Maxie didn't arrive until late that night and Mr. Hearne only came on Saturday morning, so there were only Mrs. Maxie, Deborah and me at dinner. I thought they seemed worried. I don't like having to say it, but I'm afraid Sally Jupp was a scheming little girl. She waited on us and I didn't like her attitude at all.' Dalgleish questioned her further but the 'attitude' as far as he could judge consisted of nothing more than a slight toss of the head when Deborah had spoken to her and a neglect to call Mrs. Maxie 'Madam'. But he did not discount Catherine's evidence as valueless. It was likely that neither Mrs. Maxie nor her daughter had been entirely oblivious to the danger in their midst.

He changed his tack and took her carefully over the events of Sunday morning. She described how she had woken with a headache after a poor night and had gone in search of aspirin. Mrs. Maxie had invited her to help herself. It was then that she had noticed the little bottle of Sommeil. At first she had mistaken the tablets for aspirin but had quickly realized that they were too small and were the wrong colour. Apart from that, the bottle was labelled. She had not noticed how many Sommeil tablets were in the bottle but she was absolutely certain that the bottle was in the drug cupboard at seven o'clock hat morning and equally certain that it was no longer there when she and Stephen Maxie had looked for it after the finding of Sally Jupp's body. The only Sommeil in the cupboard then had been an unopened and sealed packet.

Dalgleish asked her to describe the finding of the body

and was surprised at the vivid picture which she was able to give.

'When Martha came to tell Mrs. Maxie that Sally hadn't got up we thought at first that she'd just overslept again. Then Martha came back to say that her door was locked and Jimmy was crying so we went to see what was wrong. There's no doubt that the door was bolted. As you know, Dr. Maxie and Mr. Hearne got in through the window and I heard one of them drawing back the bolt. I think it must have been Mr. Hearne because he opened the door. Stephen was standing near the bed looking at Sally. Mr. Hearne said, "I'm afraid she's dead." Someone screamed. It was Martha, I think, but I didn't look round to see. I said, "She can't be! She was all right last night!" We had moved over to the bed then and Stephen had drawn the sheet down from her face. Before that it had been up to her chin and folded quite neatly. I thought that it looked as if someone had tucked her up comfortably for the night. As soon as we saw the marks on her neck we knew what had happened. Mrs. Maxie closed her eyes for a moment. I thought that she was going to faint so I went over to her. But she managed to keep on her feet and stood at the bottom of the bed gripping the rail. She was shaking violently, so much that the whole bed was shaking. It is only a light single bed as you will have seen, and the shaking made the body bounce very gently up and down. Stephen said very fondly, "Cover her face", but Mr. Hearne reminded him that we had better not touch anything more until the police came. Mr. Hearne was the calmest of us all, I thought, but I suppose that he is used to violent death. He looked more interested than shocked. He bent over Sally and lifted one of her eyelids. Stephen said roughly, "I shouldn't worry, Hearne. She's dead all right." Mr. Hearne replied, "It isn't that. I'm wondering why she didn't struggle." Then he dipped his little finger into the mug of cocoa on the bedside table. It was just over half full and a skin had formed on the top. The skin stuck to his finger and he scraped it off against the side of the mug before putting the finger in his mouth. We were all looking at him as if he were going to demonstrate something wonderful to us. I thought that Mrs. Maxie looked – well, rather hopeful.

Rather like a child at a party. Stephen said, "Well, what is it?" Mr. Hearne shrugged his shoulders and said, "That's for the analyst to say. I think she's been doped." Just then Deborah gave a kind of gasp and fumbled towards the door. She was deathly white and was obviously going to be sick. I tried to get to her, but Mr. Hearne said quite sharply, "All right. Leave her to me." He guided her out of the room, and I think they went into the maid's bathroom next door. I wasn't surprised. I would have expected Deborah to break down like that. That left Mrs. Maxie and Stephen in the room with me. I suggested that Mrs. Maxie should find a key so that the room could be locked and she replied, "Of course. I believe that is usual. And oughtn't we to telephone the police? The extension in the dressing-room would be best." I suppose she meant that it would be most private. I remember thinking, "If we 'phone from the dressing-room the maids won't overhear", forgetting that "the maids" meant Sally and that Sally wouldn't be overhearing anything again.'

'Do you mean that Miss Jupp was in the habit of listening to other people's conversation?' interrupted the inspector.

'I certainly always had that impression, Inspector. But I always thought she was sly. She never seemed the least grateful for all that the family had done for her. She hated Mrs. Riscoe, of course. Anyone could see that. I expect you've been told about the affair of the copied dress?'

Dalgleish expressed himself interested in this intriguing title and was rewarded with a graphic description of the incident and the reaction it had provoked.

'So you can see the type of girl she was. Mrs. Riscoe pretended to take it calmly, but I could see what she was feeling. She could have killed Sally.' Catherine Bowers pulled her skirt down over her knees with complacent mock modesty. She was either a very good actress or she was unconscious of her solecism. Dalgleish continued the questioning with a feeling that he might be facing a more complex personality than he had at first recognized.

'Will you tell me please what happened when Mrs. Maxie, her son and you reached the dressing-room?'

'I was just coming to that, Inspector. I had picked up

Jimmy from his cot and was still holding him in my arms. It seemed terrible to me that he should have been alone in that room with his dead mother. When we all burst in he stopped crying and I don't think any of us thought about him for a time. Then suddenly I noticed him. He had pulled himself up by the bars of his cot and was balancing there with his wet nappy hanging around his ankles and such an interested look on his face. Of course, he is too young to understand, thank God, and I expect he just wondered what we were all doing round his mother's bed. He had become perfectly quiet and he came to me quite willingly. I carried him with me into the dressing-room. When we got there Dr. Maxie went straight to the medicine cupboard. He said, "It's gone!" I asked him what he meant and he told me about the missing Sommeil. That was the first time I heard about it. I was able to tell him that the bottle had been there when I went to the cupboard for aspirin that morning. While we were talking Mrs. Maxie had gone through to her husband's room. She was only there for a minute and when she got back she said, "He's all right. He's sleeping. Have you got the police yet?" Stephen went across to the telephone and I said that I would take Jimmy with me while I dressed and then give him his breakfast. No one replied so I went to the door. Just before I went out I turned round. Stephen had his hand on the receiver and suddenly his mother placed her hand over his and I heard her say, "Wait. There's one thing I must know." Stephen replied, "You don't have to ask. I know nothing about it. I swear that." Mrs. Maxie gave a little sigh and put her hand up to her eyes. Then Stephen picked up the receiver and I left the room.'

She paused and looked up at Dalgleish as if expecting or inviting his comment. 'Thank you,' he said gravely, 'Please go on.'

'There isn't really much more to tell you, Inspector. I took Jimmy to my room, collecting a clean nappy from the small bathroom on my way. Mrs. Riscoe and Mr. Hearne were still there. She had been sick and he was helping to bathe her face. They didn't seem very pleased to see me. I said, "When you feel better I daresay your mother would like some attention. I'm looking after

71

Jimmy." Neither of them replied. I found the nappies in the airing cupboard and went to my room and changed Jimmy. Then I let him play on my bed while I dressed. That only took about ten minutes. I took him to the kitchen and gave him a lightly boiled egg with bread and butter fingers and some warm milk. He was perfectly good the whole time. Martha was in the kitchen getting breakfast but we didn't speak. I was surprised to find Mr. Hearne there, too. He was making coffee. I suppose Mrs. Riscoe was with her mother. Mr. Hearne didn't seem inclined to talk either. I suppose he was annoyed with me for saying what I did to Mrs. Riscoe. She can do no wrong in his eyes as you've probably guessed. Well, as they didn't seem inclined to discuss what should be done next I decided to take matters into my own hands and I went into the hall with Jimmy and telephoned Miss Liddell. I told her what had happened and asked her to take back the baby until things had been sorted out. She came round by taxi within about fifteen minutes and, by then, Dr. Epps and the police had arrived. The rest you know.'

'That has been a very clear and useful account, Miss Bowers. You have the advantage of being a trained observer, but not all trained observers can present their facts in logical sequence. I won't keep you very much longer. I just want to go back to the earlier part of the night. So far you have described very clearly for me the events of yesterday evening and this morning. What I want to establish now is the sequence of events from ten p.m. onwards. At that time I believe you were still in the business room with Mrs. Maxie, Dr. Epps and Miss Liddell. Could you please go on from there.'

For the first time Dalgleish discerned a trace of hesitation in his suspect's response. Until now she had responded to his questioning with a ready fluency which had impressed him as being too spontaneous for guile. He could believe that, so far, Catherine Bowers had not found the interview unpleasant. It was difficult to reconcile such uninhibited outpourings with a guilty conscience. Now, however, he sensed the sudden withdrawal of confidence, the slight tensing to meet an unwelcome change of emphasis. She confirmed that Miss Liddell and Dr. Epps had left the business room to go home at about

72

ten-thirty. Mrs. Maxie had seen them off and had then returned to Catherine. Together they had tidied the papers and locked the money in the safe. Mrs. Maxie had not mentioned seeing Sally. Neither of them had discussed her. After locking away the money they had gone to the kitchen. Martha had retired for the night, but had left a saucepan of milk on the top of the stove and a silver tray of beakers on the kitchen table. Catherine remembered noting that Mrs. Riscoe's Wedgwood beaker wasn't there and thought it strange that Mr. Hearne and Mrs. Riscoe could have come in from the garden without anyone knowing. It never occurred to her that Sally might have taken the beaker although, of course, one could see that it was just the sort of thing she might do. Dr. Maxie's mug had been there, together with a glass one in a holder which belonged to Mrs. Maxie and two large cups with saucers which had been put out for the guests. There was a bowl of sugar on the table and tins of two milk drinks. There was no cocoa. Mrs. Maxie and Catherine had collected their drinks and taken them up to Mr. Maxie's dressing-room where his wife was to spend the night. Catherine had helped her to make the invalid's bed and had then stopped to drink her Ovaltine before the dressing-room fire. She had offered to sit up with Mrs. Maxie for a time but the offer had not been accepted. After about half an hour Catherine had left to go to her own room. She was sleeping on the opposite side of the house from Sally. She had seen no one on the way to her room. After undressing she had visited the bathroom in her dressing-gown and had been back in her room by about a quarter past eleven. As she was closing the door she thought she heard Mrs. Riscoe and Mr. Hearne coming up the stairs but she couldn't be sure. She had seen or heard nothing of Sally up to that time. Here Catherine paused and Dalgleish waited patiently, but with a quickening of interest. In the corner Sergeant Martin turned over a page of his notebook in practised silence and cast a quick sidelong glance at his chief. Unless he was much mistaken the old man's thumbs were pricking now. 'Yes, Miss Bowers,' prompted Dalgleish inexorably. His witness went bravely on. 'I'm afraid this part you may find rather strange but it all seemed perfectly natural at the time. As

73

you can understand the scene before dinner had been a great shock to me. I couldn't believe that Stephen and this girl were engaged. It wasn't he who had broken the news after all, and I don't think for one moment that he had really proposed to her. Dinner had been a terrible meal as you can imagine and, afterwards, everyone had gone on behaving as if nothing had happened. Of course, the Maxies never do show their feelings but Mrs. Riscoe went off with Mr. Hearne and I've no doubt they had a good talk about it and what could be done. But no one said anything to me although, in a sense, I was the one who was most concerned. I thought that Mrs. Maxie might have discussed it with me after the other two guests had left, but I could see that she didn't mean to. When I got to my room I realized that if I didn't do something no one would. I couldn't bear to lie there all night without knowing the worst. I felt I just had to find out the truth. The natural thing seemed to be to ask Sally. I thought that if she and I could only have a private talk together I might be able to get it all straightened out. I knew that it was late but it seemed the only chance. I had been lying there in the dark for some time but, when I had made up my mind, I put on the bedside lamp and looked at my watch. It said three minutes to midnight. That didn't seem so very late in the mood I was in. I put on my dressing-gown and took my pocket torch with me and went to Sally's room. Her door was locked but I could see that the light was on because it was shining through the keyhole. I knocked on the door and called her softly. The door is very strong as you know, but she must have heard me because the next thing I heard was the sound of the bolt being shot home and the light from the keyhole was suddenly obscured as she stood in front of it. I knocked and called once more but it was obvious that she wasn't going to let me in, so I turned and went back to my room. On the way there I suddenly thought I had to see Stephen. I couldn't face going back to bed in the same uncertainty. I thought that he might be wanting to confide in me. So I turned back from my own bedroom door and went to his. The light wasn't on so I knocked gently and went in. I felt that if only I could see him everything would be all right.'

'And was it?' asked Dalgleish.

This time the air of cheerful confidence had gone. There could be no mistaking the sudden pain in those unattractive eyes.

'He wasn't there, Inspector. The bed was turned down ready for the night but he wasn't there.' She made a sudden effort to return to her former manner and gave him a smile which was almost pathetic in its artificiality. 'Of course, I know now that Stephen had been to see Bocock, but it was very disappointing at the time.'

'It must have been,' agreed Dalgleish gravely.

5

Mrs. Maxie seated herself quietly and composedly, offered him whatever facilities he needed and only hoped that the investigation could be carried out without disturbing her husband who was gravely ill and incapable of realizing what had happened. Watching her across the desk Dalgleish could see what her daughter might become in thirty years' time. Her strong, capable, jewelled hands lay inertly in her lap. Even at that distance he could see how alike they were to the hands of her son. With greater interest he noticed that the nails, like the nails on the surgeon's fingers, were cut very short. He could detect no sign of nervousness. She seemed rather to personify the peaceful acceptance of an inevitable trial. It was not, he felt, that she had schooled herself to endurance. Here was a true serenity based on some kind of central stability which would take more than a murder investigation to disturb. She answered his questions with a deliberate thoughtfulness. It was as if she was setting her own value on every word. But there was nothing new that she could tell. She corroborated the evidence of Catherine Bowers about the discovery of the body and her account of the previous day agreed with the accounts already given. After the departure of Miss Liddell and Dr. Epps at about half past ten, she had locked up the house with the exception of the drawing-room window and the back door. Miss Bowers had been with her. Together they had collected their mugs of milk from the kitchen – only her

75

son's then remained on the tray — and together they had gone up to bed. She had spent the night half sleeping and half watching her husband. She had heard and seen nothing unusual. No one had come near her until Miss Bowers had arrived early and had asked her for aspirin. She had known nothing of the tablets said to have been discovered in her husband's bed and found the story very difficult to believe. In her view it was impossible for him to have hidden anything in his mattress without Mrs. Bultitaft finding it. Her son had told her nothing of the incident, but had mentioned that he had substituted a medicine for the pills. She had not been surprised at this. She had thought that he was trying some new preparation from the hospital and was confident that he would have prescribed nothing without the approval of Dr. Epps.

Not until the patient probing questions on her son's engagement was her composure shaken. Even then it was irritation rather than fear which gave an edge to her voice. Dalgleish sensed that the smooth apologies with which he usually prefaced embarrassing questions would be out of place here, would be resented more than the questions themselves. He asked bluntly :

'What was your attitude, madam, to this engagement between Miss Jupp and your son?'

'It hardly lasted long enough to be dignified with that name surely. And I'm surprised that you bother to ask, Inspector. You must know that I would disapprove strongly.'

'Well, that was frank enough,' thought Dalgleish. 'But what else could she say? We would scarcely believe that she liked it.'

'Even though her affection for your son could have been genuine?'

'I am paying her the compliment of assuming that it was. What difference does that make? I would still have disapproved. They had nothing in common. He would have had to support another man's child. It would have hindered his career and they would have disliked each other within a year. These King Cophetua marriages seldom work out. How can they? No girl of spirit likes to think she's been condescended to and Sally had plenty of spirit even if she chose not to show it. Furthermore, I fail

76

to see what they would have married on. Stephen has very little money of his own. Of course I disapproved of this so-called engagement. Would you wish for such a marriage for your son?'

For one unbelievable second Dalgleish thought that she knew. It was a commonplace, almost banal argument which any mother faced with her circumstances might casually have used. She could not possibly have realized its force. He wondered what she would say if he replied, 'I have no son. My only child and his mother died three hours after he was born. I have no son to marry anyone – suitable or unsuitable.' He could imagine her frown of well-bred distaste that he should embarrass her at such a time with a private grief at once so old, so intimate, so unrelated to the matter at hand. He replied briefly :

'No. I should not wish it either. I'm sorry to have taken up so much of your time with what must seem no one's business but your own. But you must see its importance.'

'Naturally. From your point of view it provides a motive for several people, myself particularly. But one does not kill to avoid social inconvenience. I admit I intended to do all I could to stop them marrying. I was going to have a talk with Stephen next day. I've no doubt we should have been able to do something for Sally without the necessity of welcoming her into the family. There must be a limit to what these people expect.'

The sudden bitterness of her last sentence roused even Sergeant Martin from the routine automatism of his note-taking. But if Mrs. Maxie realized that she had said too much she did not aggravate her error by saying more. Watching her, Dalgleish thought how like a picture she was, an advertisement in water-colour for toilet water or soap. Even the low bowl of flowers on the desk between them emphasized her serene gentility as if placed there by the cunning hand of a commercial photographer. 'Picture of an English lady at home,' he thought, and wondered what the Chief Superintendent would make of her and, if it ever came to that, what a jury would make of her. Even his mind, accustomed to finding wickedness in strange as well as high places, could not easily reconcile Mrs. Maxie with murder. But her last words had been revealing.

77

He decided to leave the marriage question at present and concentrate on other aspects of the investigation. Again he went over the account of the preparation of the nightly hot drinks. There could be no confusion about the ownership of the different mugs. The Wedgwood blue one found at Sally's side belonged to Deborah Riscoe. The milk for the drinks was placed on top of the stove. It was a solid-fuel stove with heavy covers on each of the hot-plates. The saucepan of milk was left on top of one of these covers where there could be no danger of its boiling over. Any of the family wanting to boil milk would transfer the saucepan to the hot-plate and replace it afterwards on top of the cover. Only the family's mugs and cups for their guests were placed on the tray. She could not say what Sally or Mrs Bultitaft usually drank at night but, certainly, none of the family drank cocoa. They were not fond of chocolate.

'It comes to this, doesn't it,' said Dalgleish. 'If, as I am now assuming, the post-mortem shows that Miss Jupp was drugged and the analysis of the cocoa shows that the drug was in her last night drink, then we are faced with two possibilities. She could have taken the drug herself, perhaps for no worse reason than to get a good sleep after the excitement of the day. Or someone else drugged her for a reason which we must discover but which is not so difficult to guess. Miss Jupp, as far as is known, was a healthy young woman. If this crime was premeditated her murderer must have considered how he – or she – could get into that room and kill the girl with the least possible disturbance. To drug her is an obvious answer. That supposes that the murderer is familiar with the evening drink routine at Martingale and knew where the drugs were kept. I suppose a member of your household or a guest is familiar with your household routine?'

'Surely then he would know that the Wedgwood beaker belonged to my daughter. Are you satisfied, Inspector, that the drug was intended for Sally?'

'Not entirely. But I am satisfied that the killer did not mistake Miss Jupp's neck for Mrs. Riscoe's. Let us assume for the present that the drug was intended for Miss Jupp. It could have been put into the saucepan of milk, the Wedgwood beaker itself either before or after the drink

78

was made, into the tin of cocoa, or into the sugar. You and Miss Bowers made your drinks from the milk in the same saucepan and sugared them from the bowl on the table without ill effects. I don't think that the drug was put in the empty beaker. It is brownish in colour and would be easily seen against the blue china. That leaves us with two possibilities. Either it was crumbled into the dry cocoa or it was dissolved in the hot drink some time after Miss Jupp made it but before she drank it.'

'I don't think the latter is possible, Inspector. Mrs. Bultitaft always puts on the hot milk at ten. At about twenty-five minutes past we saw Sally carrying her mug up to her room.'

'Who do you mean by "we", Mrs. Maxie?'

'Dr. Epps, Miss Liddell and myself saw her. I'd been upstairs with Miss Liddell to fetch her coat. When we came back into the hall Dr. Epps joined us from the business room. As we stood there together Sally came from the kitchen end of the house and went up the main staircase carrying the blue Wedgwood beaker on its saucer. She was wearing pyjamas and a dressing-gown. We all three saw her but no one spoke. Miss Liddell and Dr. Epps left at once.'

'Was it usual for Miss Jupp to use that staircase?'

'No. The back one leads more directly from the kitchen to her room. I think she was trying to make some kind of gesture.'

'Although she couldn't have known that she would meet anyone in the hall?'

'No. I don't see how she could have known that.'

'You say that you noticed that Miss Jupp was carrying Mrs. Riscoe's beaker. Did you mention this to either of your guests or remonstrate to Miss Jupp about it?'

Mrs. Maxie smiled faintly. For the second time the delicate claw was unsheathed.

'What old-fashioned ideas you have, Inspector! Did you expect me to tear it from her grasp to the embarrassment of my guests and the satisfaction of Sally herself? What an exciting and exhausting world yours must be.'

Dalgleish pursued his question undeterred by this gentle irony. But he was interested to know that his witness could be provoked.

'What happened after Miss Liddell and Dr. Epps left?'

'I rejoined Miss Bowers in the business room where we tidied up the papers and locked away the bags of money in the safe. We then went to the kitchen and made our drinks. I had hot milk and Miss Bowers made Ovaltine. She likes it very sweet and added sugar from the bowl set ready. We carried our drinks to the dressing-room next to my husband's bedroom where I spend the nights when I am on duty nursing him. Miss Bowers helped me to remake my husband's bed. I suppose we spent about twenty minutes together. Then she said "good night" and left.'

'Having had her Ovaltine?'

'Yes. It was too hot to drink at once but she sat down and finished it before she left me.'

'Did she go to the drug cupboard while she was with you?'

'No. Neither of us did. My son had given his father something earlier to make him sleep and he appeared to be dozing. There was nothing to do for him except make his bed as comfortable as possible. I was glad of Miss Bowers's help. She is a trained nurse and, together, we were able to tidy the bed without disturbing him.'

'What were Miss Bowers's relations with Dr. Maxie?'

'As far as I know Miss Bowers is a friend of both my children. That is the kind of question which it would be better to ask them and her.'

'She and your son are not engaged to be married as far as you know?'

'I know nothing about their personal affairs. I should have thought it unlikely.'

'Thank you,' said Dalgleish. 'I will see Mrs. Riscoe now if you will be good enough to send her in.'

He rose to open the door for Mrs. Maxie but she did not move. She said, 'I still believe that Sally took that drug herself. There's no reasonable alternative. But if someone else did administer it then I agree with you that it must have been put into the dry cocoa. Forgive me — but wouldn't you be able to tell that from an examination of the tin and its contents?'

'We might have been,' replied Dalgleish gravely. 'But the empty tin was found in the dustbin. It had been rinsed out. The inner paper lining isn't there. It was probably burnt in the kitchen stove. Someone was making assurance doubly sure.'

'A very cool lady, sir,' said Sergeant Martin when Mrs. Maxie had left them. He added with unaccustomed humour, 'She sat there like a Liberal candidate waiting for the recount.'

'Yes,' agreed Dalgleish dryly. 'But with every confidence in her Party organization. Well, let's hear what the rest of them have to tell us.'

6

It was a very different room from the last time, thought Felix, but that room, too, had been quiet and peaceful. There had been pictures and a heavy mahogany desk not unlike the one Dalgleish was sitting at now. There had been flowers, too, a small posy arranged in a bowl hardly larger than a teacup. Everything about the room had been homely and comfortable, even the man behind the desk with his plump white hands, his smiling eyes behind the thick spectacles. The room had retained that look. It was surprising how many procedures there were for the extracting of truth which did not shed blood, were calculatedly unmessy, did not require very much in the way of apparatus. He wrenched memory back and made himself look at the figure at the desk. The folded hands were leaner, the eyes dark and less kind. There was only one other person in the room and he, too, was an English policeman. This was Martingale. This was England.

So far it had not gone too badly. Deborah had been absent for half an hour. When she returned she walked to her seat without looking at him and he, just as silently, got up and followed the uniformed policeman into the business room. He was glad that he had resisted the desire to have a drink before his questioning. and that he had refused Dalgleish's proffered cigarette. That was an old one! They couldn't catch him that way! He wasn't going to make them a present of his nervousness. If only he could keep his temper all would be well.

The patient man behind the desk looked at his notes.

'Thank you. That's clear so far. Now may we please go back a little? After coffee you went with Mrs. Riscoe to help wash up the dinner things. At about nine-thirty you both returned to this room where Mrs. Maxie, Miss Liddell, Miss Bowers and Dr. Epps were counting the money taken at the fête. You told them that you and Mrs. Riscoe were going out and you said "good night" to Miss Liddell and Dr. Epps, who would probably have left Martingale by the time you returned. Mrs. Maxie said that she would leave one of the french windows in the drawing-room open for you and asked you to lock it when you had come in. This arrangement was heard by everyone who was in the room at the time?'

'As far as I know it was. No one commented on it and, as they were busy counting money, I doubt whether they took it in.'

'I find it surprising that the drawing-room window was left unlatched for you when the back door was also open. Isn't that a Stubbs on the wall behind you? This house has several very fine things which are easily portable.'

Felix did not turn his head.

'The cultured cop! I thought they were peculiar to detective novels. Congratulations! But the Maxies don't advertise their possessions. There's no danger from the village. People have been wandering in and out of this house pretty freely for the last three hundred years. The locking-up here is rather haphazard except for the front door. That is ritually bolted and barred every night by Stephen Maxie or his sister almost as if it had some esoteric significance. Apart from that, they aren't thorough. In that, as in other matters, they appear to rely on our wonderful police.'

'Right! You went out into the garden with Mrs. Riscoe at about nine-thirty p.m. and walked there together. What did you talk about, Mr. Hearne?'

'I asked Mrs. Riscoe to marry me. I am going out to our Canadian house in two months' time and I thought it might be pleasant to combine business with a honeymoon.'

'And Mrs. Riscoe accepted?'

'It's charming of you to be interested, Inspector, but I'm afraid I must disappoint you. Inexplicable as it must seem to you, Mrs. Riscoe was not enthusiastic.'

The memory flooded back in a wave of emotion. Darkness, the cloying scent of roses, the hard urgent kisses which were the expression of some compelling need in her but not, he felt, of passion. And afterwards the sick weariness in her voice. 'Marriage, Felix? Hasn't there been enough talk of marriage in this family? God, how I wish she were dead!' He knew then that he had been betrayed into speaking too soon. The time and the place had both been wrong. Had the words been wrong too? What exactly was it that she wanted? Dalgleish's voice recalled him to the present.

'How long did you stay in the garden, sir?'

'It would be gallant to pretend that time ceased to exist. In the interest of your investigation, however, I will admit that we came in through the drawing-room window at ten-forty-five p.m. The chimney clock on the mantelpiece struck the three-quarters as I closed and bolted the window.'

'That clock is kept five minutes fast, sir. Would you go on please.'

'Then we returned at ten-forty p.m. I did not look at my watch. Mrs. Riscoe offered me a whisky which I declined. I also declined a milk drink and she went to the kitchen to get her own. She came back in a few minutes and said that she'd changed her mind. She also said that, apparently, her brother was still out. We talked for a little time and arranged to meet to ride together at seven this morning. Then we went to bed. I had a reasonably good night. As far as I know Mrs. Riscoe had, too. I had dressed and was waiting for her in the hall when I heard Stephen Maxie calling down to me. He wanted my help with the ladder. The rest you know.'

'Did you kill Sally Jupp, Mr. Hearne?'

'Not so far as I am aware.'

'What do you mean by that?'

'Merely that I suppose I could have done it while in a state of amnesia, but that is hardly a practical supposition.'

'I think we can dismiss that possibility. Miss Jupp was killed by someone who knew what he, or she, was doing. Have you any idea who?'

'Do you expect me to take that question seriously?'

'I expect you to take all my questions seriously. This young mother was murdered. I intend to find out who

83

killed her without wasting too much of my own time or anyone else's and I expect you to co-operate with me.'

'I have no idea who killed her and I doubt whether I should tell you if I had. I haven't your evident passion for abstract justice. However, I'm prepared to co-operate to the extent of pointing out some facts which, in your enthusiasm for lengthy interrogations of your suspects, you may possibly have overlooked. Someone had got through that girl's window. She kept .glass animals on the ledge and they had been scattered. The window was open and her hair was damp. It rained last night from half-past twelve until three. I deduce that she was dead before twelve-thirty or she would have closed the window. The child did not awake until its normal time. Presumably then the visitor made little noise. It is unlikely that there was a violent quarrel. I imagine that Sally herself let in her visitor through the window. He probably used the ladder. She would know where it was kept. He probably came by appointment. Your guess is as good as mine as to why. I didn't know her but, somehow, she never struck me as being highly sexed or promiscuous. The man was probably in love with her and, when she told him about her intention to marry Stephen Maxie, he killed her in a sudden access of jealousy or anger. I can't believe that this was a premeditated crime. Sally had locked the door to secure their privacy and the man got out through the window without unlocking it. He may not have realized it was bolted. Had he done so he would not probably have unbolted it and made his exit with more care. That bolted door must be a great disappointment to you, Inspector. Even you can hardly visualize any of the family pounding up and down a ladder to get in and out of their own house. I know how excited you must be about the Maxie-Jupp engagement but you don't need me to point out that, if we had to commit murder to get out of an unwelcome engagement the mortality rate among women would be very high.'

Even as he was speaking Felix knew that it was a mistake. Fear had trapped him into garrulity as well as anger. The police sergeant was looking at him with the resigned and slightly pitying look of a man who has seen too many men make fools of themselves to be surprised, but still rather wishes that they wouldn't do it. Dalgleish spoke mildly.

'I thought that you had a good night. Yet you noticed that it rained from half past twelve until three.'

'It was a good night for me.'

'You suffer from insomnia then? What do you take for it?'

'Whisky. But seldom in other people's houses.'

'You described earlier how the body was discovered and how you went into the adjoining bathroom with Mrs. Riscoe while Dr. Maxie 'phoned the police. After a time Mrs. Riscoe left you to go to her mother. What did you do after that?'

'I thought I had better see if Mrs. Bultitaft was all right. I didn't suppose that anyone would feel like breakfast, but it was obvious that we should need plenty of hot coffee, and that sandwiches would be a good idea. She seemed stunned and kept repeating that Sally must have killed herself. I pointed out as gently as I could that that was anatomically impossible and that seemed to upset her more. She gave me one curious look as if I were a stranger and then burst into loud sobbing. By the time I had managed to calm her Miss Bowers had arrived with the child and was being rather obviously capable with its breakfast. Martha took herself in hand and we got on with the coffee and with Mr. Maxie's breakfast. By that time the police had arrived and we were told to wait in the drawing-room.'

'When Mrs. Bultitaft burst into tears, was that the first sign of grief that she had shown?'

'Grief?' The pause was almost imperceptible. 'She was obviously very much shocked, as we all were.'

'Thank you, sir. That has been very helpful. I will have your statement typed and later I will ask you to read it over and, if you agree with it, sign it. If you have anything else you want to tell me there'll be plenty of opportunity. I shall be about the place. If you are going back to the drawing-room will you ask Mrs. Bultitaft if she will come in next.'

It was a command not a request. As he reached the door Felix heard the quiet voice speaking again.

'You will scarcely be surprised to hear that your account of things tallies almost exactly with that of Mrs. Riscoe. With one exception. Mrs. Riscoe says that you spent almost the whole of last night in her room, not your own. She says, in fact, that you slept together.'

Felix stood for a moment facing the door and then turned round and faced the man behind the desk.

'That was very sweet of Mrs. Riscoe, but it makes things difficult for me, doesn't it? I'm afraid you will have to make up your mind, Inspector, as to which of us is lying.'

'Thank you,' said Dalgleish. 'I have already done so.'

7

Dalgleish had met a number of Marthas in his time and had never supposed them to be complicated people. They were concerned with the comfort of the body, the cooking of food, the unending menial tasks which someone must carry out before the life of the mind can have any true validity. Their own undemanding emotional needs found fulfilment in service. They were loyal, hard-working and truthful and made good witnesses because they lacked both the imagination and the practice necessary for successful lying. They could be a nuisance if they decided to shield those who had gained their loyalty but this was an overt danger which could be anticipated. He expected no difficulty with Martha. It was with a sense of irritation that Dalgleish realized that someone had been talking to her. She would be correct, she would be respectful, but any information he extracted would be gained the hard way. Martha had been coached and it was not hard to guess by whom. He pressed patiently on.

'So you do the cooking and help with the nursing of Mr. Maxie. That must be a heavy load. Did you suggest to Mrs. Maxie that she should employ Miss Jupp?'

'No.'

'Do you know who did?'

Martha was silent for several seconds as if wondering whether to chance an indiscretion.

'It may have been Miss Liddell. Madam may have thought of it herself. I don't know.'

'But I presume that Mrs. Maxie talked it over with you before she employed the girl.'

'She told me about Sally. It was for Madam to decide.'

Dalgleish began to find this servility irritating but his voice did not change. He had never been known to lose his temper with a witness.

'Had Mrs. Maxie ever employed an unmarried mother before?'

'It would never have been thought of in the old days. All our girls came with excellent references.'

'So that this was a new venture. Do you think it was a success? You had most to do with Miss Jupp. What sort of a girl was she?'

Martha did not reply.

'Were you satisfied with her work?'

'I was satisfied enough. At first anyway.'

'What caused you to change your mind? Was it her late rising?' The heavy-lidded, obstinate eyes slewed suddenly from side to side.

'There are worse things than lying abed.'

'Such as?'

'She began to get cheeky.'

'That must have been trying for you. I wonder what caused Miss Jupp to get cheeky.'

'Girls are like that. They start quietly enough and then begin to act as if they are mistresses in the house.'

'Suppose Sally Jupp were beginning to think that she might be mistress here one day?'

'Then she was out of her mind.'

'But Dr. Maxie did propose marriage to her on Saturday evening.'

'I know nothing of that. Dr. Maxie couldn't have married Sally Jupp.'

'Someone seems to have made that certain, don't they? Have you any idea who?'

Martha did not reply. There was, indeed, nothing to be said. If Sally Jupp really had been killed for that reason the circle of suspects was not large. Dalgleish began to take her with tedious thoroughness over the events of Saturday afternoon and evening. There was little she could say about the fête. She had apparently taken no part in it except to walk once round the garden before giving Mr. Maxie his evening meal and making him comfortable for the night. When she returned to the kitchen Sally had evidently given Jimmy his tea and taken him up for his bath because the pram was in the scullery and the child's plate and mug were in the sink. The girl did not appear and Martha had wasted no time in looking for her. The family had waited on themselves at dinner which was a cold meal and Mrs. Maxie had not rung for her. Afterwards Mrs. Riscoe and Mr. Hearne had come into the kitchen to help wash up. They hadn't asked whether Sally was back. No one had mentioned her. They had talked mostly about the fête. Mr. Hearne had laughed and joked with Mrs. Riscoe while they washed up. He was a very amusing gentleman. They hadn't helped to get the hot drinks ready. That was done later. The cocoa tin was in a cupboard with the other dry provisions and neither Mrs. Riscoe nor Mr. Hearne had been to the cupboard. She had stayed in the kitchen all the time that they were there.

After they left she turned on the television for half an hour. No, she hadn't worried about Sally. The girl would come in when she felt like it. At about five minutes to ten Martha had put a saucepan of milk to heat slowly at the side of the stove. That was done most nights at Martingale so that she could get early to bed. She had put out the mugs on a tray. There were large cups and saucers put out for any guest who liked a hot drink at night. Sally knew very well that the blue beaker belonged to Mrs. Riscoe. Everyone at Martingale knew. After seeing to the hot milk Martha had gone to bed. She was in bed before half past ten and had heard nothing unusual all night. In the morning she had gone to wake up Sally and had found the door bolted. She had gone to tell Madam. The rest he knew.

It took over forty minutes to extract this unremarkable information but Dalgleish showed no sign of impatience. Now they came to the actual finding of the body. It was important to discover how far Martha's account agreed with that of Catherine Bowers. If it agreed, then at least one of his tentative theories might prove correct. The account did agree. Patiently he went on to inquire about the missing Sommeil. But here he was less successful. Martha Bultitaft did not believe Sally had found any tablets in her master's bed.

'Sally liked to make out that she nursed the master. Maybe she took a turn at nights if Madam was extra tired. But he never liked anyone about him but me. I do all the heavy nursing. If there was anything hidden in the bed I should have found it.'

It was the longest speech she had made. Dalgleish felt that it carried conviction. Finally he questioned her about the empty cocoa tin. Here, again, she spoke quietly but with unemphatic certainty. She had found the empty tin on the kitchen table when she came down to make the early morning tea. She had burned the inside paper, rinsed the tin and put it in the dustbin. Why had she rinsed it first? Because Madam disliked sticky or greasy tins being put in the dustbin. The cocoa tin hadn't been greasy, of course, but that didn't signify. All used tins were rinsed at Martingale. And why had she burned the inside wrapper? Well, she couldn't rinse the inside of the tin with the paper lining still there, could she? The tin was empty so she rinsed it out and threw it away. Her tone suggested that no reasonable person could have done otherwise.

For the life of him Dalgleish couldn't see how her story could be effectively countered. His heart sank at the thought of interrogating Mrs. Maxie on the usual method of disposal of the family's used tins. But, once again he suspected that Martha had been coached. He was seeing the beginning of a pattern. The infinite patience of the last hour had been well worth while.

CHAPTER FIVE

1

Sᴛ. ᴍᴀʀʏ's ʀᴇꜰᴜɢᴇ was about a mile from the main part of the village, an ugly red-brick house with a multiplicity of gables and turrets which was set back from the main road behind a discreet shield of laurel bushes. The gravel drive led to a front door whose worn knocker gleamed with much polishing. The net curtains were snowy white at each of the windows. Shallow stone steps at the side of the house led down to a square lawn where several prams were clustered together. A maid in cap and apron admitted them, probably one of the mothers Dalgleish thought, and showed them into a small room at the left of the hall. She seemed uncertain what to do and could not catch Dalgleish's name although he repeated it twice. Large eyes stared at him uncomprehendingly through the steel-frame spectacles as she hovered miserably in the doorway. 'Never mind,' said Dalgleish kindly, 'just let Miss Liddell know that there are two policemen to see her from Martingale. She'll know all about us.'

'Please, I have to have the name. I'm being trained for a house parlourmaid.' She hovered in desperate persistence, torn between fear of Miss Liddell's censure and embarrassment at being in the same room as two strange men, and both of them policemen at that. Dalgleish handed her his card. 'Just give her this then. That will be even more proper and correct. And don't worry. You'll make a very nice house parlourmaid. Nowadays they're prized above rubies you know.'

'Not saddled with an illegitimate kid, they aren't,' said Sergeant Martin as the slight figure disappeared through the door with what might have been a whispered 'Thank you'.

'Funny to see a plain little thing like that here, sir. A bit missing by the way she acted. Someone took advantage of her I suppose.'

'She's the kind of person who gets taken advantage of from the day she's born.'

'Properly scared, too, wasn't she? I suppose this Miss Liddell treats the girls all right, sir?'

'Very well, I imagine, according to her own lights. It's easy to get sentimental over her job, but she has to deal with a pretty mixed bunch. What you want here is hope, faith and charity to an unlimited degree. In other words you want a saint and we can hardly expect Miss Liddell to measure up to that standard.'

'Yes, sir,' said Sergeant Martin. On second thoughts he felt that 'No, sir' would have been more appropriate. Unconscious of having uttered any unorthodoxy Dalgleish moved slowly about the room. It was uncomfortable but unostentatious and was furnished, he thought, with many of Miss Liddell's personal possessions. All the wood glowed with polishing. The spinet and the rosewood table both looked as if they would have struck warm to the touch from the vigour and energy spent on them. The one large window which overlooked the lawn was curtained with flower-patterned cretonne now drawn against the sun. The carpet, although showing signs of age, was not the kind provided by official bodies however voluntary and public-spirited. The room was as much Miss Liddell's in spirit as if she had owned the house. Along the walls were photographs of babies. Babies lying naked on rugs, their heads reared towards the camera in helpless absurdity. Babies smiling toothlessly from prams and cradles. Woollen-clad babies held in their mothers' arms. There were even one or two lying lumpily in the arms of an embarrassed man. These presumably were the lucky ones, the ones who had achieved an official father at last. Above a small mahogany desk was the framed print of a woman at a spinning-wheel with a plaque attached to the base of the frame. 'Presented by the Chadfleet and District Committee for Moral Welfare to Miss Alice Liddell in commemoration of twenty years' devoted service as Warden of St. Mary's Refuge.' Dalgleish and Martin looked at it together. 'I don't know that I'd call this place a refuge exactly,' said the Sergeant. Dalgleish looked again at the furniture, the carefully tended legacies from Miss Liddell's childhood.

'It might well be to a single woman of Miss Liddell's age. She's made this place her home for over twenty years. She might do a great deal to prevent herself being driven out of it.'

Sergeant Martin was prevented from replying by the entrance of the lady. Miss Liddell was always most at ease on her own ground. She shook hands composedly and apologized for keeping them waiting. Looking at her Dalgleish deduced she had spent the time in applying powder to her face and resolution to her mind. She was obviously determined to treat this as a social call as far as possible and she invited them to sit down with all the conscious charm of an inexperienced hostess. Dalgleish declined her offer of tea, carefully avoiding the reproachful eye of his sergeant. Martin was perspiring freely. His own view was that punctilio towards a possible suspect could be carried too far and that a nice cup of tea on a hot day had never yet obstructed justice.

'We shall try not to keep you too long, Miss Liddell. As I'm sure you have realized, I am investigating the death of Sally Jupp. I understand that you dined at Martingale yesterday evening. You were also at the fête during the afternoon and you did, of course, know Miss Jupp while she was with you here at St. Mary's. There are one or two matters which I am hoping you may be able to explain.' Miss Liddell started at the use of his last word. As Sergeant Martin drew out his notebook with something akin to resignation, Dalgleish noted her quick moistening of her lips and the almost imperceptible tensing of her hands and knew that she was on her guard.

'Anything you care to ask, of course, Inspector. It is Inspector, isn't it? Of course I knew Sally very well and the whole thing is a dreadful shock to me. It is to us all. But I'm afraid I'm not likely to be of much help. I'm not very clever at noticing and remembering things, you know. It's rather a disadvantage sometimes, but we can't all be detectives can we?' The nervous laugh was a little too high to be natural. 'We've got her scared all right,' thought Sergeant Martin. 'Might be something here after all.'

'Perhaps we could begin with Sally Jupp herself,' said Dalgleish gently. 'I understand that she lived here during the last five months of her pregnancy and came back to you when she left the hospital after the birth. She stayed here until she started the job at Martingale which she did when her baby was four months old. Until that time she helped here with the household duties. You must have got to know her very well during this time. Did you like her, Miss Liddell?'

'Like her?' The woman laughed nervously. 'Isn't that rather a funny question, Inspector?'

'Is it? In what way?'

She made an effort to conceal her embarrassment and to give the question the compliment of careful thought.

'I hardly know what to say. If you had asked me that question a week ago I should have had no hesitation in saying that Sally was an excellent little worker and a most deserving girl who was doing her best to atone for her mistake. But now, of course, I can't help wondering whether I was wrong about her, whether she was really genuine after all.' She spoke with the sorrow of a connoisseur whose previously infallible judgment has at last been proved at fault. 'I suppose now that we shall never know whether she was genuine or not.'

'By genuine, I assume you mean whether she was sincere in her affection for Mr. Stephen Maxie.'

Miss Liddell shook her head sadly. 'The appearances were against it. I was never more shocked in my life, Inspector, never. Of course she had no right to accept him whatever she felt for him. She looked positively triumphant when she stood in that window and told us. He was horribly embarrassed of course, and went as white as a sheet. It was a dreadful moment for poor Mrs. Maxie. I'm afraid I shall always blame myself for what happened. I recommended Sally to Martingale, you know. It seemed such a wonderful chance for her in every way. And now this.'

'You believe, then, that Sally Jupp's death is the direct result of her engagement to Mr. Maxie?'

'Well, it does look like that, doesn't it?'

'I agree that her death was highly convenient for anyone who had a reason to dislike the proposed marriage. The Maxie family for instance.'

Miss Liddell's face flamed. 'But that's ridiculous, Inspector. It's a terrible thing to say. Terrible. Of course, you don't know the family as we do, but you must take it from me that the whole suggestion is fantastic. You can't have thought that I meant that! It's perfectly plain to me what happened. Sally had been playing fast and loose with some man we don't know about and when he heard of the engagement – well, he lost control of himself. He got through the window, didn't he? That's what Miss Bowers told me. Well, that proves it wasn't the family.'

'The murderer probably got out of the room through the window. We have no knowledge as yet how he or she got in.'

'You surely can't imagine Mrs. Maxie climbing down that wall. She couldn't do it!'

'I imagine nothing. There was a ladder in the customary place for anyone who cared to use it. It could have been put in place ready even if the murderer got in through the door.'

'But Sally would have heard! Even if the ladder were placed there very gently. Or she might look out of her window and see it!'

'Perhaps. If she were awake.'

'I don't understand you, Inspector. You seem determined to suspect the family. If only you knew what they've done for that girl.'

'I should like to be told. And you must not misunderstand me. I suspect everyone who knew Miss Jupp and who has no alibi for the time she was killed. That is why I am here now.'

'Well, you know about my movements presumably. I've no wish to make a secret of them. Dr. Epps brought me back here in his car. We left Martingale at about half past ten. I wrote in this room for a little while and then took a stroll in the garden. I went to bed at about eleven which is rather late for me. I heard about this dreadful thing while I was finishing my breakfast. Miss Bowers 'phoned and asked if I could take Jimmy back for a while until they knew what was to happen to him. Naturally I left my deputy, Miss Pollack, in charge of the girls and went round at once. I telephoned George Hopgood and told him to bring round his taxi.'

'You said a little earlier that you thought the news of Miss Jupp's engagement to Mr. Maxie was the reason for her death. Was that news known outside the household? I was given to understand that Mr. Maxie only proposed on Saturday night so that no one who was not at Martingale after that time could have been told.'

'Dr. Maxie may have proposed on Saturday, but no doubt the girl had made up her mind to have him before then. Something had been happening, I'm sure of it. I saw her at the fête and she was flushed with excitement all the afternoon. And were you told how she copied Mrs. Riscoe's dress?'

'You are hardly suggesting that that constituted another motive.'

'It showed which way her mind was working. Make no mistake about it, Sally asked for what she got. I'm only desperately sorry that the Maxies should have been involved in all this trouble on her account.'

'You have told me that you went to bed about eleven after a stroll in the garden. Have you anyone to confirm that statement?'

'No one saw me as far as I know, Inspector. Miss Pollack and the girls are in bed by ten. I have my own key of course. It was an unusual thing for me to have gone out again like that but I was disturbed. I couldn't help thinking about Sally and Mr. Maxie and I knew I shouldn't get to sleep if I went to bed too early.'

'Thank you. There are just two other questions. Where in the house do you keep your private papers? I mean documents referring to the administration of this Home. Letters from the committee for example.'

Miss Liddell walked over to the rosewood desk.

'They are kept in this drawer, Inspector. Naturally I keep it locked although only the most trustworthy girls are allowed to look after this room. The key is kept in this little compartment at the top.'

She lifted the desk lid as she spoke and indicated the place. Dalgleish reflected that only the dullest or least curious housemaid could have missed the hidden key if she had had sufficient nerve to look. Miss Liddell was obviously used to dealing with girls who had too fearful a respect for papers and official documents to tamper with them voluntarily. But Sally Jupp had been neither dull nor, he suspected, incurious. He suggested as much to Miss Liddell and, as expected, the image of Sally's picking fingers and amused ironic eyes roused her to even greater resentment than his earlier questions about the Maxies.

'You mean that Sally may have pried about among my things? I would never have believed that once, but you could be right. Oh, yes. I see it now. That was why she liked to work in here. All that docility, that politeness was so much pretence! And to think that I trusted her! I really thought that she cared for me, that I was helping her. She confided in me, you know. But I suppose all those stories were lies. She must have been laughing at me all the time. I suppose you think I'm a fool too. Well, I may be, but I've done nothing to be ashamed of. Nothing! They've told you about that scene in the Maxie dining-room no doubt. She couldn't frighten me. There may have been little difficulties here in the past. I'm not very clever with figures and accounts. I've never pretended to be. But I've done nothing wrong. You can ask any member of the committee. Sally Jupp could pry as much as she liked. A lot of good it's done her.'

She was shaking with anger and made no attempt to hide the bitter satisfaction behind her last words. But Dalgleish was unprepared for the effect of his last question.

'One of my officers has been to see the Proctors, Sally Jupp's next-of-kin. Naturally we hoped that they might be able to give us some information about her life which might help us. Their young daughter was there and she volunteered some information. Can you tell me, Miss Liddell, why it was you telephoned Mr. Proctor early on Saturday morning – the morning of the fête? The child said she answered the telephone.' The transformation from furious resentment to complete surprise was almost ludicrous. Miss Liddell gazed at him literally open-mouthed.

'Me? Telephoned Mr. Proctor? I don't know what you mean! I haven't been in touch with the Proctors since Sally first went to Martingale. They never took an interest

96

in her. What on earth would I telephone Mr. Proctor about?'

'That,' said Dalgleish, 'was what I had been wondering.'

'But it's ridiculous! If I had telephoned Mr. Proctor I should have no objection to admitting it. But I didn't. The child must be lying.'

'Someone is lying, certainly.'

'Well, it isn't me,' retorted Miss Liddell stoutly if ungrammatically. Dalgleish, on this point at least, was disposed to believe her. As she accompanied him to the door he asked casually:

'Did you tell anyone about the events at Martingale when you go home, Miss Liddell? If your deputy were still up no doubt it would be natural to mention Sally's engagement to her.'

Miss Liddell hesitated then said defensively, 'Well, the news was bound to get around, wasn't it? I mean, the Maxies could hardly expect to keep it secret. Actually, I did mention it to Miss Pollack. Mrs. Pullen was here, too. She came over from Rose Cottage to return some teaspoons which we'd lent for the fête teas. She was still here chatting to Miss Pollack when I got back from Martingale. So Mrs. Pullen knew and you're surely not suggesting that telling her had anything to do with Sally's death.'

Dalgleish replied non-committally. He was not so sure.

2

By dinner-time the activity of the day at Martingale seemed to be slowing down. Dalgleish and the sergeant were still working in the business room from which the sergeant occasionally emerged to speak to the man on duty at the door. The police cars still mysteriously appeared, disgorged their uniformed or mackintoshed passengers and, after a short wait, bore them away again. The Maxies and their guests watched these comings and goings from the windows, but no one had been sent for since the late afternoon and it looked as if the questioning was over for the day and that the party could think about dinner with some prospect of being able to eat undisturbed. The house had suddenly become very quiet and, when Martha nervously and half-heartedly sounded the gong at half past seven it boomed out like a vulgar intrusion into the silence of grief, sounding unnaturally loud to the family's heightened nerves. The meal itself passed almost in silence. The ghost of Sally moved from door to sideboard, and when Mrs. Maxie rang and the door opened to admit Martha, no one looked up. Martha's own preoccupations were shown in the poverty of the meal. No one had any hunger and there was nothing to tempt hunger. Afterwards they all moved as if by unspoken but common summons into the drawing-room. It was a relief when they saw Mr. Hinks pass the window and Stephen went out to welcome him in. Here at least was a representative of the outside world. No one could accuse the vicar of murdering Sally Jupp. Presumably he had come to offer spiritual guidance and comfort. The only kind of comfort which would have been welcome to the Maxies was the assurance that Sally was not after all dead, that they had been living through a brief nightmare from which they could now awake, a little tired and distressed by the lack of sleep but raised into joy by the glorious realization that none of it was true. But if this could not be, it was at least reassuring to talk with someone who stood outside the shadow of suspicion and who could give this dreadful day the semblance of normality. They found that they had even been speaking in whispers and Stephen's call to the vicar rang out like a shout. Soon he was with them and, as he entered with Stephen behind him, four pairs of eyes looked up inquiringly as if anxious to know the verdict on them of the world outside.

'Poor girl,' he said. 'Poor little girl. And she was so happy yesterday evening.'

'Did you speak to her after the fête then?' Stephen could not succeed in hiding the urgency in his voice.

'No, not after the fête. I get so muddled about times. Stupid of me. Now that you mention it I didn't speak to her at all yesterday, although, of course, I did see her about the gardens. Such a pretty white dress she was wearing. No, I spoke to her on Thursday evening. We walked up the road together and I asked about Jimmy. I think it was Thursday. Yes, it must have been because I was at home all the evening on Friday. Thursday evening was the last time we spoke. She was so happy. She told me about her marriage and how Jimmy was to have a father. But you know all about that, I expect. It was a surprise to me, but, of course, I was glad for her. And now this. Have the police any news yet?'

He looked round in gentle inquiry seeming oblivious of the effect of his words. No one spoke for a moment and then Stephen said, 'You may as well know, Vicar, that I had asked Sally to marry me. But she couldn't have told you about it on Thursday. She didn't even know then. I never mentioned marriage to her until seven-forty p.m. on Saturday.'

Catherine Bowers laughed shortly and then turned away in embarrassment as Deborah turned and looked at her. Mr. Hinks creased worried brows but his gentle old voice was firm.

'I do get times muddled I know, but it was certainly Thursday when we met. I was coming out of church after Compline and Sally was passing with Jimmy in his push-chair. But I couldn't be mistaken about the conversation. Not the exact words, but the general gist. Sally said that Jimmy was soon to have a father. She asked me not to tell anyone and I said I wouldn't, but that I was very glad for her. I asked whether I knew the bridegroom but she just laughed and said she would rather let it be a surprise. She was very excited and happy. We only walked a little way together as I left her at the vicarage and I suppose she came on here. I'm afraid I rather assumed that you knew all about it. Is it important?'

'Inspector Dalgleish will probably think so,' said Deborah wearily. 'I suppose you ought to go and tell him. There isn't much choice really. The man has an uncanny facility for extracting uncomfortable truths.'

Mr. Hinks looked troubled, but was saved from the necessity of replying by a quick knock at the door and the appearance of Dalgleish. He held out his hand towards Stephen. Loosely wrapped in a man's white handkerchief was a small mud-caked bottle.

'Do you recognize this?' he asked.

Stephen went across and looked at it for a moment but did not try to touch it.

'Yes. It's the bottle of Sommeil from Father's drug cupboard.'

'There are seven three-grain tablets left. Do you confirm that three tablets are missing since you put them in this bottle?'

'Naturally I do. I told you. There were ten three-grain tablets.'

'Thank you,' said Dalgleish and turned again to the door.

Deborah spoke just as his hand reached for the door-knob :

'Are we permitted to ask where that bottle was found?' she asked.

Dalgleish looked at her as if the question really needed his serious consideration.

'Why not? It is probable that at least one of you would genuinely like to know. It was found by one of the men working with me, buried in that part of the lawn which was used for a treasure hunt. As you know, the turf has been cut about fairly intensively there, presumably by hopeful competitors. There are several sods still lying on the surface. The bottle had been placed in one of the holes and the turf pressed down over it. The person responsible had even been considerate enough to mark the place with one of the named wooden pegs which were lying about. Curiously enough it was yours, Mrs. Riscoe. Your mug with the drugged cocoa; your peg marking the hidden bottle.'

'But why? Why?' said Deborah.

'If any of you can answer that question I shall be in the business room for an hour or two yet.' He turned courteously to Mr. Hinks. 'I think you must be Mr. Hinks, sir. I was hoping to see you. If it is convenient perhaps you could spare me a few minutes now.'

The vicar looked around at the Maxies in puzzled pity. He paused and seemed about to speak. Then, without a word, he followed Dalgleish from the room.

3

It was not until ten o'clock that Dalgleish got round to interviewing Dr. Epps. The doctor had been out nearly all day seeing cases that might or might not have been urgent enough to warrant a Sunday visit, but which had certainly provided him with an excuse to postpone questioning. If he had anything to hide he had presumably decided on his tactics by now. He was not an obvious suspect. It was difficult, for one thing, to imagine a motive. But he was the Maxie family doctor and a close family friend. He would not willingly obstruct justice but he might have unorthodox ideas about what constituted justice and he would have the loop-hole of professional discretion if he wanted to avoid inconvenient questions. Dalgleish had had trouble with that kind of witness before. But he need not have worried. Dr. Epps, as if conceding some semi-medical recognition to the visit, invited him willingly enough into the red-brick surgery which had been misguidedly added to his pleasant Georgian house, and squeezed himself into a swivel-chair at his desk. Dalgleish was waved towards the patients' chair, a large Windsor of disconcerting lowness in which it was difficult to appear at ease or to take the initiative. He almost expected the doctor to begin on a string of personal and embarrassing questions. And, in fact, Dr. Epps had obviously decided to do most of the talking. This suited Dalgleish who knew very well when he might learn most by silence. The doctor lit a large and peculiarly shaped pipe.

'Won't offer you a smoke. Or a drink for that matter. Know you don't usually drink with suspects.' He darted a sharp glance at Dalgleish to see his reaction but, receiving no comment, he established his pipe with a few vigorous sucks and began to talk.

'Won't waste your time saying what an appalling thing this is. Difficult to believe really. Still, someone killed her. Put his hand round her neck and throttled her. Terrible for Mrs. Maxie. For the girl, too, of course, but naturally I think of the living. Stephen called me in at about seven-thirty. No doubt the girl was dead, of course. Had been for seven hours as far as I could judge. The police surgeon knows more about that than me. Girl wasn't pregnant. I doctored her for the odd spot of trouble and I do know that. It'll be one in the eye for the village though. They do like to hear the worst. And it would have been a motive I suppose – for someone.'

'If we're thinking about motive,' replied Dalgleish, 'we could start with this engagement to Mr. Stephen Maxie.'

The doctor shifted uncomfortably in his chair.

'Lot of rot. The boy's a fool. He hasn't a bean except what he earns and God knows that's little enough. Of course, there will be something when his father dies, but these old families, living and keeping up property on capital, well, it's a wonder they haven't had to sell. The government's doing its best to tax them out of existence. And that fellow Price surrounds himself with accounts and grows fat on untaxed expenses! Makes you wonder if we've all gone mad! Still, that's not your problem. You can take it from me, though, that Maxie isn't in a position to marry anyone at present. And where did he think Sally was going to live? Stay on at Martingale with her mother-in-law? Silly fool wants his head examined.'

'All of which makes it plain,' said Dalgleish, 'that this projected match would have been calamitous for the Maxies. And that gives several people an interest in seeing that it didn't happen.'

The doctor leaned across the desk at him challengingly.

'At the cost of killing the girl? By making that child motherless as well as fatherless? What sort of people do you think we are?'

Dalgleish did not reply. The facts were incontrovertible. Someone had killed Sally Jupp. Someone who had not even been deterred by the presence of her sleeping child. But he noted how the doctor's cry allied him with the Maxies. 'What sort of people do you think we are?' There was no doubt where Dr. Epps's allegiance lay.

It was growing dark in the little room. Grunting with the slight effort, the doctor heaved himself across his desk and turned on a lamp. It was jointed and angled and he adjusted it carefully so that a pool of light fell on his hands but left his face in shadow. Dalgleish was beginning to feel weary but there was much to be done before his working day was over. He introduced the main object of his visit.

'Mr. Simon Maxie is your patient, I believe?'

'Of course. Always has been. Not much to be done for him now, of course. Just a matter of time and good nursing. Martha sees to that mostly. But, yes, he's my patient. Quite helpless. Advanced arteriosclerosis with other complications of one kind and another. If you're thinking that he crawled upstairs to do in the maid, well, you're wrong. I doubt if he knew she existed.'

'I believe you've been prescribing some special sleeping tablets for him for the last year or so?'

'Wish you wouldn't keep on saying you believe this, that and the other. You know damn well I have. There's no secret about them. Can't see what they've got to do with this business though.' He stiffened suddenly. 'You don't mean she was doped first?'

'We haven't the post-mortem report yet, but it looks very like it.'

The doctor did not pretend that he did not understand. 'That's bad.'

'It does rather narrow down the field. And there are other disquieting features.'

Dalgleish then told the doctor about the missing Sommeil, where Sally was alleged to have found it, what Stephen did with the ten tablets and the finding of the bottle in the treasure-hunt plot. When he had finished there was a silence for a moment. The doctor was sagging back into the chair which had at first seemed too small to withstand his cheerful and comfortable rotundity. When he spoke the deep rumbling voice was suddenly an old and tired voice.

'Stephen never told me. Not much chance with the fête, of course. Might have changed his mind though. Probably thought I wouldn't be much help. I ought to have known, you see. He wouldn't overlook carelessness like that. His father . . . my patient. I've known Simon Maxie for thirty years. Brought his children into the world. You ought to know your patients, know when they want help. I just left the prescription week after week. Didn't even go up to him very often recently. Didn't seem much point in it. Can't think what Martha was doing though. She nursed him, did everything. She must have known about those tablets. That is, if Sally was telling the truth.'

'It's difficult to imagine her making the whole thing up. Besides, she had the tablets. I presume they can only be obtained by a doctor's prescription?'

'Yes. Can't just walk into a chemist's and buy them. Oh, it's true all right. Never doubted it really. I blame myself. Should have seen what was happening at Martingale. Not only to Simon Maxie. To all of them.'

'So he thinks one of them did it,' thought Dalgleish. 'He can see clearly enough which way things are moving and he doesn't like it. Small blame to him. He knows this is a Martingale crime all right. The thing is, does he know for certain? And if so, which one?'

He asked about the Saturday evening at Martingale. Dr. Epps's account of Sally's appearance before dinner and the disclosure of Stephen's proposal was considerably less dramatic than that of Catherine Bowers or Miss Liddell, but the versions fundamentally agreed. He confirmed that neither he nor Miss Liddell had left the business room during the counting of the money and that he had seen Sally Jupp mounting the main staircase as he and his hostess were passing through the hall to the front door. He thought Sally was wearing a dressing-gown and carrying something, but he couldn't recall what. It might have been a cup and saucer or perhaps a beaker. He had not spoken to her. That was the last time he had seen her alive.

Dalgleish asked who else in the village had been pre-scribed Sommeil.

'I'll have to look up my records if you want accuracy. May take half an hour or so. It wasn't a common prescrip-tion. I can remember one or two patients who had it. May be others, of course. Sir Reynold Price and Miss Pollack at St. Mary's had it, I know. Mr. Maxie, of course. By the way, what's happening about his medicine now?'

'We're holding the Sommeil. I understand that Dr. Maxie has prescribed its equivalent. And now, Doctor, perhaps I might have a word with your housekeeper before I go.'

It was a full minute before the doctor seemed to hear. Then he shuffled out of his chair with a muttered apology and led the way from the surgery into the house. There Dalgleish was able tactfully to confirm that the doctor had arrived home at 10.45 the evening before and had been called out to a confinement at 11.10. He hardly expected to hear otherwise. He would have to check with the patient's family, but no doubt they would provide an alibi for the doctor up to 3.30 in the morning when he had finally left Mrs. Baines of Nessingford in proud possession of her first-born son. Dr. Epps had been busy helping life into the world for most of Saturday night, not choking it out of Sally Jupp.

The doctor muttered something about a late visit and walked with Dalgleish to the gate, first protecting himself from the evening air by an opulent and voluminous coat at least a size too large for him. When they were at the gate the doctor, who had plunged his hands into his pockets, gave a little start of surprise and opened his right hand to reveal a small bottle. It was nearly full of small brown tablets. The two men looked at it in silence for a moment. Then Dr. Epps said, 'Sommeil.'

Dalgleish took a handkerchief, wrapped up the bottle and slipped it into his own pocket. He noted with interest the doctor's first instinctive gesture of resistance.

'That would be Sir Reynold's stuff, Inspector. Nothing to do with the family. This was Price's coat.' His tone was defensive.

'When did the coat come into your possession, Doctor?' asked Dalgleish. Again there was a long pause. Then the doctor seemed to remember that there were facts which it was pointless to try to hide.

'I bought it on Saturday. At the church fête. I bought it rather as a joke between myself and . . . and the stall-holder.'

'And that was . . . who?' asked Dalgleish inexorably.

Dr. Epps did not meet his eyes as he answered dully, 'Mrs. Riscoe.'

4

Sunday had been secularized and timeless, its legacy a week so out-of-joint that Monday dawned without any colour or individuality, a mere limbo of a day. The post was heavier than usual, a tribute to the efficiency both of the ubiquitous telephone and to those subtler and less scientific methods of country communications. Presumably tomorrow's post would be heavier still when the news of the Martingale murder reached those who depended on print for their information. Deborah had ordered half a dozen papers. Her mother wondered whether this extravagance was a gesture of defiance or a sop to genuine curiosity.

The police were still using the business room, although they had notified their intention of moving to the Moonraker's Arms later in the day. Mrs. Maxie privately wished them joy of the cooking. Sally's room was kept locked. Only Dalgleish held the key and he gave no explanation for his frequent visits there nor of what he had found or hoped to find.

Lionel Jephson had arrived early in the morning, fussy, scandalized and ineffectual. The family only hoped that he was being as big a nuisance to the police as he was to them. As Deborah predicted he was at a loss in a situation so divorced from his normal concerns and experience. His obvious anxiety and reiterated admonitions suggested that he had either grave doubts of his clients' innocence or little faith in the efficiency of the police. It was a relief to the whole household when he scurried back to town before luncheon to consult with a colleague.

At twelve o'clock the telephone rang for the twentieth time.

Sir Reynold Price's voice boomed across the wire to Mrs. Maxie.

'But it's disgraceful, my dear lady. What are the police doing?'

'I think at the moment they're trying to trace the baby's father.'

'Good God! Whatever for? I should think they'd do better to concentrate on finding who killed her.'

'They seem to think there could be a connection.'

'Damn silly ideas they would get. They've been here, you know. Wanted to know about some pills that Epps prescribed for me. Must have been months ago. Fancy him remembering after all that time. Now why do you suppose they worried about those? Most extraordinary thing. Not going to arrest me yet, Inspector, I said. You could see he was amused.' Sir Reynold's hearty laughter crackled unpleasantly in Mrs. Maxie's ear.

'How very tiresome for you,' said Mrs. Maxie. 'I am afraid this sad business is causing a lot of trouble to everyone. Did you send them away happy?'

'The police? My dear lady, the police are never happy. I told them plainly that it's no use expecting to find anything in this house. Maids tidy up everything that isn't actually kept under lock and key. Fancy looking for a bottle of tablets which I had months ago. Damn silly idea. The inspector seemed to think I ought to remember just how many I took and what happened to the others. Well, I ask you! I told him that I was a busy man with something better to do with my time. They were asking, too, about that spot of bother we had at St. Mary's about two years ago. The inspector seemed very interested in it. Wanted to know why you had resigned from the committee and so on.'

'I wonder how they got on to that?'

'Some fool's been talking too much, I suppose. Funny how people can't keep their mouths shut, especially to the police. That chap Dalgleish said to me that it was a funny thing you weren't on the St. Mary's committee when you ran practically everything else in the village. I told him you'd resigned two years ago when we had that spot of trouble and, naturally, he wanted to know what spot of trouble. Asked why we hadn't got rid of Liddell at the time. I said to him, "My dear chap, you just can't just chuck a woman out after twenty-five years' service. It's not as if there was actual dishonesty." I take my stand on that, you know. Always have. Always will. Carelessness and general muddle with the accounts, maybe, but that's a far cry from deliberate dishonesty. I told the man that we'd had her before the committee – all very hushed up and tactful of course – and sent her a letter confirming the new financial arrangements so that there couldn't be any misunderstanding. Damn stiff letter, too, all things considered. I know you thought at the time that we should have turned over the Home to the diocesan welfare committee or one of the national associations for unmarried mothers, instead of keeping it on as a private charitable concern, and so I told the inspector.'

'I thought it was time we handed over a difficult job to trained and experienced people, Sir Reynold.' Even as she spoke Mrs. Maxie cursed the unwariness which had trapped her into this recapitulation of old history.

'That's what I mean. I told Dalgleish, "Mrs. Maxie

may well have been right. I'm not saying she wasn't. But Lady Price was keen on the Home – practically founded it, in fact – and naturally I wasn't keen to hand it over. Not enough of these small individual places left now. Personal touch is what counts. No doubt, though, that Miss Liddell had made a nonsense of the accounts. Too much worry for her. Figures not really woman's work." He agreed of course. Had quite a laugh about it.'

Mrs. Maxie could well believe it. The picture was not a pretty one. No doubt this facility for being all things to all men was a prerequisite for success as a detective. When the hearty man-to-man amusement had died down Mrs. Maxie had no doubt that Dalgleish's mind was busy with a new theory. Yet how was it possible? The mugs and cups for those last night drinks had certainly been placed ready by ten. After that Miss Liddell had never been out of her hostess's sight. Together they had stood in the hall and watched that glowing triumphant figure carrying Deborah's beaker up to bed. Miss Liddell might possibly have a motive if Sally's taunt had any significance, but there was no evidence that she had the means, and certainly not that she had had the opportunity. Mrs. Maxie, who had never liked Miss Liddell, was still able to hope that the half-forgotten humiliations of two years ago could remain hidden and that Alice Liddell, not very efficient, not very intelligent, but fundamentally kind and well-meaning would be left in peace.

But Sir Reynold was still speaking.

'And by the way, I wouldn't take any notice of these extraordinary rumours that are going round the village. People are bound to talk you know, but it will all die down as soon as the police get their man. Let's hope they get a move on. Now don't forget, let me know if there's anything I can do. And mind you lock up carefully at night. It might be Deborah or yourself next. And there's another thing.' Sir Reynold's voice became hoarsely conspiratorial and Mrs. Maxie had to strain to hear. 'It's about the boy. Nice little fellow as far as I could see. Was watching him in his pram at the fête, you know. Thought this morning I'd like to do something there. Not much fun losing your mother. No real home. Someone ought to keep an eye on him. Where is he now? With you?'

'Jimmy's back at St. Mary's. It seemed best that way. I don't know what will be arranged for him. It's early yet, of course, and I don't know if anyone's given much thought to it.'

'Time they did, dear lady. Time they did. Perhaps they'll put him up for adoption. Better get on the list, eh? Miss Liddell would be the person to ask, I suppose.'

Mrs. Maxie was at a loss for an answer. She was more familiar with the laws of adoption than Sir Reynold and doubted whether he could be considered the most suitable applicant to have charge of a child. If Jimmy were to be adopted his situation would ensure that there were plenty of offers. She herself had already given thought to the child's future. She did not mention this, however, but contented herself by pointing out that Sally's relations might yet accept the boy and that nothing could be done until their views were known. It was possible, even, that the father would be traced. Sir Reynold dismissed this possibility with a hoot of derision but promised to do nothing in a hurry. With renewed warnings against homicidal maniacs he rang off. Mrs. Maxie wondered whether anyone could be as stupid as Sir Reynold appeared to be and what could have prompted his sudden concern for Jimmy.

She replaced the receiver with a sigh and turned to the day's letters. Half a dozen were from friends who, obviously in some social embarrassment, expressed their sympathy with the family and their confidence in Maxie innocence by invitations to dine. Mrs. Maxie found this demonstration of support more diverting than reassuring. The next three envelopes bore unfamiliar handwriting and she opened them reluctantly. Perhaps it would be better to destroy them unread but one never knew. Some information of value might be lost that way. Besides, it was more courageous to face unpleasantness and Eleanor Maxie had never lacked courage. But the first two letters were less objectionable than she had feared. One, indeed, was meant to be heartening. It contained three little printed texts with robins and roses in unseasonable proximity and an assurance that whosoever endured to the end would be saved. It asked for a contribution to enable this good news to be spread and suggested that the texts should be copied and distributed to those friends who were also in trouble. Most of Mrs. Maxie's friends were discreet about their troubles but, even so, she felt a tinge of guilt as she dropped the texts into the waste-paper basket. The next letter was in a mauve scented envelope from a lady who claimed psychic powers and was prepared, for a fee, to organize a séance at which Sally Jupp might be expected to appear and name her murderer. The assumption that Sally's disclosures would be completely acceptable to the Maxies did at least suggest that the writer gave them the benefit of the doubt. The last communication bore the local postmark and merely inquired, 'Why weren't you content to work her to death, you dirty murderess?' Mrs. Maxie looked at the writing carefully but could not remember seeing it before. But the postmark was clear and she recognized a challenge. She decided to go down to the village and do some shopping.

The little village store was rather busier than usual and the buzz of talk which stopped as soon as she appeared left her in no doubt as to the subject of conversation. Mrs. Nelson was there, Miss Pollack, old Simon from the Weir cottage who was claimed as the oldest inhabitant and seemed to think that this absolved him from any effort at personal hygiene, and one or two of the women from the new agricultural cottages whose faces and personalities, if any, were still strange to her. There was a general murmur of 'Good morning' in reply to her own greeting and Miss Pollack went so far as to say, 'Lovely day again, isn't it?' before hurriedly consulting her shopping list and trying to conceal her red face behind the barricades of breakfast cereal. Mr. Wilson himself left the invoicing which was concerning him behind the scenes and came forward, quietly deferential as ever, to attend to Mrs. Maxie. He was a tall, lean, cadaverous-looking man with a face of such startling unhappiness that it was difficult to believe that he was not on the brink of bankruptcy instead of the owner of a flourishing little business. He heard more gossip than almost anyone in the village, but expressed an opinion himself so rarely that his pronouncements were listened to with great respect and commonly remembered. So far he had been uniformly silent on the subject of Sally

110

Jupp, but it was not therefore supposed that he considered it an unsuitable subject for comment or was restrained by any reverence in the face of sudden death. Sooner or later, it was felt, Mr. Wilson would pronounce judgment, and the village would be very surprised if the judgment of the Law itself, given later and with more ceremony, were not substantially the same. He accepted Mrs. Maxie's order in silence and occupied himself with serving his most valued customer, while one by one the little group of women muttered their good-byes and crept or swept out of his shop.

When they had gone Mr. Wilson gave a conspiratorial glance around, cast his watery eyes upwards as if seeking guidance and then leaned across the counter towards Mrs. Maxie.

'Derek Pullen,' he said. 'That's who.'

'I'm afraid I don't know what you mean, Mr. Wilson.' Mrs. Maxie spoke the truth. She might have added that she had no particular desire to know.

'I'm saying nothing, mind you, madam. Let the police do their own work I say. But if they bother you at Martingale, ask them where Derek Pullen was going last Saturday night. Ask them that. He passed here at twelve or thereabouts. Saw him myself from the bedroom window.'

Mr. Wilson drew himself up with the self-satisfied air of a man who has pronounced a final unanswerable argument and returned with a complete change of mood to the business of totalling Mrs. Maxie's bill. She felt that she ought to say that any evidence he possessed or thought that he possessed should be communicated to the police, but she could not bring herself to say words to this effect. She remembered Derek Pullen as she had last seen him, a small, rather spotty youth who wore over-cut city suits and cheap shoes. His mother was a member of the Women's Institute and his father worked for Sir Reynold on the larger of his two farms. It was too silly and unfair. If Wilson couldn't keep his mouth shut there would be the police at the Pullens' cottage before nightfall and it was anyone's guess what they would ferret out. The boy looked timid and would probably be scared out of the few wits he looked as if he possessed. Then Mrs. Maxie remembered that someone had been in Sally's room that night.

111

It could have been Derek Pullen. If Martingale were to be saved any further suffering she must keep her allegiance clear. 'If you have information, Mr. Wilson,' she said, 'I think you should give it to Inspector Dalgleish. In the meantime you might harm a great many innocent people by making accusations of that kind.'

Mr. Wilson received this mild rebuke with the liveliest satisfaction as if it were the only confirmation needed of his own theories. He had obviously said all he intended to and the subject was now closed. 'Four and five and ten and nine and one pound one shilling is one pound sixteen and two, if you please, madam,' he intoned. Mrs. Maxie paid.

5

Meanwhile Johnnie Wilcox, a grubby and under-sized twelve-year-old, was being interviewed by Dalgleish in the business room. He had presented himself at Martingale with the announcement that the vicar had sent him to see the inspector and please it was important. Dalgleish received him with grave courtesy and invited him to sit down and tell his story in comfort. He told it clearly and well and it was the most intriguing piece of evidence that Dalgleish had heard for some time.

Apparently Johnnie had been detailed with other members of his Sunday school class to help with the teas and the washing-up. There had been some feeling over this arrangement which was generally felt by the boys to be domestic, degrading and, frankly, not much fun. True, there had been promises of feasting later with the leftovers but the teas were always popular and last year several helpers had arrived to lend a belated hand and to share the meagre spoils with those who had borne the heat of the day. Johnnie Wilcox had seen no advantage in lingering longer than necessary and as soon as enough children had arrived to make his absence less noticeable he had possessed himself of two fish sandwiches, three chocolate buns and a couple of jam tarts and had borne them off to Bocock's stable loft in the confidence that Bocock was safely occupied giving pony rides.

Johnnie had been sitting peacefully in the loft munching and reading his comic for some time – it was useless to expect him to estimate for how long but only one bun remained – when he had heard footsteps and voices. He had not been alone in a desire for privacy and two other people were coming into the stable. He did not wait to see whether they were also intending to climb into the loft, but took the sensible precaution of removing himself and his bun to a corner where he hid behind a large bale of straw. This action did not seem unnecessarily timid. In Johnnie's world a great deal of unpleasantness from spankings to going to bed at an early hour was avoided by the simple expedient of knowing when not to be seen. This time his caution was again justified. The footsteps did come up into the hay loft and he heard the soft thud of the trap-door being replaced. After that he was forced to sit in silence and some boredom, nibbling quietly at his bun and trying to make it last out until the visitors should depart. There were only two of them, he was certain of that – and one of them was Sally Jupp. He had caught a brief glimpse of her hair as she came through the trap-door, but had been forced to dodge back before she was in full view. But there was no doubt about it. Johnnie knew Sally well enough to be quite certain that he had both seen and heard her in the hay loft on Saturday afternoon. But he had not seen nor recognized the man with her. Once Sally had entered the loft it would have been risky to peer round the bundle of hay since even the smallest movement caused an unexpectedly loud rustling, and Johnnie had employed all his energies in keeping perfectly, and most unnaturally, still. Partly because the heavy hay bundle had muffled the voices and partly because he was used to finding the conversations of grown-up people both boring and incomprehensible, he made no effort to understand what was being said. All that Dalgleish could count on as reliable was that the two visitors had been arguing, but in low voices, that there was some mention of forty pounds, and that Sally Jupp had ended up by saying something about there being no risk if he kept his head and 'watching for the light'. Johnnie said that there had been a great deal of talk but most of it was spoken quietly and quickly. Only those few phrases remained in his memory. He could not say how long the three of them remained in the loft.

It had seemed a dreadfully long time and he was stiff and thoroughly bored before he heard the sound of the trap-door being banged back and the girl and her companion left the loft. Sally had gone first and the man had followed. Johnnie had not felt safe in peering from his hiding-place until the sound of their footsteps was heard disappearing down the steps. Then he was in time to see a brown gloved hand replacing the trap-door. He had waited another few minutes himself then had run back to the fête where his absence had aroused very little interest. That, indeed, was the sum total of Johnnie Wilcox's Saturday afternoon adventure and it was irritating to consider how a few changes in circumstances might have added to its value. If Johnnie had been a little more adventurous he might have seen the man. If he had been a few years older or of a different sex he certainly would have considered this clandestine meeting in a more intriguing light than the mere interruption of a feast and would certainly have listened to and remembered as much of the conversation as possible. Now it was difficult to place any interpretation on the scraps he had overheard. He seemed an honest and reliable little boy, but ready enough to admit that he might have made a mistake. He thought that Sally had talked about 'the light' but he might have imagined it. He hadn't really been listening and they were speaking quietly. On the other hand he had no doubt at all that it was Sally he had seen and was equally firm in his belief that it was not a friendly meeting. He couldn't be sure of the time when he left the stable. Teas began about half past three and lasted as long as people wanted them and the food held out. Johnnie thought it must have been about half past four when he first made his escape from Mrs. Cope. He couldn't remember how long he was hidden in the stable. It had seemed a very long time. With that Dalgleish had to be content. The whole thing was suspiciously like a case of blackmail and it seemed likely that another assignation had been made. But the fact that Johnnie had not recognized the man's voice seemed to prove conclusively that it could not have been either Stephen Maxie or a local man, most of whom would be well known to him. That at least supported the theory that there was another man to be considered. If Sally were

114

blackmailing this stranger and he was actually at the church fête, then things looked brighter for the Maxies. As he thanked young Johnnie, warned him against talking to anyone else about his experience, and dismissed him to the comforting pleasure of revealing all that had passed to the vicar, Dalgleish's mind was already busy with new evidence.

CHAPTER SIX

1

THE inquest was fixed for three o'clock on Tuesday and the Maxies found they were almost looking forward to it as at least one known obligation which might help to speed the slow, uncomfortable hours. There was a sense of constant unease like the tension of a thundery day when the storm is inevitable and yet will not break. The tacit assumption that no one at Martingale could be a murderer precluded any realistic discussion of Sally's death. They were all afraid of saying too much or of saying it to the wrong person. Sometimes Deborah wished that the household could get together and at least decide on some solid basis of strategy. But when Stephen hesitantly voiced the same wish she drew back in sudden panic. Stephen talking about Sally was not to be borne.

Felix Hearne was different. With him it was possible to discuss almost anything. He did not fear death for himself nor was he shy of it and he apparently saw no breach of good taste in discussing Sally Jupp's death dispassionately and even lightly. At first Deborah took part in these conversations in a spirit of bravado. Later she realized that humour was only a feeble attempt to denigrate fear. Now, before Tuesday luncheon, she paced between the roses at Felix's side while he poured out his spate of blessedly foolish chatter, provoking her to an equally dispassionate and diverting flow of theories.

'Seriously though, Deborah. If I were writing a book I should make it one of the village boys. Derek Pullen, for example.'

'But he didn't. Anyway, he hasn't a motive.'

'Motive is the last thing to look for. You can always find a motive. Perhaps the corpse was blackmailing him. Perhaps she was pressing him to marry her and he wouldn't. She could tell him that there was another baby

116

on the way. It isn't true, of course, but he wasn't to know that. You see, they had been having the usual passionate *affaire*. I should make him one of the quiet, intense kind. They're capable of anything. In fiction anyway.'

'But she didn't want him to marry her. She had Stephen to marry. She wouldn't want Derek Pullen if she could have Stephen.'

'You speak, if I may say so, with the blind partiality of a sister. But have it your own way. Whom do you suggest?'

'Suppose we make it Father.'

'You mean the elderly gentleman, tied to his bed?'

'Yes. Except that he wasn't. It could be one of those Grand Guignol plots. The elderly gentleman didn't want his son to marry the scheming hussy so he crawled upstairs step by step and strangled her with his old school tie.'

Felix considered this effort and rejected it.

'Why not make it the mysterious visitor with a name like a cinema cat. Who is he? Where does he come from? Could he be the father of her child?'

'Oh, I don't think so.'

'Well, he was. He had met the corpse when she was an innocent girl at her first job. I shall draw a veil over that painful episode but you can imagine his surprise and horror when he meets her again, the girl he has wronged, in the home of his fiancée. And with his child too!'

'Has he a fiancée?'

'Of course. An extremely attractive widow whom he is determined to snare. Anyway, the poor wronged girl threatens to tell all so he has to silence her. I should make him one of those cynical, unlikable characters so that no one would worry when he got copped.'

'You don't think that would be rather sordid? What about making it the Warden of St. Mary's? It could be one of those psychological thrillers with highbrow quotations at the beginning of the chapters and a lot of Freud.'

'If it's Freud you fancy I'd put my money on the corpse's uncle. Now there would be a fine excuse for some deep psychological stuff. You see, he was a hard, narrow-minded man who had turned her out when he heard about the baby. But like all Puritans in fiction, he was just as bad himself. He had been carrying on with a simple

117

little girl whom he met singing in the choir and she was in the same Home as the corpse having her baby. So the whole horrible truth came out and, of course, Sally was blackmailing him for thirty bob a week and nothing said. Obviously he couldn't risk exposure. He was far too respectable for that.'

'What did Sally do with the thirty bob?'

'Opened a savings account in the baby's name of course. All that will come to light in due course.'

'It would be nice if it did. But aren't you forgetting about the corpse's prospective sister-in-law? No difficulty about motive there.'

Felix said easily, 'But she wasn't a murderess.'

'Oh, damn you, Felix! Must you be so blatantly tactful?'

'Since I know very well that you didn't kill Sally Jupp, do you expect me to go about registering embarrassment and suspicion just for the fun of it?'

'I did hate her, Felix. I really hated her.'

'All right, my sweet. So you really hated her. That is bound to put you at a disadvantage with yourself. But don't be too anxious to confide your feelings to the police. They are worthy men, no doubt, and their manners are beautiful. They may, however, be limited in imagination. After all, their great strength is their common sense. That is the basis of all sound detective work. They have the method and the means so don't go handing them the motive. Let them do some work for the taxpayers money.'

'Do you think Dalgleish will find out who did it?' asked Deborah after a little pause.

'I think he may know now,' replied Felix calmly. 'Getting enough evidence to justify a charge is a different matter. We may find out this afternoon how far the police have got and how much they're prepared to tell. It may amuse Dalgleish to keep us in suspense but he's bound to show his hand sooner or later.'

But the inquest was both a relief and a disappointment. The coroner sat without a jury. He was a mild-voiced man with the face of a depressed St. Bernard dog who gave the impression of having wandered into the proceedings by mistake. For all that, he knew what he wanted and he wasted no time. There were fewer villagers present than the Maxies had expected. Probably they were conserving time and energy for the better entertainment of the funeral. Certainly, those present were little wiser than they were before. The coroner made it all seem deceptively simple. Evidence of identification was given by a nervous, insignificant little woman who proved to be Sally's aunt. Stephen Maxie gave evidence and the factual details of finding the body were briefly elicited. The medical evidence showed that death was caused by vagal inhibition during manual strangulation and had been very sudden. There were about one and a half grains of barbiturate acid derivative in the stomach. The coroner asked no questions other than those necessary to establish these facts. The police asked for an adjournment and this was granted. It was all very informal, almost friendly. The witnesses crouched on the low chairs used by the Sunday school children while the coroner drooped over the proceedings from the superintendent's dais. There were jam jars of summer flowers on the window-sills and a flannelgraph on one wall showed the Christian's journey from baptism to burial in crayoned pictures. In these innocent and incongruous surroundings the law, with formality but without fuss, took note that Sarah Lillian Jupp had been feloniously done to death.

2

Now there was the funeral to face. Here, unlike the inquest, attendance was optional and the decision whether or not to appear was one which none but Mrs. Maxie found easy. She had no difficulty and made it clear that she had every intention of being present. Although she did not discuss the matter, her attitude was obvious. Sally Jupp had died in their house and in their employ. Her only relations had obviously no intentions of forgiving her for being as embarrassing and unorthodox in death as she had been in life. They would have no part in the funeral and it would take place from St. Mary's and at the expense of that institution. But, apart from the need for someone to be there, the Maxies had a responsibility. If people died in your house the least you could do was to attend the funeral. Mrs. Maxie did not express herself in these words, but her son and daughter were unmistakably given to understand that such attendance was mere courtesy and that those who extended to others the hospitality of their homes should, if it unfortunately proved necessary, extend that hospitality to seeing them safely into their graves. In all her private imaginings of what life at Martingale would be during a murder investigation Deborah had never considered the major part which comparatively minor matters of taste or etiquette would play. It was strange that the overriding anxiety of all their futures would be, temporarily at least, less urgent than the worry of whether or not the family should send a wreath to the funeral, and if so, what appropriate condolence should be written on the card. Here again the question did not worry Mrs. Maxie who merely inquired whether they wished to club together or whether Deborah would send a wreath of her own.

Stephen, it appeared, was exempt from these obsequies. The police had given him permission to return to hospital after the inquest and he would not be at Martingale again until the following Saturday night, except for fleeting visits. No one expected him to provide a chaste wreath for the delectation of the village gossips. He had every excuse for returning to London and carrying on with his job. Even Dalgleish could not expect him to hang about at Martingale indefinitely for the convenience of the police.

If Catherine had almost as valid an excuse for returning to London she did not avail herself of it. Apparently she still had seven days of her annual leave in hand and was willing and happy to stay at Martingale. Matron had been approached and was sympathetic. There would be absolutely no difficulty if she could help Mrs. Maxie in any way. Undeniably she could. There was still the heavy nursing of Simon Maxie to be coped with, there was the continual interruption of household routine caused by Dalgleish's investigation, and there was the lack of Sally.

Once it was established that her mother intended to be at the funeral, Deborah set about subduing her natural abhorrence of the whole idea and announced abruptly that she would be there. She was not surprised when

120

Catherine expressed a similar intention, but it was both unexpected and a relief to find that Felix meant to go with them.

'It's not in the least necessary,' she told him angrily. 'I can't think what all the fuss is about. Personally I find the whole idea morbid and distasteful, but if you want to come and be gaped at, well, it's a free show.' She left the drawing-room quickly but returned a few minutes later to say with the disconcerting formality which he found so disarming in her : 'I'm sorry I was so rude, Felix. Please do come if you will. It was sweet of you to think of it.'

Felix felt suddenly angry with Stephen. It was true that the boy had every excuse for returning to work, but it was nevertheless typical and irritating that he should have so ready and simple an excuse for evading responsibility and unpleasantness. Neither Deborah nor her mother, of course, would see it that way and Catherine Bowers, poor besotted fool, was ready to forgive Stephen anything. None of the women would intrude their troubles or difficulties on Stephen. But, thought Felix, if that young man had disciplined his more quixotic impulses none of this need have happened. Felix prepared for the funeral in a mood of cold anger and fought resolutely against the suspicion that part of his resentment was frustration and part was envy.

It was another wonderful day. The crowd were dressed in summer dresses, some of the girls in clothes which would have been more suitable on a bathing-beach than in a cemetery. A large number had evidently been picnicking and had only heard of the better entertainment to be offered in the churchyard by chance. They were laden with the remains of their feasts and some were actually still engaged in finishing their sandwiches or oranges. They were perfectly well behaved once they got near to the grave. Death has an almost universal sobering effect and a few nervous giggles were soon repressed by the outraged glances of the more orthodox. It was not their behaviour that enraged Deborah, it was the fact that they should be there at all. She was filled with a cold contempt and an anger that was frightening in its intensity.

Afterwards she was glad of this since it left no room for grief or embarrassment.

The Maxies, Felix Hearne and Catherine Bowers stood together at the open graveside with Miss Liddell and a handful of girls from St. Mary's bunched behind them. Opposite them stood Dalgleish and Martin. Police and suspects faced each other across the open grave. A little way away another funeral was in progress taken by some alien clergyman from another parish. The little group of mourners were all in black and huddled so close to the grave in a tight circle that they seemed engaged in some secret and esoteric rite that was not for the eyes of others. No one took any notice of them and the voice of their priest could not be heard above the minor rustlings of Sally's crowd. Afterwards they went quietly away. They, thought Deborah, had at least buried their dead with some dignity. But now Mr. Hinks was speaking his few words. Wisely he did not mention the circumstances of the girl's death, but said gently that the ways of Providence were strange and mysterious, an assertion which few of his listeners were competent to disprove, even though the presence of the police suggested that some at least of this present mystery was the work of human agency.

Mrs. Maxie took an active interest in the whole ceremony, her audible 'Amens' sounded emphatic agreement at the end of each petition, she found her way about the Book of Common Prayer with capable fingers and helped two of the St. Mary's girls to find the place when they were too overcome with grief or embarrassment to manage their books themselves. At the end of the service she stepped up to the grave and stood for a moment gazing down at the coffin. Deborah felt rather than heard her sigh. What it meant no one could have told from the composed face that turned itself again to confront the crowd. She pulled on her gloves and leaned down to read one of the mourning-cards before joining her daughter.

'What an appalling crowd. One would think people had something better to do. Still, if that poor child Sally were half the exhibitionist she seems to have been, this funeral would meet with her approval. What is that boy doing? Is this your mother? Well, surely your little boy knows that one doesn't jump about on graves. You must control him better if you want to bring him into the churchyard. This is consecrated ground, not the school playground. A funeral isn't suitable entertainment for a child anyway.'

The mother and child gaped after them, two pale astounded faces with the same sharp noses, the same scrawny hair. Then the woman pulled her child away with a frightened backward glance. Already the bright splurge of colour was dispersing, the bicycles were being dragged from among the Michaelmas daisies by the churchyard wall, the photographers were packing up their cameras. One or two little groups still waited about, whispering together and watching an opportunity to snoop among the wreaths. The sexton was already picking up the legacy of orange peel and paper bags, muttering under his breath. Sally's grave was a sheet of colour. Reds, blues and gold spread over the piled turfs and wooden planks like a gaudy patchwork quilt and the scent of rich earth mixed with the scent of the flowers.

3

'Isn't that Sally's aunt?' asked Deborah. A thin, nervous-looking woman with hair which might once have been red was talking to Miss Liddell. They walked away together towards the churchyard gate. 'Surely it's the same woman who identified Sally at the inquest. If it is the aunt perhaps we could drive her home. The buses are dreadfully infrequent at this time of day.'

'It might be worth while having a word with her,' said Felix consideringly. Deborah's suggestion had originally been prompted by simple kindness, the wish to save someone a long wait in the hot sun. But now the practical advantages of her proposal asserted themselves.

'Do get Miss Liddell to introduce you, Felix. I'll bring the car round. You might find out where Sally worked before she got pregnant, and who Jimmy's father is and whether Sally's uncle really liked her.'

'In two or three moments of casual conversation? I hardly think so.'

'We should have all the drive to pump her. Do try, Felix.'

123

Deborah sped after her mother and Catherine with as much speed as decency permitted, leaving Felix to his task. The woman and Miss Liddell had reached the road now and were pausing for a few last words. From a distance the two figures seemed to be excuting some kind of ceremonial dance. They moved together to shake hands, then bobbed apart. Then Miss Liddell, who had turned away, swung back with some fresh remark and the figures drew together again.

As Felix moved towards them they turned to watch him and he could see Miss Liddell's lips moving. He joined them and the inescapable introductions were made. A thin hand, gloved in cheap black rayon, held his hand timidly for a brief second and then dropped. Even in that apathetic and almost imperceptible contact he sensed that she was shaking. The anxious grey eyes looked away from his as he spoke.

'Mrs. Riscoe and I were wondering if we might drive you home,' he said gently. 'There will be a long wait for a bus and we should be very glad of the drive.' That at least was the truth. She hesitated. Just as Miss Liddell had apparently decided that the offer, although unexpected, could not in decency be ignored and might even be safely accepted and had begun to urge this course, Deborah drew up beside them in Felix's Renault and the matter was settled. Sally's aunt was introduced to her as Mrs. Victor Proctor and was comfortably ensconced beside her in the front of the car before anyone had time for argument. Felix settled himself in the back, aware of some distaste for the enterprise but prepared to admire Deborah in action. 'Painless extractions a speciality' he thought as the car swung away down the hill. He wondered how far they were going and whether Deborah had bothered to tell her mother how long they would be away. 'I think I know roughly where you live,' he heard her saying. 'It's just outside Canningbury, isn't it? We go through it on our way to London. But I shall have to rely on you for the road. It's very sweet of you to let us drive you home. Funerals are so awful. It really is a relief to get away for a time.' The result of this was unexpected. Suddenly Mrs. Proctor was crying, not noisily, hardly even without moving her face. Almost as if her tears were without any

124

possibility of control she let them slide in a stream down her cheeks and fall on to her folded hands. When she spoke her voice was low but clear enough to be heard above the engine. And still the tears fell silently and without effort.

'I shouldn't have come really. Mr. Proctor wouldn't like it if he knew I'd come. He won't be back when I get home and Beryl is at school, so he won't know. But he wouldn't like it. She's made her own bed so let her lie on it. That's what he says and you can't blame him. Not after what he's done for her. There was never any difference between Sally and Beryl. Never. I'll say that to the day I die. I don't know why it had to happen to us.'

This perennial cry of the unfortunate struck Felix as unreasonable. He was not aware that the Proctors had accepted any responsibility for Sally since her pregnancy and they had certainly succeeded in dissociating themselves from her death. He leaned forward to hear more clearly. Deborah may have made some kind of encouraging sound, he could not be sure. But there was to be no question of pumping this witness. She had been keeping things to herself for too long. 'We brought her up decently. No one can say we didn't. It hasn't always been easy. She did get the scholarship but we still had to feed her. She wasn't an easy child. I used to think it was the bombing but Mr. Proctor wouldn't have that. They were with us at the time, you know. We had a house in Stoke Newington then. There hadn't been many raids and somehow we felt safe with the Anderson shelter and everything. It was one of those V1 rockets that did for Lil and George. I don't remember anything about it nor about being dug out. They never told me about Lil for a week afterwards. They got us all out but Lil was dead and George died in hospital. We were the lucky ones. At least I suppose we were. Mr. Proctor was really bad for a long time and, of course, he's got his disability. But they said we were the lucky ones.'

'Like me,' thought Felix bitterly. 'One of the lucky ones.'

'And then you took Sally and brought her up,' prompted Deborah.

'There wasn't anyone else really. Mother couldn't have

125

taken her. She wasn't fit for it. I tried to think that Lil
would have liked it, but those sort of thoughts can't help
you to love a child. She wasn't loving really. Not like
Beryl. But then Sally was ten before Beryl arrived and I
suppose it was hard on her after being the only one for so
long. But we never made a difference. They always had
the same, piano lessons and everything. And now this. The
police came round after she died. They weren't in uniform
or anything, but you could see who they were. Everyone
knew about it. They asked who the man was but, of
course, we couldn't say.'

'The man who killed her?' Deborah sounded incredulous.

'Oh no. The father of the baby. I suppose they thought
he might have done it. But we couldn't tell them anything.'

'I suppose they asked a lot of questions about where
you were on the night.'

For the first time Mrs. Proctor seemed aware of her
tears. She fumbled in her handbag and wiped them away.
Interest in her story seemed to have assuaged whatever
grief she was indulging. Felix thought that it was unlikely
that she wept for Sally. Was it the resurrected memory of
Lil, of George and of the helpless child they had left
behind which had caused those tears, or was it just weariness and a sense of failure? Almost as if she sensed his
question she said, 'I don't know why I'm crying. Crying
can't bring back the dead. I suppose it was the service.
We had that hymn for Lil. "The King of Love my Shep-
herd Is". It doesn't seem right for either of them really.
You were asking about the police. I suppose you've had
your share of them, too. They came to us all right. I told
them I was at home with Beryl. They asked if we went
to the fête at Chadfleet. I told them we didn't know anything about it. Not that we would have gone. We didn't
see Sally ever and we didn't want to come nosing around
where she worked. I could remember the day all right. It
was funny really. Miss Liddell telephoned in the morning
to talk to Mr. Proctor which she hadn't done since Sally
took her new job. Beryl answered the 'phone and it made
her feel quite queer. She thought something must have
happened to Sally for Miss Liddell to 'phone. But it

126

was only to say that Sally was doing all right. It was funny though. She knew we didn't want to hear.'

It must have struck Deborah as strange, too, for she asked. 'Had Miss Liddell telephoned before to tell you how Sally was getting on?'

'No. Not since Sally went to Martingale. She telephoned to tell us that. At least I think she did. She may have written to Mr. Proctor, but I can't be sure. I suppose she thought that we ought to know about Sally leaving the Home, Mr. Proctor being her guardian. At least he used to be, but now she's over twenty-one and on her own it's nothing to us where she goes. She never cared for us not for any of us, not even Beryl. I thought I'd better come today because it looks queer if no one from the family's there, whatever Mr. Proctor may say. But he was right really. You can't help the dead by being there and it's only upsetting. All those people, too. They ought to have something better to do.'

'So Mr. Proctor hadn't seen Sally since she left your house?' pursued Deborah.

'Oh, no. There wouldn't be any point in it, would there?'

'I expect the police asked him where he was on the night she died. They always do. Of course it's only a formality.'

If Deborah had been afraid of causing offence she was worrying unnecessarily.

'It's funny the way they go on. You'd have thought we knew something about it by the way they talked. Asking questions about Sally's life and whether she had any expectations and who her friends were. Anyone would think she was someone important. They had Beryl in to ask about the telephone call from Miss Liddell. They even asked Mr. Proctor what he was doing the night Sally died. Not that we were likely to forget that night. It was the one he had his cycle accident. He wasn't home till twelve and he was in a proper bad state with his lip all swollen and the cycle bent up. He lost his watch, too, which was up-setting as his father left it to him and it was real gold. Very valuable they always told us. We aren't likely to for-get that night in a hurry I can tell you.'

Mrs. Proctor had now recovered completely from the

emotional effects of the funeral and was chatting away with the eagerness of someone who is more accustomed to listening than to getting a hearing. Deborah was making light work of the driving. Her hands lay gently on the wheel and her blue eyes gazed steadily on the road ahead, but Felix had little doubt that most of her mind was on other matters. She made sympathetic sounds in reply to Mrs. Proctor's story and replied, 'What a horrid shock for you both! You must have been terribly worried when he was so late. How did it happen?'

'He came off at the bottom of a hill somewhere Finch-worthy way. I don't know exactly where. He was coming down fast and someone had left broken glass in the road. Of course it ripped the front tyre and he lost control and went into the ditch. He might have been killed as I told him, or badly injured, and if he had, goodness knows what would have happened because those roads are very lonely. You could lie there for hours and no one come by. Mr. Proctor doesn't like the busy roads for cycling and I don't wonder. There's no peace if you don't get away by yourself.'

'Is he fond of cycling?' asked Deborah.

'Cycling mad. Always has been. Of course he doesn't go in for the real road work now. Not since the war and being bombed. He did a lot of it when he was young though. But he still likes to get about and we don't usually see much of him on Saturday afternoons.'

Mrs. Proctor's voice held a shade of relief which was not lost on either of her listeners. A bicycle and an accident can be a useful alibi, thought Felix, but he can't be a serious suspect if he was indoors by twelve. It would take him at least an hour to get home from Martingale even if the accident were faked, and he had the use of the bicycle all the way. It was difficult, too, to imagine an adequate motive since Proctor had obviously found no reason to murder his niece before her admission to St. Mary's and had apparently had no contact with her since. Felix's mind played with the possibility of a future inheritance for Sally which, at her death, would conveniently devolve upon Beryl Proctor. But in his heart he knew that he was looking not for the murderer of Sally Jupp but for someone with sufficient motive and opportunity to divert the police investigation from more likely suspects. It seemed a forlorn hope so far as the Proctors were concerned, but Deborah had obviously made up her mind that there was something to be discovered from them. The time factor was apparently worrying her, too.

'Did you wait up for your husband, Mrs. Proctor? You must have been getting pretty desperate by midnight unless he was usually late.'

'Well, he was usually a bit late and he always said not to wait up so I didn't. I go to the pictures most Saturdays with Beryl. We've got the telly, of course, and we sometimes watch that, but it makes a change to get out of the house once a week.'

'So you were in bed when your husband returned?' Deborah insisted gently.

'He had his own key, of course, so there wasn't any point in waiting up. If I'd known he was going to be so late it would have been different. I usually go up to bed about ten when Mr. Proctor's out. Mind you, there's not the same rush on a Sunday morning, but I was never one for late nights. That's what I told the police. "I was never one for late nights", I said. They were askiing about Mr. Proctor's accident, too. The inspector was very sympathetic. "Not home until nearly twelve", I told them. They could see it had been a worrying night without Sally getting herself murdered like that.'

'I expect Mr. Proctor woke you when he arrived home. It must have been terribly worrying to see him in that condition.'

'Oh, it was! I heard him in the bathroom and when I called out he came in to me. His face looked awful, a terrible green colour streaked with blood, and he was shaking all over. I don't know how he got home. I got up to make him a cup of tea while he had a bath. I remember the time because he called down to ask me what it was. He'd lost his watch you see after the accident, and we'd only got the little kitchen clock and the one in the front room. That said ten minutes past midnight and the kitchen one said the same. It was a shock to me I can tell you. It must have been half past twelve before we were back in bed and I never thought he'd be fit to get up the next morning. But he did, the same as usual. He always goes down first and makes the tea. He thinks no one can make tea like him and he does bring up a good cup. But I never thought he'd get up early that Sunday, not after what he looked like the night before. He's still shaken up by it even now. That's why he didn't go to the inquest. And then to have the police arriving that morning to tell us about Sally. We shan't forget that night in a hurry.'

4

They had reached Canningbury now and there was a long wait at the traffic lights which regulated the surge of traffic meeting at the High Road and the Broadway. It was obviously a popular shopping afternoon in this over-crowded suburb of east London. The pavements were spilling with housewives who every now and then, as if propelled by some primeval urge, streamed with mad-dening slowness across the path of the traffic. The shops on both sides of the road had once been a row of houses and their grandiose windows and frontages were in incon-gruous contrast to the modest roofs and windows above. The town hall, which looked as if it had been designed by a committee of morons in an excess of alcohol and civic pride, stood in isolated splendour bounded by two bombed sites where rebuilding had only just begun.

Closing his eyes against the heat and the noise Felix reminded himself sternly that Canningbury was one of the more enlightened suburbs with an enviable record of good public services and that not everyone wanted to live in a quiet Georgian house in Greenwich where the mist came up from the river in white fingers and only the most per-sistent friends found their way to his door. He was glad when the traffic lights changed and, under Mrs. Proctor's guidance, they moved forward in a series of gentle jerks and turned left away from the main road. Here was the backwash of the shopping centre, the women walking home with their laden baskets, the few smaller gown-shops and hairdressers with pseudo-French names over the con-verted front-room windows. After a few minutes they turned again into a quiet street where a row of identical houses stretched as far as the eye could see. Although they

130

were identical in structure, however, they were very different in appearance for hardly two of the small front gardens were alike. All were carefully sown and tended. A few householders had expressed their individuality with monkey-puzzle trees, coy stone gnomes fishing from basins or spurious rock gardens, but the majority had contented themselves by creating a little show of colour and fragrance which shamed the dull nonentity of the house behind. The curtains showed signs of careful if misguided choosing and of frequent washings, and were supplemented by additional half-curtains of draped lace or net which were carefully drawn against the curiosity of a vulgar world. Windermere Crescent had the respectable look of a street that is a cut above its neighbours and whose inhabitants are determined to maintain that superiority.

This then had been the home of Sally Jupp who had fallen so lamentably from its standards. The car drew in to the kerb at the gate of number 17 and Mrs. Proctor clutched her black shapeless handbag to her chest and began to fumble at the door. 'Let me,' said Deborah, and leaned across her to release the catch. Mrs. Proctor extricated herself and began her profuse thanks which Deborah cut short.

'Please don't. We were very glad to come. I wonder if I might bother you for a glass of water before we leave. It's silly, I know, but driving is so thirst-making in this heat. Really only water. I hardly ever drink anything else.'

'Don't you, by God!' thought Felix as the two women disappeared into the house.

He wondered what Deborah was up to now and hoped that the wait wouldn't be too long. Mrs. Proctor had been offered no choice about inviting her benefactor into the house. She could hardly have brought a glass of water out to the car. Nevertheless Felix was certain that she had not welcomed the intrusion. She had glanced anxiously up the road before they went in and he guessed that the time was getting dangerously late and that she was desperately anxious that the car should be gone before her husband came home. Some of the anxiety she had shown when they first met her in the churchyard had returned. He felt a momentary spasm of irritation with Deborah. The exercise

131

was unlikely to be useful and it was a shame to worry that pathetic little woman.

Deborah, untouched by such nice refinement of feeling, was being shown into the front room. A schoolgirl was arranging her music on the piano in evident preparation for her practice but was bundled out of the room with a hasty injunction to 'Fetch a glass of water, dear' spoken in the falsely bright tone often used by parents in the presence of strangers. The child went out rather reluctantly Deborah thought and not without giving her a long and deliberate stare. She was a remarkably plain child, but the likeness to her dead cousin was unmistakable. Mrs. Proctor had not introduced her and Deborah wondered whether this was an oversight due to nervousness or a deliberate wish to keep the child in ignorance of her mother's afternoon's activities. If so, presumably some story would be concocted to explain the visit, although Mrs. Proctor had not struck her as possessing much inventive faculty.

They sat down in opposite armchairs, each with its embroidered chair-back of a crinolined and bonneted female gathering hollyhocks and its plump unsullied cushions. This was obviously the best room, used only for entertaining or for piano practice. It had the faint musty smell compounded of wax polish, new furniture and seldom-opened windows. On the piano were two photographs of young girls in ballet dresses, their graceless bodies bent into unnatural and angular poses and their faces set into determined smiles beneath the wreaths of artificial roses. One of them was the child who had just left the room. The other was Sally. It was strange how, even at that age, the same family colouring and similar bone structure should have produced in one an essential distinction and in the other a heavy plainness that held little promise for the future. Mrs. Proctor saw the direction of her glance.

'Yes,' she said, 'we did everything for her. Everything. There was never any difference made. She had piano lessons, too, the same as Beryl although she never had Beryl's gift. But we always treated them alike. It's a dreadful thing that it's all ended like this. That other photo is the group we had took after Beryl's christening. That's me and Mr. Proctor with the baby and Sally. She was a pretty little thing then, but it didn't last.'

132

Deborah moved over to the photograph. The group had been stiffly posed in heavy carved chairs and against a contrived background of draped curtains which made the photograph look older than it was. Mrs. Proctor, younger and more buxom, held her child awkwardly and looked ill at ease in her new clothes.

Sally looked sulky. The husband was posed behind them, his gloved hands leaning proprietorially on the backs of the chairs. There was something unnatural in his stance, but his face gave nothing away. Deborah looked at him carefully. Somewhere she was certain that she had seen that face before, but the recognition was tenuous and unsatisfactory. It was, after all, an unremarkable face and the photograph was more than ten years old. She turned away from the photograph with a sense of disappointment. It had told her very little and she hardly knew what else she had expected to gain from it.

Beryl Proctor came back with the glass of water, one of the best glasses carried on a small papier mâché tray. No introductions were made and Deborah was conscious as she drank that both of them wished her away. Suddenly she wished nothing more herself than to be out of the house and free of them. Her coming in had been an incomprehensible impulse. It had been prompted partly by boredom, partly by hope and very largely by curiosity. Sally dead had become more interesting than Sally alive and she had wanted to see from what sort of home Sally had been rejected. That curiosity now seemed presumption and her entry into the house an intrusion which she did not want to prolong.

She said her 'good-byes' and rejoined Felix. He took the wheel and they did not speak until the town was behind them and the car was shaking free of the suburban tentacles and climbing into the country.

'Well,' said Felix at last, 'was the exercise in detection worth while? Are you sure you want to go on with it?'

'Why not?'

'Only that you might discover facts which you would prefer not to know.'

'Such as my family contains a murderer?'

'I didn't say that.'

'You have been studiously careful not to say it, but I

133

would prefer honesty to tact. That is what you think, isn't it?'

'Speaking as a murderer myself, I admit that it's a possibility.'

'You're thinking of the Resistance. That wasn't murder. You didn't kill women.'

'I killed two. I admit it was by shooting, not by strangulation, and it seemed at the time to be expedient.'

'This killing was expedient all right – for someone,' said Deborah.

'Then why not leave it to the police? Their greatest difficulty will be to get enough evidence to justify a charge. If we start interfering we may only hand them the evidence they want. The case is wide open. Stephen and I got through Sally's window. So could almost anyone else. Most people in the village must have known where that ladder was kept. The evidence of that locked door is incontrovertible. However her murderer got in he didn't go out through the door. There's only the Sommeil to connect this crime with Martingale and the two need not be related. Other people had access to the stuff even if they are.'

'Aren't you relying too much on coincidence?' asked Deborah coldly.

'Coincidences happen every day. An average jury will be able to think up half a dozen instances in their own experience. The most likely interpretation of the facts so far is that someone known to Sally got in through her window and killed her. He may or may not have used the ladder. There are scratches on the walls as if he slid down by the stack-pipe and lost his hold when he was nearly at the ground. The police must have noticed these, but I don't see how they can prove when the scratches were made. Sally may have been admitting callers that way on previous occasions.'

'It seems a curious thing to say but somehow I can't believe that. It's not in character. I'd like to believe it for all our sakes, but I don't. I never liked Sally, but I don't believe that she was promiscuous. I don't want safety at the price of blackening the poor little devil's reputation further now that she isn't here to defend herself.'

'I think you are right about her,' said Felix. 'But I

don't advise you to make the inspector a present of your opinion. Let him make his own psychological assessment of Sally. The whole case may run into the sand if we keep our heads cool and our mouths shut. The Sommeil is the greatest danger. The hiding of that bottle makes the two things seem connected. Even so, the drug was put into your drinking-mug. It could have been put there by anyone.'

'Even by me.'

'Even by you. It could have been put there by Sally. She may have taken the mug to annoy you. I think she did. But she may have put the drug in her cocoa for no more sinister reason than the desire for a good night. It wasn't a lethal dose.'

'In which case, why was the bottle hidden?'

'Let us say that it was hidden either by someone who erroneously believed that the drugging and the murder were connected and who wanted to conceal that fact, or by someone who knew that they weren't but who wanted to implicate the family. As your stake marked the hiding-place we may assume that such a person specifically wished to implicate you. That's a pleasant thought for you to be going on with.'

They were cresting the hill above Little Chadfleet now. Below them lay the village and there was a glimpse of the tall grey chimneys of Martingale above the trees. With the return home the oppression and fear which the drive had only partially relieved fell like a black cloud.

'If they never solve this crime,' said Deborah, 'can you really imagine us living on happily at Martingale? Don't you ever feel that you must know the truth? Do you honestly never convince yourself that Stephen did it, or I?'

'You? Not with those hands and finger-nails. Didn't you notice that very considerable force was used and that her neck was bruised, but not scratched? Stephen is a possibility. So are Catherine and your mother and Martha. So am I. The superfluity of suspects is our greatest protection. Let Dalgleish take his pick. As for not living on at Martingale with an unsolved crime hanging over you – I imagine that the house has seen its share of violence in the past three hundred years. Not all your ancestors lived such

135

well-regulated lives even if their deaths were with benefit of clergy. In two hundred years the death of Sally Jupp will be one of the legends told on All-Hallows to frighten your great grandchildren. And if you really can't stand Martingale there will always be Greenwich. I won't bore you with that again, but you know what I feel.'

His voice was almost expressionless. His hands lay lightly on the wheel and his eyes still looked at the road ahead with easy and unstrained concentration. He must have known what she was thinking for he said :

'Don't let it worry you. I shan't complicate things more than I can help. I just don't want any of those beefy types you run around with to misunderstand my interest.'

'Would you want me, Felix, if I were running away?'

'Isn't that being melodramatic? What else have most of us been doing for the last ten years? But if you want marriage as an escape from Martingale you may yet find the sacrifice unnecessary. As we left Canningbury we passed Dalgleish and one of his minions on the way in. My guess is that they were on the same errand. Your instinct about Proctor may not have been so far wrong after all.'

They garaged the car in silence and passed into the coolness of the hall. Catherine Bowers was mounting the stairs. She was carrying a linen-covered tray and the white nylon overall which she usually wore when nursing Simon Maxie looked cool, efficient and not unbecoming. It is never agreeable to see another person competently and publicly performing duties which conscience suggests are one's own and Deborah was honest enough to recognize the reason for her spasm of irritation. She tried to hide it by an unusual burst of confidence.

'Wasn't the funeral awful, Catherine? I'm terribly sorry that Felix and I ran off like that. We drove Mrs. Proctor home. I had a sudden urge to fix the murder on the wicked uncle.'

Catherine was unimpressed.

'I asked the inspector about the uncle when he questioned me for the second time. He said that the police are satisfied that Mr. Proctor couldn't have killed Sally. He didn't explain why. I should leave the job to him. Goodness knows there's enough work here.'

She went on her way. Looking after her, Deborah said:

'I may be uncharitable, but if anyone at Martingale killed Sally I should prefer it to have been Catherine.'

'It isn't likely, though, is it?' said Felix. 'I can't see her capable of murder.'

'And the rest of us are, even Mother?'

'She particularly, I think, if she felt it were necessary.'

'I don't believe it,' said Deborah. 'But even if it were true, can you see her saying nothing while police overrun Martingale and people like Miss Liddell and Derek Pullen are suspected?'

'No,' replied Felix. 'No, I can't see that.'

CHAPTER SEVEN

1

ROSE COTTAGE on the Nessingford Road was a late-eighteenth-century labourer's cottage with enough superficial charm and antiquity to tempt the passing motorist to an opinion that something could be made of it. In the Pullens' hands something had, a replica of a thousand urban council houses. A large plaster model of an Alsatian dog occupied all the window space in the front room. Behind it the lace curtains were elegantly draped and tied with blue ribbon. The front door opened straight into the living-room. Here the Pullens' enthusiasm for modern décor had outrun discretion and the result was curiously irritating and bizarre. One wall was papered with a design of pink stars against a blue background. The opposite wall was painted in matching pink. The chairs were covered with blue striped material obviously carefully chosen to tone with the paper. The haircord carpet was a pale pink and had suffered from the inevitable comings and goings of muddy feet. Nothing was clean, nothing made to last, nothing was simple or honest. Dalgleish found it all profoundly depressing.

Derek Pullen and his mother were at home. Mrs. Pullen showed none of the normal reactions to the arrival of police officers engaged in a murder investigation, but greeted them with a spate of welcoming miscellanea, as if she had stayed at home specially to receive them and had long awaited their arrival. The phrases tumbled against one another. Delighted to see them . . . her brother a police constable . . . perhaps they had heard of him . . . Joe Pullen over at Barkingway . . . always better to tell the truth to the police . . . not that's there's anything to tell . . . poor Mrs. Maxie . . . couldn't hardly believe it when Miss Liddell told her . . . come home and told Derek and he didn't believe it neither . . . not the sort of girl a decent man would want . . . very proud the Maxies were . . . a girl like that asked for trouble. As she spoke the pale eyes wavered over Dalgleish's face but with little comprehension. In the background stood her son, braced to the inevitable.

So Pullen had known about the engagement late on Saturday night although, as the police had already ascertained, he had spent the evening at the Theatre Royal, Stratford, with a party from his office and had not been at the fête.

Dalgleish had difficulty in persuading the voluble Mrs. Pullen to retire to her kitchen and leave the boy to answer for himself but he was helped by Pullen's fretful insistence that she should leave them alone. He had obviously been expecting the visit. When Dalgleish and Martin were announced he had risen from his chair and faced them with the pathetic courage of a man whose meagre reserves have scarcely carried him through the waiting period. Dalgleish dealt with him gently. He might have been speaking to a son. Martin had seen this technique in use before. It was a cinch with the nervous, emotional types, especially if they were burdened with guilt. Guilt, thought Martin, was a funny thing. This boy, now, had probably done nothing worse than meet Sally Jupp for a bit of kiss and cuddle but he wouldn't feel at peace until he'd spilt the beans to someone. On the other hand he might be a murderer. If he were, then fear would keep his mouth shut for a little longer. But in the end he'd crack. Before long he would see in Dalgleish, patient, uncensorious and omnipotent, the father confessor whom his conscience craved. Then it would be difficult for the shorthand writer to catch up with the spate of self-accusation and guilt. It was a man's own mind which betrayed him in the end and Dalgleish knew that better than most. There were times when Sergeant Martin, not the most sensitive of men, felt that a detective's job was not a pretty one.

But, so far, Pullen was standing up well to the questioning. He admitted that he had walked past Martingale late on Saturday night. He was studying for an examination and liked to get some air before going to bed. He often went for a late walk. His mother could confirm that. He took the Venezuelan envelope found in Sally's

139

room, pushed a pair of bent spectacles up on his forehead and peered short-sightedly at the scribbled dates. Quietly he admitted that the writing was his. The envelope had come from a pen friend in South America. He had used it to jot down the times when he could meet Sally Jupp. He couldn't remember when he had given it to her but the dates referred to their meetings last month.

'She used to lock her door and then come down the stack-pipe to you, didn't she?' asked Dalgleish. 'You needn't be afraid of breaking her confidence. We found her palm-marks on the pipe. What did you do when you had those meetings?'

'We went for walks in the garden once or twice. Mostly we sat in the old stable block opposite her room and talked.' He must have fancied that he saw incredulity in Dalgleish's face for he flushed and said defensively :

'We didn't make love if that's what you're thinking. I suppose all policemen have to cultivate dirty minds but she wasn't like that.'

'What was she like?' asked Dalgleish gently. 'What did you talk about?'

'Anything. Everything really. I think she was lonely for someone her own age. She wasn't happy when she was at St. Mary's but there were the other girls to have a laugh with. She was a wonderful mimic. I could almost hear Miss Liddell talking. She talked about her home too. Her parents were killed in the war. Everything would have been different for her if they had lived. Her father was a university don and she would have had a different kind of home from her aunt's. Cultured and . . . well, different.'

Dalgleish thought that Sally Jupp had been a young woman who enjoyed exercising imagination and in Derek Pullen she had at least found a credulous listener. But there was more in these meetings than Pullen was choosing to say. The girl had been using him for something. But for what?

'You looked after her child for her, didn't you, when she went up to London on the Thursday before she died?'

It was a complete shot in the dark but Pullen did not even seem surprised that he knew.

'Yes, I did. I work in a local government office and I can take a day's leave now and then. Sally said that she

140

wanted to go up to town and I didn't see why she shouldn't. I expect she wanted to see a flick or go shopping. Other mothers can.'

'It seems strange that Sally didn't leave her child at Martingale if she wanted to go up to London. Mrs. Bultitaft would probably have been willing to look after him occasionally. All this secrecy was surely rather unnecessary.'

'Sally liked it that way. She liked things to be secret. I think that was half the attraction of sneaking out at night. I had a feeling sometimes that she wasn't really enjoying it. She was worried about the baby or just plain sleepy. But she had to come. It made her pleased to know next day that she had done it and got away with it.'

'Didn't you point out that it would make trouble for both of you if it were discovered?'

'I don't see how it could affect me,' said Pullen sulkily.

'I think you're pretending to be a great deal more simple than you are, surely. I'm ready to believe that you and Miss Jupp weren't lovers because I like to think I know when people are telling the truth and because it fits in with what I know so far of you both. But you can't honestly believe that other people would be so accommodating. The facts bear one obvious interpretation and that is the one most people would put on them, especially in the circumstances.'

'That's right. Just because the kid had an illegitimate child then she must be a nymphomaniac.' The boy used this last word self-consciously as if it were one he had only recently known and had not used before.

'You know, I doubt whether they'd understand what that word means. Perhaps people have rather nasty minds, but then it's surprising how often the nastiness is justified. I don't think Sally Jupp was being very fair to you when she used those stables as a retreat from Martingale. Surely you must have thought that, too?'

'Yes, I suppose so.' The boy looked away unhappily and Dalgleish waited. He felt that there was still something to be explained but that Pullen was enmeshed in his own inarticulateness and frustrated with the difficulty of explaining the girl he had known, alive, gay and foolhardy, to two officers of police who had never even met her. The difficulty was easily understood. He had no doubt how Pullen's story would look to a jury and was glad that it would never be his job to convince twelve good men and true that Sally Jupp, young, pretty and already lapsed from grace, had been sneaking out of her bedroom at night and leaving her baby alone, however briefly, for the sole pleasure of intellectual discussion with Derek Pullen.

'Did Miss Jupp ever suggest to you that she was afraid of anyone or had an enemy?' he asked.

'No. She wasn't important enough to have enemies.'

'Not until Saturday night, perhaps,' thought Dalgleish.

'She never confided in you about her child, who the father was, for example?'

'No.' The boy had mastered some of his terror and his voice was sullen.

'Did she tell you why she wanted to go to London last Thursday afternoon?'

'No. She asked me to look after Jimmy because she was sick of carting him around the forest and wanted to get away from the village. We arranged where she was to hand him over at Liverpool Street Station. She brought the folding pram and I took him to St. James's Park. In the evening I handed him back and we travelled home separately. We weren't going to give the village tabbies anything else to gossip about.'

'You never thought she might be falling in love with you?'

'I knew damn well she wasn't.' He gave Dalgleish one quick direct glance and then said, as if the confidence surprised him:

'She wouldn't even let me touch her.'

Dalgleish waited for a moment and then said quietly:

'Those aren't your normal spectacles, are they? What happened to the ones you usually wear?'

The boy almost snatched them from his nose and closed his hands over the lenses in a gesture which was pathetic in its futility. Then, realizing the significance of that instinctive gesture, he dug in his pocket for a handkerchief and made a show of cleaning the lenses.

His hands shook as he pushed the spectacles back on his nose where they rested lopsidedly, his voice croaked with fright:

'I lost them. That is, I broke them. I'm having them mended.'

'Did you break them at the same time as you got that bruise over your eye?'

'Yes. I knocked into a tree.'

'Indeed. The trees around here seem curiously hazardous. Dr. Maxie grazed his knuckle on the bark of one, I'm told. Could it have been the same tree?'

'Dr. Maxie's troubles are nothing to do with me. I don't know what you mean.'

'I think you do,' said Dalgleish gently. 'I'm going to ask you to think over what we've said and later I shall want you to make a statement and sign it. There isn't any tremendous hurry. We know where to find you if we want you. Talk it over with your father when he comes in. If either of you want to see me let me know. And remember this: someone killed Sally. If it wasn't you, then you've got nothing to fear. Either way, I hope you'll find the courage to tell us what you know.' He waited for a moment but his eyes met only the glazed stare of fear and resolution. After a minute he turned away and beckoned Martin to follow.

Half an hour later the telephone rang at Martingale. Deborah, carrying her father's tray through the hall, paused, balanced it on her hip, and lifted the receiver. A minute later she put her head round the drawing-room door.

'It's for you, Stephen. The 'phone. Derek Pullen of all people.'

Stephen, home unexpectedly for a few hours only, did not look up from his book but Deborah could see the sudden arrest of movement and the slight tensing of his back.

'Oh Lord, what does he want?'

'He wants you. He sounds pretty worried.'

'Tell him I'm busy, Deb.'

Deborah translated this message into the semblance of civility. The voice at the end of the line rose into incoherence. Holding the receiver away from her ear Deborah made soothing noises and felt the well of hysterical laughter which nowadays was never far submerged. She went back to the drawing-room.

'You'd better come, Stephen. He really is in a bad way.

143

What on earth have you been up to? He says the police have been with him.'

'Is that all? He's not the only one. Tell him they've been with me for about six hours all told. And they haven't finished yet. Tell him to keep his mouth shut and stop flapping.'

'Hadn't you better tell him yourself?' suggested Deborah sweetly. 'I'm not in your confidence and I'm certainly not in his.'

Stephen swore softly and went to the telephone. Pausing in the hall to balance her tray, Deborah could hear his quick impatient expostulations.

'All right. All right. Tell them if you want to. I'm not stopping you. They're probably listening in to this conversation anyway. . . . No, as a matter of fact I didn't, but don't let that influence you . . . Quite the little gentleman, aren't you. . . . My dear man, I don't care a damn what you tell them, or when or how, only for God's sake don't be such a bore about it. Good-bye.'

Moving out of earshot along the gallery, Deborah thought sadly, 'Stephen and I have grown so far apart that I could ask him outright whether he killed Sally without being certain what answer I'd get.'

2

Dalgleish and Martin sat in the small parlour of The Moonraker's Arms in that state of repletion without satisfaction which commonly follows a poor meal. They had been assured that Mrs. Piggott who, with her husband, kept the inn, was noted for her good plain cooking and plenty of it. The expression had struck ominously on the ears of men whose travels had inured them to most of the vagaries of good plain English fare. It is probable that Martin suffered most. His war service in France and Italy had given him a taste for continental food which he had been indulging ever since on holidays abroad. Most of his spare time and all of his spare money was spent in this way. He and his cheerful, enterprising wife were enthusiastic and unsophisticated travellers, confident of their ability to be understood, tolerated and well fed in almost any corner of Europe. So far, strangely enough, they had never been disappointed. Sitting in deep abdominal distress Martin let his mind ramble on *cassoulet de Toulouse* and remembered with yearning the *poularde en vessu* he had first eaten in a modest hotel in the Ardèche. Dalgleish's needs were at once simpler and more exacting. He merely craved simple English food properly cooked.

Mrs. Piggott was reputed to take some trouble with her soups. This was true in so far as the packaged ingredients had been sufficiently well mixed to exclude lumps. She had even experimented with flavours and today's mixture of tomato (orange) and oxtail (reddish brown), thick enough to support the spoon unaided, was as startling to the palate as to the eye. Soup had been followed by a couple of mutton chops nestling artistically against a mound of potato and flanked with tinned peas larger and shinier than any peas which had ever seen pod. They tasted of soya flour. A green dye which bore little resemblance to the colour of any known vegetable seeped from them and mingled disagreeably with the gravy. An apple and blackcurrant pie had followed in which neither of the fruits had met each other nor the pastry until they had been arranged on the plate by Mrs. Piggott's careful hand and liberally blanketed with synthetic custard.

Martin wrenched his mind from a contemplation of these culinary horrors and fixed it on the matter in hand.

'It's curious, sir, that Dr. Maxie should have fetched Mr. Hearne to help with the ladder. It's one that a strong man can manage on his own. The quickest way to the old stable block would have been down the back stairs. Instead of that, Maxie goes to find Hearne. It looks as if he wanted a witness to the finding of the body.'

'That's possible, of course. Even if he didn't kill the girl he may have wanted a witness to whatever was to be found in that room. Besides that, he was in pyjamas and dressing-gown. Hardly the most convenient garb for climbing up ladders and through windows.'

'Sam Bocock confirmed Dr. Maxie's story to some extent. Not that it means much until the time of death is established. Still, it does prove he was telling the truth on one point.'

'Sam Bocock would confirm anything the Maxies said.

That man would be a gift to the defending counsel. Apart from his natural gift for saying little while creating an impression of absolute and incorruptible veracity he honestly believes that the Maxies are innocent. You heard him. "They're good people up at the house." A simple statement of truth. He would maintain it against the evidence of God Almighty at the Judgment Seat itself. The Old Bailey isn't likely to frighten him.'

'I thought him an honest witness, sir.'

'Of course you did, Martin. I would have liked him better if he hadn't looked at me with that curious expression, half amused, half pitying, which I've noticed before on the faces of old country people. You're a countryman yourself. No doubt you can explain it.'

No doubt Martin could, but his was a nature in which discretion had long taken precedence over valour.

'He seemed a very musical old gentleman. That was a fine record-player he had. It looked funny seeing a hi-fi instrument in a cottage like that.'

The player, with its surrounding racks of long-play records, had indeed struck an incongruous note in the cottage sitting-room where almost every other article was a legacy from the past. Bocock evidently shared the normal countryman's respect for fresh air. The two small windows were shut; showed, indeed, no signs of ever having been opened. The wallpaper bore the entwined and faded roses of another era. Hung in erratic profusion were the trophies and mementoes of the First World War, a posse of mounted cavalrymen, a small glass frame of medals, a luridly coloured reproduction of King George V and his Queen. There were the family photographs, relations whom no casual observer could hope to identify. Was the serious bewhiskered young man with his Edwardian bride Bocock's father or grandfather? Could he really have a personal memory of a family loyalty for these sepia groups of bowler-hatted countrymen in their Sunday best with their solid-bosomed wives and daughters? Above the mantelpiece were the newer photographs. Stephen Maxie, proud on his first shaggy pony with an unmistakable but younger Bocock by his side. A pigtailed Deborah Maxie bending from the saddle to receive her rosette. For all its conglomeration of old and new, the room bore evidence

146

of an old soldier's disciplined care of his personal chattels.

Bocock had welcomed them in with an easy dignity. He had been having his tea. Although he lived alone he had the woman's habit of putting everything edible on the table at once, presumably to provide for any sudden whim of taste. There had been a loaf of crusty bread, a pot of jam supporting its spoon, an ornate glass jar of sliced beetroot and one of spring onions, and a cucumber stuck precariously in a small jug. In the middle of the table a bowl of lettuce disputed with a large and obviously home-baked cake for pride of place. Dalgleish had recalled that Bocock's daughter was married to a farmer in Nessingford and kept an eye on her father. The cake was probably a recent offering of filial duty. In addition to this bounty there was evidence by sight and smell that Bocock had just finished a meal of fried fish and chipped potatoes.

Dalgleish and Martin were ensconced in the heavy armchairs which flanked the fireplace – even on that warm July day there was a small fire burning, its faint incandescent flame hardly visible in a shaft of sunlight from the western window, and were offered a cup of tea. This done, Bocock obviously felt that the obligations of hospitality had been met and that it was the duty of his guests to announce their business. He carried on with his tea, snapping off pieces of bread with lean brown hands and casting them absent-mindedly into his mouth where they were chewed and turned in silent concentration. He volunteered no remarks of his own, answered Dalgleish's questions with a deliberation which gave the impression of lack of interest rather than any unwillingness to co-operate and he regarded both policemen with that frank amused appraisal which Dalgleish, his thighs prickled by the horsehair and his face sweating with the heat, found a little disconcerting and more than a little irritating.

The slow catechism had produced nothing new, nothing unexpected. Stephen Maxie had been at the cottage the previous evening. He had arrived during the nine o'clock news. Bocock couldn't say when he had left. It had been latish. Mr. Stephen would know. Very late? 'Aye. After eleven. Maybe later. Maybe a goodish bit later.' Dalgleish remarked dryly that no doubt Mr. Bocock would remember more precisely when he had had time to think about it. Bocock admitted the force of this possibility. What had they talked about? 'Listened to Beethoven mostly. Mr. Stephen wasn't much of a one for talking.' Bocock spoke as if deploring his own volubility and the distressing garrulity of the world at large and of policemen in particular. Nothing else emerged. He had not noticed Sally at the fête except during the latish part of the afternoon when she gave the baby a ride in her arms on one of the horses, and about six o'clock when one of the Sunday school children's balloon had got caught in an elm and Mr. Stephen had fetched the ladder to get it down. Sally had been with him then with her child in the pram. Bocock remembered her holding the foot of the ladder. Apart from that he hadn't noticed her about. Yes, he had seen young Johnnie Wilcox. That was at ten to four or thereabouts. Sneaking away from the tea-tent he was with as suspicious-looking a bundle as Bocock had seen. No, he hadn't stopped the boy. Young Wilcox was a good enough lad. None of the boys liked helping with the teas. Bocock hadn't much cared for it in his young days. If Wilcox said he left the tent at four-thirty he was a bit out, that's all. That lad hadn't put in more than thirty minutes' work at most. If the old man wondered why the police should be interested in Johnnie Wilcox and his peccadilloes he gave no sign. All Dalgleish's questions were answered with equal composure and apparent candour. He knew nothing of Mr. Maxie's engagement and had heard no talk of it in the village, either before or after the murder. 'Some folks'll say anything. You've no call to mind village talk. They're good people up at the house.' That had been his final word. No doubt, if and when he had talked to Stephen Maxie and knew what was wanted he would remember more clearly the time when Maxie had left him the previous night. At the moment he was wary. But his allegiance was clear. They had left him still eating, sitting in solitary and impressive state among his music and his memories.

'No,' said Dalgleish. 'We're not likely to get anything helpful about the Maxies out of Bocock. If young Maxie was looking for an ally he knew where to go. We've gained something though. If Bocock is right about times, and he's certainly more likely to be accurate than Johnnie Wilcox, the meeting in the loft probably took place before four-thirty. That would fit in with what we know of Jupp's subsequent movements, including the scene in the tea-tent when she appeared in a duplicate of Mrs. Riscoe's dress. Jupp hadn't been seen in it before four-thirty p.m. so that she must have changed after the interview in the stable loft.'

'It was a funny thing to do, sir. And why wait until then?'

'She may have bought the dress with the idea of wearing it publicly on some occasion or other. Perhaps something happened at that interview which freed her from any future dependence on Martingale. She could afford to make a last gesture. On the other hand, if she knew before last Saturday that she was going to marry Maxie, she was presumably free to make her gesture whenever the fancy took her. There's a curious conflict of evidence about that proposal of marriage. If we are to believe Mr. Hinks – and why not? – Sally Jupp certainly knew that she was to marry someone when she met him on the previous Thursday. I find it difficult to believe that she had two prospective bridgrooms and there isn't a surfeit of obvious candidates. And while we're considering young Maxie's love life here's something you haven't seen.'

He handed over a thin sheet of official-looking writing-paper. It bore the name of a small coastal hotel.

Dear Sir,

Although I have my reputation to think of and am not particularly anxious to be mixed up in police matters, I think it my duty to inform you that a Mr. Maxie stayed at this hotel last May 24th with a lady he signed for as his wife. I have seen a photograph in the *Evening Clarion* of Dr. Maxie who is mixed up in the Chadfleet murder case and who the papers say is a bachelor and it is the same one. I have not seen any photographs of the dead girl so could not swear to her, but I thought it my duty to bring the above to your notice. Of course it may not mean anything and I do not wish to be mixed up in anything unpleasant so I would be grateful if my name could be kept out of this. Also the name of my hotel which has always catered for a very good class of people. Mr. Maxie only stayed for one night and they were a very quiet couple, but my husband thinks it our duty to bring this information to your notice. It is, of course, entirely without prejudice.

Yours faithfully,

LILY BURWOOD (Mrs.)

'The lady seems curiously concerned with her duty,' said Dalgleish, 'and it is a little difficult to see what she can mean by "without prejudice". I feel that her husband had a great deal to do with this letter, including the phraseology, without quite managing to bring himself to signing it. Anyway, I sent that eager young fledgling, Robson, down to investigate and I've no doubt he enjoyed himself hugely. He managed to convince them that the night in question has nothing to do with the murder and that the best interests of the hotel will be served by forgetting the whole thing. It isn't quite as simple as that, though. Robson took some photographs down with him, one or two of those taken at the fête, and they confirmed a rather interesting little theory. Any idea who young Maxie's partner in sin was?'

'Would it be Miss Bowers, sir?'

'It would. I hoped that might surprise you.'

'Well, sir, if it had to be someone from here she was the only one. There isn't any evidence that Dr. Maxie and Sally Jupp had been carrying on. And that was nearly a year ago.'

'So you aren't inclined to pay much attention to it?'

'Well, the young today don't seem to make so much of it as I was taught to.'

'It's not that they sin less but that they bear their sins more lightly. But we have no evidence that Miss Bowers feels the same. She may easily have been very hurt by what happened. She doesn't strike me as an unconventional person and she is very much in love and not particularly clever at concealing the fact. I think she is desperately anxious to marry Dr. Maxie and her chances have, after all, increased since Saturday night. She was present at the scene in the drawing-room. She knew what she had to lose.'

'Do you think it's still going on, sir?' Sergeant Martin could never bring himself to be more explicit about these

150

sins of the flesh. He had seen and heard enough in thirty years of police work to have shattered most men's illusions, but he was of a tough yet gentle disposition and could never believe that men were either as wicked or as weak as the evidence consistently proved them to be.

'I should think it very unlikely. That week-end was probably the only excursion into passion. Perhaps it wasn't particularly successful. Perhaps it was, as you rather unkindly suggest, a mere bagatelle. It's a complication. Catherine Bowers is the sort of woman who tells her man that she will do anything for him, and sometimes does.'

'Could she have known about the tablets though, sir?'

'No one admits to having told her and I think she was telling the truth when she said she knew nothing. Sally Jupp might have told her but they weren't on particularly good terms, in fact they weren't on any terms at all as far as I can see, and it seems unlikely. But that proves nothing. Miss Bowers must have known that there were sleeping tablets of some kind in the house and where they were likely to be kept and the same thing applies to Hearne.'

'It seems strange that he's able to stay around.'

'That probably means that he thinks one of the family did it and wants to be on the spot to see that we don't get the same idea. He may actually know who did it. If so, he's not likely to slip up, I'm afraid. I got Robson on to him, too. His report, stripped of a lot of psychological jargon about everyone he interviewed, is much what I expected. Here we are. All the details on Felix Georges Mortimer Hearne. He has a fine war record, of course. God knows how he did it or what it did to him. Ever since 1945 he seems to have flitted around doing a little writing and not much else. He is a partner in Hearne and Illingworth the publishers. His great-grandfather was old Mortimer Hearne who founded the firm. His father married a French woman, Mlle Annette D'Apprius in 1919. The marriage brought more money into the family. Felix was born in 1921. Educated in the usual and expensive places. Met Deborah Riscoe through her husband who was at school with him, although considerably his junior, and as far as Robson can tell, never saw Sally Jupp until he met her in this house. He has a very pleasant little house in Greenwich, still true to type you see, and an ex-batman to look after him. Gossip says that he and Mrs. Riscoe are lovers, but there's no evidence, and Robson says you would get nothing out of the manservant. I doubt whether there's anything to get. Mrs. Riscoe was certainly lying when she said they spent all Saturday night together. I suppose Felix Hearne might have murdered Sally Jupp to save Deborah Riscoe from embarrassment, but a jury wouldn't believe it and neither would I.'

'There's no mention of his having the drug in his possession?'

'None at all. I don't think that there's much doubt that the Sommeil used to drug Sally Jupp came from the bottle which was taken from Mr. Maxie's cupboard. Still, other people did have the stuff. The Martingale bottle could have been hidden in that melodramatic way as a blind. According to Dr. Epps he prescribed Sommeil for Mr. Maxie, Sir Reynold Price and Miss Pollack of St. Mary's. None of these insomniacs can account for the correct dose. I'm not surprised at that. People are very careless about medicines. Where's that report? Yes, here we are. Mr. Maxie we know all about. Sir Reynold Price. His Sommeil was prescribed in January of this year and dispensed by Goodliffes of the City on January 14th. He had twenty three-gr. tablets and says that he took about half and then forgot all the rest. Apparently his insomnia was quickly overcome. Taking the common-sense view his was the bottle of nine tablets left in his overcoat pocket and found by Dr. Epps. Sir Reynold is ready enough to claim them without being able to remember putting them in his pocket. It's not a very likely place to keep sleeping-tablets, but he spends nights away from home and says that he probably picked them up in a hurry. We know all about Sir Reynold Price, our local business man *cum* farmer, making a calculated loss on the second activity to compensate for his profits on the first. He fumes against what he calls the desecration of Chadfleet New Town from a Victorian pseudo-castle so ugly that I'm surprised someone hasn't formed a trust to preserve it. Sir Reynold is a philistine, no doubt, but not, I think, a murderer. Admittedly he has no alibi for last Saturday night and all we know from his staff is that he left home in his car at about ten p.m. and didn't return until early Sunday morning. Sir Reynold is being so guilty and embarrassed by his absence, is so patently trying to preserve a gentlemanly reticence, that I think we can take it that there's a "little woman" in the case. When we really put on the pressure and he appreciates that there's a murder charge involved I think we shall get the lady's name. These one-night excursions are fairly regular with him and I don't think they had anything to do with Jupp. He would hardly make himself conspicuous by taking his Daimler on a surreptitious visit to Martingale.

'We know about Miss Pollack. She seems to have regarded the tablets as a cocaine addict ought to regard cocaine, but so seldom does. She wrestled long with the twin evils of temptation and insomnia and ended by trying to put the Sommeil down the w.c. Miss Liddell dissuades her and returns them to Dr. Epps. Dr. Epps, according again to Robson, thinks he may have had them back but isn't sure. There weren't enough to be a really dangerous dose and they were labelled. Shockingly careless of someone I suppose, but then people are careless. And Sommeil, of course, isn't on the D.D.A. Besides, it only took three tablets to drug Sally Jupp and, taking the common-sense view, those tablets came from the Martingale bottle.'

'Which leads us back to the Maxies and their guests.'

'Of course. And it's not such a stupid crime as it appears on the face of it. Unless we can find those tablets and get some evidence that one of the Maxies administered them, there's no hope of getting a conviction. You can see how it would go. Sally Jupp knew about the tablets. She might have taken them herself. They were put into Mrs. Riscoe's mug. No evidence to show they were meant for Sally Jupp. Anyone could have got into the house during the fête and lain in wait for the girl. No adequate motive. Other people had access to Sommeil. And as far as I know at present he might be right.'

'But if the murderer had used more of the tablets and killed the girl that way there might have been no suspicion of murder.'

'It couldn't be done. Those barbiturates are notoriously slow-acting if you want to kill. The girl might have been in a coma for days and then recovered. Any doctor would know that. On the other hand it would be difficult to

153

smother a strong and healthy girl, or even to get into her bedroom unobserved, unless she were drugged. The combination was risky for the murderer, but not as risky as one method on its own. Besides, I doubt whether anyone would swallow a fatal dose without suspecting something. Sommeil is supposed to be less bitter than most of these sleeping-tablets, but it's not tasteless. That is probably why Sally Jupp left most of the cocoa. She could hardly have felt sleepy with so small a dose in her, and yet she still died without a struggle. That's the curious part of it. Whoever entered that bedroom must have been either expected by Jupp or at least not feared. And if that were so, why the drugging? They may be unconnected but it's really too much of a coincidence that someone should put a dangerous dose of barbiturate in her drink on the same night as someone else chooses to throttle her. Then there is the curious distribution of finger-prints. Someone went down that stack-pipe, but the only prints are those of Jupp herself and they're possibly not recent. The cocoa tin was found empty in the dustbin with the paper lining missing. The tin bore the prints of Jupp and Bultitaft. The lock of the bedroom has a print of Jupp only, although it's badly smudged. Hearne says that he protected the lock with his handkerchief when he opened the door which, considering the circumstances, shows some presence of mind. Perhaps too much presence of mind. Hearne of all these people is the one least likely to lose his head in an emergency or to overlook any essential points.'

'Something had rattled him pretty badly by the time he came to be questioned, though.'

'It had indeed, Sergeant. I might have reacted more positively to his offensiveness if I hadn't known it was only pure funk. It takes some people that way. The poor devil was almost pitiable. It was a surprising exhibition coming from him. Even Proctor put up a better show and heaven knows he was scared enough.'

'We know Proctor couldn't have done it.'

'So presumably does Proctor. Yet he was lying about a number of things and we shall break him when the time's right. I think he was telling the truth about that telephone call, though, or at least part of the truth. It was unlucky for him that his daughter took the call. If he had answered the 'phone I doubt whether we should have been told about it. He still maintains that the call was from Miss Liddell and Beryl Proctor confirms that the caller gave that name. First of all Proctor tells his wife and us that she was merely ringing to give him news of Sally. When we question him again and tell him that Liddell denies making the call he still persists that the call was either from her or from someone impersonating her, but admits that she told him that Sally was engaged to be married to Stephen Maxie. That would certainly be a more reasonable motive for the call than a general report on his niece's progress.'

'It's interesting how many people claim to have known about this engagement before it actually took place.'

'Or before Maxie admits that it took place. He still insists that he proposed as a result of an impulse when they met in the garden at about seven-forty p.m. on Saturday night and that he had never previously considered asking her to marry him. That doesn't mean that she hadn't considered it. She may even have expected it. But surely it was asking for trouble to spread the glad news in advance. And what possible motive had she for telling her uncle unless it was an understandable urge to gloat over him or disconcert him? Even so, why pretend to be Miss Liddell?'

'You're satisfied that Sally Jupp made that call then, sir?'

'Well – we've been told, haven't we, what a good mimic she was? I think we can be certain that Jupp made that call and it's significant that Proctor isn't yet willing to admit as much. Another minor mystery, which we'll very likely never solve, is where Sally Jupp spent the hours between putting her child to bed on Saturday night and her final appearance on the main staircase at Martingale. No one admits to having seen her.'

'Doesn't that make it likely that she stayed in her room with Jimmy and then went to get her last night drink when she knew that Martha would have gone to bed and the coast be clear?'

'It's certainly the likeliest explanation. She would hardly have been welcome either in the drawing-room or the kitchen. Perhaps she wanted to be alone. God knows, she must have had plenty to think about!'

155

They sat in silence for a moment. Dalgleish pondered on the curious diversity of the clues which he felt were salient in the case. There was Martha's significant reluctance to dwell on one of Sally's shortcomings. There was the bottle of Sommeil pressed hastily into the earth. There was an empty cocoa tin, a golden-haired girl laughing up at Stephen Maxie as he retrieved a child's balloon from a Martingale elm, an anonymous telephone call and a gloved hand briefly glimpsed as it closed the trap-door into Bocock's loft. And at the heart of the mystery, the clue which would make all plain, lay the complex personality of Sally Jupp.

CHAPTER EIGHT

1

THE Thursday morning list at St. Luke's had been a heavy one and it was not until he sat down for lunch that Stephen Maxie remembered Sally. Then, as always, the remembrance came down like a knife severing appetite, cutting him off from the careless and undemanding pleasure of everyday life. The talk at table sounded false; a barrage of trivialities put up to cover his colleagues' embarrassment in his presence. The newspapers were too tidily folded away in case a chance headline should draw attention to the presence among them of a suspected murderer. They included him too carefully in their conversation. Not too much in case he should think they were sorry for him. Not too little in case he should think they were avoiding him. The meat on his plate was as tasteless as cardboard. He forced down a few more mouthfuls – it would never do if the suspect went right off his food – and made a show of despising the pudding. The need for action was upon him. If the police could not bring this thing to a head perhaps he could. With a murmured apology he left the residents to their speculation. And why not? Was it so very surprising that they wanted to ask him the one crucial question? His mother, her hand over his on the telephone, her ravaged face turned to him in desperate inquiry had wanted to ask the same. And he had replied, 'You don't have to ask. I know nothing about it. I swear it.'

He had a free hour and he knew what he wanted to do. The secret of Sally's death must lie in her life, and probably in her life before she came to Martingale. Stephen had the conviction that the baby's father would hold the key if only he could be found. He did not analyse his motives, whether this urge to find an unknown man had its roots in logic, curiosity or jealousy. It was enough to find relief in action, however fruitless its results.

157

He remembered the name of Sally's uncle but not the full address and it took some time to hunt through the Proctors in search of a Canningbury number. A woman answered in the stilted, artificial voice of one unused to the telephone. When he announced himself there was a silence so long that he thought they must have been cut off. He sensed her distrust like a physical impulse along the wire and tried to propitiate it. When she still hesitated he suggested that she might prefer him to ring later and speak to her husband. The proposal was not meant as a threat. He had merely imagined that she was one of those women who are incapable of even the simplest independent action. But the result of his suggestion was surprising. She said quickly, 'Oh, no! No! There wasn't any need for that. Mr. Proctor didn't want to talk about Sally. It wouldn't do to telephone Mr. Proctor. After all it couldn't do any harm to tell Mr. Maxie what he wanted to know. Only it would be better if Mr. Proctor didn't know that he had 'phoned.' Then she gave the address Stephen wanted. When she became pregnant, Sally had been working for the Select Book Club, at Falconer's Yard in the City.

The Select Book Club had its offices in a courtyard near St. Paul's Cathedral. It was approached through a narrow passage, dark and difficult to find, but the courtyard itself was full of light and as quiet as a provincial cathedral close. The grinding crescendo of city traffic was muted to a faint moan like the far sound of the sea. The air was full of the river smell. There was no difficulty in finding the right house. On the sunlit side of the court a small bay window was dressed with the Select Book Club choices arranged with carefully contrived casualness against a draped back-cloth of purple velvet. The Club had been carefully named. Select Books catered for that class of reader which likes a good story without caring much who writes it, prefers to be spared the tedium of personal choice, and believes that a bookcase of volumes equal in size and bound in exactly the same colour gives tone to any room. Select Books preferred virtue to be rewarded and vice suitably punished. They eschewed salacity, avoided controversy and took no risks with unestablished writers. Not surprisingly they often had to look far back in the publishers' lists to produce a current choice. Stephen noticed that only a few of the selected volumes had originally borne the imprint of Hearne and Illingworth. He was surprised that there were any.

The front door steps were scrubbed white and the open door led into a small office obviously furnished for the convenience of those customers who preferred to collect their monthly book in person. As Stephen entered an elderly clergyman was suffering the prolonged and sprightly farewells of the woman in charge who was determined that he should not escape until the merits of the current choice, including details of the plot and the really astonishing surprise ending, had been explained in detail. This done, there were the members of his family to inquire for and his opinion of last month's choice to be solicited. Stephen waited in patience until this was concluded and the woman was free to turn her determinedly bright glance on him. A small framed card on the desk proclaimed her as Miss Titley.

'I'm sorry to have kept you waiting. You're a new customer, aren't you? I don't think I've had the pleasure before? I get to know everyone in time and they all know me. That was Canon Tatlock. A very dear customer. But he won't be hurried, you know. He won't be hurried.'

Stephen exerted all his charm and explained that he wanted to see whoever was in charge. The matter was personal and very important. He wasn't trying to sell anything and would honestly not take long. He was sorry that he couldn't be more explicit but it really was important. 'To me, anyway,' he added with a smile.

The smile was successful. It always had been. Miss Titley, flustered into normality by the unusual, retired to the back of her office and made a furtive telephone call. It was a little prolonged. She gave several glances at him during her conversation as if to reassure herself as to his respectability. Eventually she replaced the receiver and came back with the news that Miss Molpas was prepared to see him.

Miss Molpas had her office on the third floor. The drugget-covered stairs were steep and narrow and Stephen and Miss Titley had to stand aside on each of the landings while women clerks passed. There were no men to be seen. When he was finally shown into Miss Molpas's room he

159

saw that she had chosen well. Three steep flights were a small price to pay for this view over city roofs, this glimpse of a silver ribbon threading down from Westminster. Miss Titley breathed an introduction which was as reverent as it was inarticulate and faded away. From behind her desk Miss Molpas rose stockily to her feet and waved him to a chair. She was a short, dark woman of remarkable plainness. Her face was round and large and her hair was cut in a thick straight fringe above her eyebrows. She wore horn-rimmed spectacles so large and heavy that they seemed an obvious aid to caricature. She was dressed in a short tweed skirt and a man's white shirt with a yellow and green woven tie which reminded Stephen unpleasantly of a squashed cabbage caterpillar. But she had one of the pleasantest speaking voices he had ever heard in a woman and the hand which she held out to him was cool and firm.

'You're Stephen Maxie, aren't you? Saw your picture in the *Echo*. People are saying that you killed Sally Jupp. Did you?'

'No,' said Stephen. 'And neither did any member of my family. I haven't come to argue about that. People can believe what they like. I want to know something more about Sally. I thought you might be able to help. It's the child I'm really worrying about. Now that he hasn't a mother it seems important to try to find his father. No one's come forward, but it did strike me that the man may not know. Sally was very independent. If he doesn't know and would like to do something about Jimmy – well, I think he should be given the chance.'

Miss Molpas pushed a packet of cigarettes across the table at him.

'D'you smoke? No? Well, I will. You're meddling a bit, aren't you? Better get your own motives straight. You can't believe the man didn't know. Why shouldn't he? He must know now anyway. There's been enough publicity. The police have been here on the same tack but I don't imagine they're interested in the child's welfare. More likely looking for a motive. They're very thorough. You'd do better to leave them to it.'

So the police had been there. It was stupid and irrational to suppose otherwise, but he found the news depressing.

160

They would always be one step ahead. It was presumptuous to suppose that there was anything significant to be discovered about Sally that the police, experienced, persevering and infinitely patient, would not already have found. The disappointment must have shown in his face for Miss Molpas gave a shout of laughter.

'Cheer up! You may beat them to it yet. Not that I can help you much. I told the police all I know and they wrote it down most conscientiously, but I could see it wasn't getting them anywhere.'

'Except to fix the guilt more firmly where they already believe it rests – on someone in my family.'

'Well, it certainly doesn't rest on anyone here. I can't even produce a possible father for the child. We haven't a man on the premises. She certainly got herself pregnant while she was working here, but don't ask me how.'

'What was she really like, Miss Molpas?' asked Stephen. He forced out the question against his own realization of its absurdity. They were all asking the same thing. It was as if, in the heart of this maze of evidence and doubt, someone would at last be found who could say, 'This was Sally'.

Miss Molpas looked at him curiously.

'You should know what she was like. You were in love with her.'

'If I were I should be the last person to know.'

'But you weren't.' It was a statement not an impertinent question and Stephen met it with a frankness which surprised him.

'I admired her and I wanted to go to bed with her. I suppose you wouldn't call that love. Never having felt more than that for any woman, I wouldn't know.'

Miss Molpas looked away from him and out towards the river.

'I should settle for that. I doubt whether you'll ever feel more. Your kind don't.' She turned towards him again and spoke more briskly:

'But you were asking what I thought of her. So did the police. The answer's the same. Sally Jupp was pretty, intelligent, ambitious, sly and insecure.'

'You seem to have known her very well,' said Stephen quietly.

'Not really. She wasn't easy to know. She worked here for three years and I knew no more about her home circumstances when she left than I did the day I engaged her. Taking her on was an experiment. You've probably noticed that we haven't any youngsters here. They're difficult to get except at double the wages they're worth and they don't keep their minds on the job. I don't blame them. They've only a few years to find a husband and this isn't a promising hunting-ground. They can be cruel, too, if you put them to work with an older woman. Have you seen young hens pecking away at an injured bird? Well, we only employ old birds here. They may be a bit slow but they're methodical and reliable. The work doesn't call for much intelligence. Sally was too good for the job. I never understood why she stayed. She worked for a secretarial agency after finishing her training and came to us as a temporary relief when we were short of staff during a 'flu epidemic. She liked the job and asked to stay on. The Club was growing and the business justified another shorthand-typist. So I took her on. As I said, it was an experiment. She was the only member of the staff who was under forty-five.'

'Staying in this job doesn't suggest ambition to me,' said Stephen. 'What made you think she was sly?'

'I watched her and listened to her. We're rather a collection of has-beens here and she must have known it. But she was clever, was our Sally. "Yes, Miss Titley. Certainly, Miss Croome. Can I get it for you, Miss Melling?" Demure as a nun and respectful as a Victorian parlourmaid. She had the poor fools eating out of her hand of course. They said how nice it was to have a young thing about the office. They bought her birthday and Christmas presents. They talked to her about her career. She even asked for advice about her clothes! As if she cared a damn what we wore or what we thought! I should have thought her a fool if she had. It was a very pretty piece of acting. It wasn't altogether surprising that, after a few months of Sally, we had an office atmosphere. That's probably not a phenomenon which you have experienced. You can take it from me that it isn't comfortable. There are tensions, whispered confidences, barbed remarks, unexplained feuds. Old allies no longer speak to each other. Incongruous

162

friendships spring up. It all plays havoc with the work, of course, although some people seem to thrive on it. I don't. I could see what the trouble was here. She'd got them all in a tizzy of jealousy and the poor fools couldn't see it. They were really fond of her. I think Miss Melling loved her. If Sally confided in anyone about her pregnancy it would have been Beatrice Melling.'

'Could I talk to Miss Melling?' asked Stephen.

'Not unless you're clairvoyant. Beatrice died following an uncomplicated operation for appendicitis the week after Sally left. Left, incidentally, without even saying "good-bye" to her. Do you believe in death from a broken heart, Dr. Maxie? No, of course you don't.'

'What happened when Sally became pregnant?'

'Nothing. No one knew. We're hardly the most likely community to spot that kind of trouble. And Sally! Meek, virtuous, quiet little Sally! I noticed that she looked wan and even thinner than usual for a few weeks. Then she was prettier than ever. There was a kind of radiance about her. She must have been about four months' pregnant when she left. She gave in her week's notice to me and asked me to tell no one. She gave me no reasons and I asked for none. Frankly, it was a relief. I had no tangible excuse for getting rid of her, but I had known for some time that the experiment was a failure. She went home one Friday and, on Monday, I told the rest of the staff that she had left. They drew their own conclusions, but no one as far as I know drew the right one. We had one glorious row. Miss Croome accused Miss Melling of having driven the girl away by her over-possessiveness and unnatural affection. To do Miss Croome justice I don't think she meant anything more sinister than that Jupp felt obliged to eat her luncheon sandwiches in Melling's company when she would rather have visited the nearest Lyons with Croome.'

'So you have no idea who the man was or where she could have met him?'

'None at all. Except that they met on Saturday mornings. I got that from the police. We work a five-day week here and the office is never open on Saturdays. Apparently Sally told her uncle and aunt that it was. She came up to town nearly every Saturday morning as if to work. It was a neat deception. They apparently took no interest

163

in her job and, even had they tried to telephone her on a Saturday morning, the assumption would be that the line had been left unattended. She was a clever little liar was Sally.'

The dislike in her voice was surely too bitter to be the result of anything but a personal hurt. Stephen wondered what else could have been told about Sally's office life.

'Were you surprised to hear of her death?' he asked.

'As surprised and shocked as one usually is when something as horrible and unreal as murder touches one's own world. When I thought about it I was less surprised. She seemed in some ways a natural murderee. What did astound me was the news that she was an unmarried mother. She struck me as too careful, too scheming for that kind of trouble. I would have said, too, that she was undersexed rather than the reverse. We had one curious incident when she had been here a few weeks. The packing was done in the basement then and we had a male packer. He was a quiet, middle-aged, undersized little man with about six children. We didn't see much of him, but Sally was sent down to the packing-room with a message. Apparently he made some kind of sexual advance to her. It can't have been serious. The man was genuinely surprised when he got the sack for it. He may only have tried to kiss her. I never did get the whole story. But from the fuss she made you'd have thought she was stripped naked and raped. It was all very estimable of her to be so shocked, but most girls today seem to be able to cope with that kind of situation without having hysterics. And she wasn't play-acting that time. It was real, all right. You can't mistake genuine fear and disgust. I felt rather sorry for Jelks. Luckily I have a brother with a business in Glasgow, which was the man's home town, and I was able to get him fixed up there. He's doing well and, no doubt, he's learnt his lesson. But, believe me, Sally Jupp was no nymphomaniac.'

That much Stephen had known for himself. There seemed nothing more to be learnt from Miss Molpas. He had already been away from the hospital for over an hour and Standen would be getting impatient. He said his 'good-byes' and made his own way back to the ground-floor office. Miss Titley was still in attendance and had just finished pacifying an aggrieved subscriber whose last three books had failed to satisfy. Stephen waited for a moment while they finished their conversation. The neat rows of maroon-backed volumes had touched a chord of memory. Someone he knew subscribed to Select Books Limited. It was no one at the hospital. Methodically he let his mind range over the bookcases of his friends and acquaintances and time brought the answer.

'I'm afraid I haven't much time for reading,' he said to Miss Titley. 'But the books look wonderful value. I think one of my friends is a member. Do you ever see Sir Reynold Price?'

Miss Titley did indeed see Sir Reynold. Sir Reynold was a dear member. He came in himself for his monthly books and they had such interesting talks together. A charming man in every way was Sir Reynold Price.

'I wonder if he ever met Miss Sally Jupp here?' Stephen asked his question diffidently. He expected it to provoke some surprise, but Miss Titley's reaction was unexpected. She was affronted. With infinite kindness but great firmness, she explained that Miss Jupp could not have met Sir Reynold at Select Books Limited. She, Miss Titley, was in charge of the public office. She had held that job for over ten years now. All the customers knew Miss Titley and Miss Titley knew them. Dealing personally with the members was a job requiring tact and experience. Miss Molpas had every confidence in Miss Titley and would never dream of putting anyone else in the public office. Miss Jupp, concluded Miss Titley, had only been the office junior. She was just an inexperienced girl.

And with this ironic parting shot Stephen had to be content.

It was nearly four when Stephen got back to the hospital. As he passed by the porter's room Colley called to him and leaned over his counter with the wariness of a conspirator. His kind old eyes were troubled. Stephen remembered that the police had been to the hospital. It was Colley they would have spoken to. He wondered how much harm the old man might have done by a too-loyal determination to give nothing away. And there was nothing to give away. Sally had only been to the hospital once.

165

Colley could only have confirmed what the police already knew. But the porter was speaking:

"There's been a telephone call for you, sir. It was from Martingale. Miss Bowers said would you please ring as soon as you came in. It's urgent, sir.'

Stephen fought down panic and made himself scan the letter-rack as if for an expected letter before replying.

'Did Miss Bowers leave a message, Colley?'

'No, sir. No message.'

He decided to telephone from the public call box in the hall. There was a greater chance of privacy there even if it did mean that he was in full view of Colley. He counted out the necessary coins deliberately before entering the box. As usual there was a slight delay in getting the Chadfleet exchange but at Martingale Catherine must have been sitting by the telephone. She answered almost before the bell had rung.

'Stephen? Thank God you're back. Look, can you come home at once? Someone's tried to kill Deborah.'

2

Meanwhile in the little front room of 17 Windermere Crescent, Inspector Dalgleish faced his man and moved relentlessly towards the moment of truth. Victor Proctor's face held the look of a trapped animal which knows that the last escape hole is barred but cannot even yet bring itself to turn and face the end. His dark little eyes moved restlessly from side to side. The propitiatory voice and smile had gone. Now there was nothing left but fear. In the last few minutes the lines from nose to mouth seemed to have deepened. In his red neck, scraggy as a chicken's, the Adam's apple moved convulsively.

Dalgleish pressed remorselessly on.

'So you admit that this return which you made to the "Help Them Now Association" in which you claimed that your niece was a war orphan without means was untrue?'

'I suppose I should have mentioned about the £2,000, but that was capital not income.'

'Capital which you had spent?'

'I had to bring her up. It may have been left to me in

166

trust for her but I had to feed her, didn't I? We've never had much to come and go on. She got her scholarship but we still had her clothes. It hasn't been easy let me tell you.'

'And you still say that Miss Jupp was unaware that her father had left this money?'

'She was only a baby at the time. Afterwards there didn't seem any point in telling her.'

'Because, by then, the trust money had been converted to your own use?'

'I used it to help keep her, I tell you. I was entitled to use it. My wife and I were made trustees and we did our best for the girl. How long would it have lasted if she'd had it when she was twenty-one? We fed her all those years without another penny.'

'Except the three grants which the "Help Them Now Association" gave.'

'Well, she was a war orphan, wasn't she? They didn't give much. It helped with her school uniform, that's all.'

'And you still deny having been in the grounds of Martingale House last Saturday?'

'I've told you. Why do you keep on badgering? I didn't go to the fête. Why should I?'

'You might have wanted to congratulate your niece on her engagement. You said that Miss Liddell telephoned early on the Saturday morning to tell you about it. Miss Liddell still denies that she did any such thing.'

'I can't help that. If it wasn't the Liddell woman it was someone pretending to be her. How do I know who it was?'

'Are you quite sure that it wasn't your niece?'

'It was Miss Liddell I tell you.'

'Did you, as a result of that telephone conversation, go to see Miss Jupp at Martingale?'

'No. No. I keep telling you. I was out cycling all day.'

Deliberately Dalgleish took two photographs from his wallet and spread them out on the table. In each a bunch of children were seen entering the vast wrought-iron gates of Martingale, their faces contorted into wide grimaces in an effort to persuade the hidden photographer that there was the 'Happiest-looking child to enter the fête'. At their backs a few adults made their less spectacular entrances. The furtive, macintoshed figure turning hands in pockets

167

towards the pay table was not very clearly in focus but was still unmistakable. Proctor half reached out his left hand as if to tear the photograph in two and then sank back in his chair.

'All right,' he said. 'I'd better tell you. I was there.'

3

It had taken a little time to arrange for his work to be covered. Not for the first time Stephen envied those whose personal problems were not always secondary to the demands of their profession. By the time the arrangements were complete and he had borrowed a car he felt something like hatred for the hospital and every one of his demanding, insatiable patients. Things would have been easier if he could have spoken frankly of what had happened, but something held him back. They probably thought that the police had sent for him, that an arrest was imminent. Well, let them. Let them all bloody well think what they liked. God, he was glad to get away from a place where the living were perpetually sacrificed to keep the half-dead alive!

Afterwards he could remember nothing of the drive home. Catherine had said that Deborah was all right. that the attempt had failed, but Catherine was a fool. What were they all doing to have let it happen? Catherine had been perfectly calm on the telephone but the details she had given, although clear, had explained nothing. Someone had got into Deborah's room early this morning and had attempted to strangle her. She had shaken herself free and screamed for help. Martha had reached her first and Felix a second later. Deborah had recovered sufficiently by then to pretend that she had awoken from a nightmare. But she had obviously been terrified and had spent the rest of the night sitting by the fire in Martha's room, with the door and windows locked and her dressing-gown collar hugged high round her neck. She had come down to breakfast with a chiffon scarf at her throat but, apart from looking pale and tired, had been perfectly composed. It was Felix Hearne who, sitting next to Deborah at luncheon, had noticed the edge of the bruise above the scarf and who had subsequently got the truth from her. He had consulted Catherine. Deborah had implored them not to worry her mother and Felix had been willing to give in to this, but Catherine had insisted on sending for the police. Dalgleish was not in the village. One of the constables thought that he and Sergeant Martin were in Canningbury. Felix had left no message except to ask that Dalgleish should visit Martingale as soon as convenient. They had told Mrs. Maxie nothing. Mr. Maxie was too ill now to be left for long and they were hoping that the bruise on Deborah's neck would have faded before her mother became suspicious. Deborah, explained Catherine, seemed more terrified of upsetting her mother than of being attacked for a second time. They were waiting for Dalgleish now, but Catherine thought that Stephen ought to know what had happened. She hadn't consulted Felix before telephoning. Probably Felix wouldn't have approved of her sending for Stephen. But it was time someone took a firm line. Martha knew nothing. Deborah was terrified that she might refuse to stay at Martingale if the truth came out. Catherine had no sympathy with that attitude. With a murderer at large Martha had the right to protect herself. It was ridiculous of Deborah to think that the attack could be kept secret much longer. But she had threatened to deny everything if the police told Martha or her mother. So would Stephen please come at once and see what he could do. Catherine really couldn't take any more responsibility herself. Stephen was not surprised. Hearne and Catherine between them seemed to have taken too much responsibility already. Deborah must be mad to try and conceal a thing like that. Unless she had her own reasons. Unless even the fear of a second attempt was better than knowing the truth. While his feet and hands worked with automatic co-ordination at brakes and throttle, wheel and gear lever, his mind, sharpened by apprehension, posed its questions. How long had it been after Deborah's scream before Martha arrived — and Felix? Martha slept next door. It was natural that she should have woken first. But Felix? Why had he agreed to hush it up? It was madness to think that murder and attempted murder could be treated like one of his wartime escapades. They all knew that

Felix was a bloody hero, but his brand of heroics wasn't wanted at Martingale. How much did they know about him anyway? Deborah had behaved strangely. It was unlike Deborah he knew to scream for help. Once she would have fought back with more fury than fear. But he remembered her stricken face when Sally's body was discovered, the sudden retching, the blind stumbling for the door. One couldn't guess how people would behave under stress. Catherine had behaved well, Deborah badly. But Catherine had more experience of violent death. And a better conscience?

The heavy front door of Martingale was open. The house was strangely quiet. He could hear only a murmur of voices from the drawing-room. As he entered four pairs of eyes looked up at him and he heard Catherine's quick sigh of relief. Deborah was sitting in one of the winged chairs before the fireplace. Catherine and Felix stood behind her, Felix upright and watchful, Catherine with her arms stretched over the back of the chair and her hands resting on Deborah's shoulders in an attitude which was half-protective, half-comforting. Deborah did not seem to resent it. Her head was thrown back. Her high-necked shirt was open and a yellow chiffon scarf dangled from her hand. Even from the door Stephen could see the purpling bruise above the thin shoulder-blades. Dalgleish was sitting opposite her, relaxed on the edge of his chair, but his eyes were watchful. He and Felix Hearne confronted each other like cats across a room. Somewhere in the background Stephen was conscious of the ubiquitous Sergeant Martin with his notebook. In the second before anyone spoke or moved the little gilded clock chimed the three-quarters, dropping each beautiful note into the silence like a crystal pebble. Stephen moved swiftly to his sister's side and bent his head to kiss her. The smooth cheek was icy cold against his lips. As he drew back her eyes met his with a look which was hard to interpret. Could it have been entreaty – or warning? He looked at Felix.

'What happened?' he asked. 'Where's my mother?'

'Upstairs with Mr. Maxie. She spends most of the day with him now. We told her that Inspector Dalgleish was making a routine visit. There's no need to add to her worries. Or Martha's either. If Martha takes fright and decides to go it will mean importing another trained nurse and we can't cope with that just now. Even if we could find one who would be willing to come.'

'Aren't you forgetting something,' said Stephen roughly. 'What about Deborah? Do we all sit back quietly and wait for another attempt?' He resented both Felix's calm assumption of responsibility for the family arrangements and the inference that someone had to cope with these matters while the son of the house put his professional responsibilities before his family. It was Dalgleish who answered :

'I am looking after Mrs. Riscoe's safety, Doctor. Would you please examine her throat and let me know what you think.'

Stephen turned to him.

'I prefer not to. Dr. Epps treats my family. Why not call him?'

'I'm asking you to look at the throat, not to treat it. This isn't the time to indulge in spurious professional scruples. Do as I say, please.'

Stephen bent his head again. After a moment he straightened up and said, 'He grasped the neck with both hands just above and behind the shoulder-blades. There is fairly extensive bruising but no nail scratches and no thumb-marks. The grip could have been with the base of the thumbs in front and the fingers behind. The larynx is almost certainly untouched. I should expect the bruises to fade in a day or two. There's no real harm done.' He added, 'Physically at any rate.'

'In other words,' said Dalgleish, 'it was rather an amateur effort?'

'If you care to put it like that.'

'I do care. Doesn't it suggest to you that this assailant knew his job rather well? Knew where to apply pressure and how much to apply without causing harm? Are we expected to believe that the person who killed Miss Jupp with such expertise couldn't do better than this? What do you think, Mrs. Riscoe?'

Deborah was buttoning up her shirt. She shrugged herself free of Catherine's proprietary grasp and rewound the chiffon scarf round her neck.

'I'm sorry you're disappointed, Inspector. Perhaps next

171

time he'll make a better job of it. He was quite expert enough for me, thank you.'

'I must say you seem to be taking it very coolly,' cried Catherine indignantly. 'If Mrs. Riscoe hadn't managed to shake herself free and scream she wouldn't be alive now. Obviously he got the best grip he could in the dark but was scared off when she called out. And this may not have been the first attempt. Don't forget that the sleeping-drug was put into Deborah's mug.'

'I haven't forgotten that, Miss Bowers. Nor that the missing bottle was found under her name stake. Where were you last night?'

'Helping to nurse Mr. Maxie. Mrs. Maxie and I were together for the whole of the night, except when we went to the bathroom. We were certainly together from midnight onwards.'

'And Dr. Maxie was in London. This attack has certainly happened at a convenient time for you all. Did you see this mysterious strangler, Mrs. Riscoe? Or recognize him?'

'No. I wasn't sleeping very deeply. I think I was having a nightmare. I woke up when I felt the first touch of his hands on my throat. I could feel his breath on my face but I couldn't recognize him. When I screamed and felt for the light switch he made off through the door. I put on the light and screamed. I was terrified. It wasn't a rational fear even. Somehow my dream and the attack had merged together. I couldn't tell where one horror ended and the other began.'

'And yet when Mrs. Bultitaft arrived you said nothing?'

'I didn't want to frighten her. We all know there's a strangler about but we've got to get on with our jobs. It wouldn't help her to know.'

'That shows a commendable concern for her peace of mind, but less for her safety. I must congratulate you all on your insouciance in the face of this homicidal maniac. For that is obviously what he is. Surely you are not trying to tell me that Miss Jupp was killed by mistake, that she was mistaken for Mrs. Riscoe?'

Felix spoke for the first time. 'We're not trying to tell you anything. It's your job to tell us. We only know what happened. I agree with Miss Bowers that Mrs. Riscoe is in

172

danger. Presumably you're prepared to offer her the protection she's entitled to.'

Dalgleish looked at him.

'What time did you reach Mrs. Riscoe's room this morning?'

'About half a minute after Mrs. Bultitaft, I suppose. I got out of bed as soon as Mrs. Riscoe called out.'

'And neither you nor Mrs. Bultitaft saw the intruder?'

'No. I presume he was down the stairs before we came out of our rooms. Naturally I made no search as I wasn't told until this afternoon what had happened. I've looked since, but there's no trace of anyone.'

'Have you any idea how this person got in, Mrs. Riscoe?'

'It could have been through one of the drawing-room windows. We went into the garden last night and must have forgotten to lock it. Martha mentioned that she found it open this morning.'

'By "we" do you mean yourself and Mr. Hearne?'

'Yes.'

'Were you wearing your dressing-gown by the time your maid arrived in your room?'

'Yes. I had just put it on.'

'And Mrs. Bultitaft accepted your story of a nightmare and suggested that you should spend the remainder of the night by the electric fire in her room?'

'Yes. She didn't want to go back to bed herself, but I made her. First of all we had a pot of tea together by her fire.'

'So it comes to this,' said Dalgleish. 'You and Mr. Hearne take an evening walk in the garden of a house where there has recently been a murder and leave a french window open when you come in. In the night some unspecified man comes to your room, makes an inexpert attempt at strangling you for no motive which you or anyone else can suggest and then vanishes, leaving no trace. Your throat is so little affected that you are able to scream with enough force to attract the people sleeping in near-by rooms yet, by the time they arrive in a matter of minutes, you have recovered from your fright sufficiently to lie about what has happened, a lie made more effective by the fact that you have taken the trouble to get out of

173

bed and put on your dressing-gown with its concealing collar. Does that strike you as rational behaviour, Mrs. Riscoe?'

'Of course it doesn't,' said Felix roughly. 'Nothing that has happened in this house since last Saturday has been rational. But even you can hardly suppose that Mrs. Riscoe tried to strangle herself. Those bruises can't have been self-inflicted, and if they weren't, who inflicted them? Do you really suppose that a jury wouldn't believe the two crimes to be related?'

'I don't think a jury will be asked to consider that possibility,' said Dalgleish evenly. 'I have nearly completed my investigation into Miss Jupp's death. What happened last night isn't likely to affect my conclusions. It has made no difference. I think it's time the matter was settled and I propose to take a short cut. If Mrs. Maxie has no objection I want to see you all together in this house at eight o'clock tonight.'

'Did you want something of me, Inspector?' They turned towards the door. Eleanor Maxie had come in so quietly that only Dalgleish had noticed her. She did not wait for the reply but moved swiftly to her son.

'I'm glad you're here, Stephen. Did Deborah telephone? I meant to myself if he didn't improve. It's difficult to tell, but I think there's a change. Could you get Mr. Hinks? And Charles, of course.'

It was natural, Stephen thought, for her to ask for the priest before the doctor.

'I'll come up myself first,' he said. 'That is, if the inspector will excuse me. I don't think there is anything more we can usefully discuss.'

'Not until eight o'clock tonight, Doctor.'

Stung by his tone Stephen wanted, not for the first time, to point out that surgeons were addressed as 'Mister'. He was saved from this pedantic pettiness by a realization of its futility and of his mother's need. For days now he had hardly thought of his father. Now there were amends which he must make. For a second Dalgleish and his investigation, the whole horror of Sally's murder, faded before this new and more immediate need. In this at least he could act like a son.

But suddenly Martha was blocking the door. She stood

174

there, white and shaking, her mouth opening and shutting soundlessly. The tall young man behind her stepped past her into the room. With one terrified glance at her mistress and a stiff little gesture of her arm which was less of ushering the stranger in than abandoning him to the company, Martha gave an animal-like moan and disappeared. The man looked back at her with amusement and then turned to face them. He was very tall, over six feet, and his fair hair, cut short all over the head, was bleached by the sun. He was dressed in brown corduroy trousers with a leather jacket. From its open neck the throat rose sunburnt and thick, supporting a head which was arresting in its animal health and virility. He was long-legged, long-armed. Over one shoulder was slung a rucksack. In his right hand he carried an airline hold-all, pristine new with its golden wings. It looked as incongruous as a woman's toy in his great brown fist. Beside him Stephen's good looks paled into a commonplace elegance and all the weariness and futility which Felix had known for fifteen years seemed at once graven on his face. When he spoke his voice, confident with happiness, held no trace of diffidence. It was a soft voice slightly American in tone, and yet there could be no doubt of his Englishness.

'It seems I've given your maid a bit of a shock. I'm sorry to butt in like this but I guess Sally never told you about me. The name's James Ritchie. She'll be expecting me all right. I'm her husband.' He turned to Mrs. Maxie. 'She never told me exactly what sort of job she's got here and I don't want to cause inconvenience, but I've come to take her away.'

4

In the years that followed when Eleanor Maxie sat quietly in her drawing-room she would often see again in her mind's eye that gangling and confident ghost from the past confronting her from the doorway and could sense again the shocked silence which followed his words. That silence could only have lasted for seconds yet, in retrospect, it seemed as if minutes passed while he looked round at them in confident ease and they gazed back at him in incredulous horror. Mrs. Maxie had time to think

175

how like a tableau it was, the very personification of surprise. She felt none herself. The last few days had drained her of so much emotion that this final revelation fell like a hammer on wool. There was nothing left to discover about Sally Jupp which had power to surprise any more. It was surprising that Sally was dead, surprising that she had been engaged to Stephen, surprising to learn that so many people were implicated in her life and death. To learn now that Sally had been a wife as well as a mother was interesting but not shocking. Detached from their common emotion she did not miss the quick glance that Felix Hearne gave Deborah. He was shaken all right but that swift appraisal held something, too, of amusement and triumph. Stephen looked merely dazed. Catherine Bowers had flushed deep red and was literally open-mouthed, the stock registration of surprise. Then she turned to Stephen as if throwing on him the burden of spokesman for them all. Finally Mrs. Maxie looked at Dalgleish and for a second their eyes held. In them she read a momentary but unmistakable compassion. She was conscious of thinking irrelevantly 'Sally Ritchie. Jimmie Ritchie. That's why she called the child Jimmy after his father. I could never understand why it had to be Jimmy Jupp. Why are they staring at him like that? Someone ought to say something.' Someone did. Deborah, white to her lips, spoke like someone in a dream:

'Sally's dead. Didn't they tell you? She's dead and buried. They say that one of us killed her.' Then she began to shake uncontrollably and Catherine, getting to her before Stephen, caught her before she fell and supported her into a chair. The tableau broke. There was a sudden spate of words. Stephen and Dalgleish moved over to Ritchie. There was a murmur of 'better in the business room' and the three of them were suddenly gone. Deborah lay back in her chair, her eyes closed. Mrs. Maxie could witness her distress without feeling more than a faint irritation and a passive curiosity as to what lay behind it all. Her own preoccupations were more compelling. She spoke to Catherine.

'I must go back to my husband now. Perhaps you would come to help. Mr. Hinks will be here soon and I don't expect Martha will be much use at present. This arrival seems to have unnerved her.' Catherine might have replied that Martha was not the only one to be unnerved, but she murmured an acquiescence and came at once. Her real usefulness and genuine care of the invalid did not blind Mrs. Maxie to her guest's self-imposed role of the cheerful little helpmate competent to cope with all emergencies. This last emergency might prove one too many but Catherine had plenty of stamina and the more Deborah weakened the more Catherine grew in strength. At the door Mrs. Maxie turned to Felix Hearne.

'When Stephen has finished talking to Ritchie I think he should come to his father. He's deeply unconscious, of course, but I think Stephen should be there. Deborah should come up, too, when she has recovered. Perhaps you would tell her.' Answering his unspoken comment, she added, 'There's no need to tell Dalgleish. His plans for tonight can stand. It will be all over before eight.' Deborah was stretched back in her chair, her eyes closed. The chiffon scarf loosened around her neck.

'What is the matter with Deborah's throat?' Mrs. Maxie sounded only vaguely interested.

'Some rather childish horseplay, I'm afraid,' replied Felix. 'It was as unsuccessful as it deserved to be.'

Without another glance at her daughter, Eleanor Maxie left them together.

5

Half an hour later Simon Maxie died. The long years of half-life were over at last. Emotionally and intellectually he had been dead for three years. His last breath was the technicality which finally and officially severed him from a world which he had once known and loved. It was not within his capacity now to die with courage or with dignity but he died without fuss. His wife and children were with him and his parish priest said the prescribed prayers as though they could be heard and shared by that stiffened grotesque figure on the bed. Martha was not there. Afterwards the family were to say that there seemed no point in asking her. At the time they knew that her sentimental weeping would have been more than they could bear. This death-bed was only the culmination of a slow process of dying. Although they stood white-faced about the bed and tried to evoke some pietas of remembrance and grief their thoughts were with that other death and their minds reached towards eight o'clock.

Afterwards all of them met in the drawing-room, except Mrs. Maxie, who was either without curiosity about Sally's husband, or who had decided to detach herself momentarily from the murder and all its ramifications. She merely instructed the family not to let Dalgleish know that her husband was dead, then walked with Mr. Hinks back to the vicarage.

In the drawing-room Stephen poured the drinks and told his story:

'It's simple enough really. Of course I had only time for the bare details. I wanted to get up to Father. Dalgleish stayed on with Ritchie after I left and I suppose he got all the information he wanted. They were married all right. They met while Sally was working in London and married there secretly about a month before he went to Venezuela, on a building job.'

'But why didn't she say?' asked Catherine. 'Why all the mystery?'

'Apparently he wouldn't have got the job abroad if the firm had known. They wanted an unmarried man. The pay was good and it would have given them a chance to set up house. Sally was mad keen to get married before he went. Ritchie rather thinks she liked the idea of putting one over on her aunt and uncle. She was never happy with them. The idea was that she would have stayed with them and kept on with her job. She planned to save £50 before Ritchie came back. Then, when she found the baby was coming, she decided to stick to her side of the bargain. Heaven knows why. But that part didn't surprise Ritchie. He said that was just the kind of thing that Sally would do.'

'It's a pity he didn't make sure that she wasn't pregnant before he left her,' Felix said dryly.

'Perhaps he did,' said Stephen shortly. 'Perhaps he asked her and she lied. I didn't question him about his sexual relationship. What business is that of mine? I was faced by a husband who had returned to find his wife murdered in this house, leaving a child he never even

178

knew existed. I don't want a half hour like that again. It was hardly the time to suggest that he might have been more careful. So might we, by God!'

He gulped down his whisky. The hand which held the glass was shaking. Without waiting for them to speak he went on:

'Dalgleish was wonderful with him. I could like him after tonight if he were here in any other capacity. He's taken Ritchie with him. They're calling in at St. Mary's to see the child and then they hope to get a room for Ritchie at The Moonraker's Arms. Apparently he hasn't any family to go to.' He paused to refill his glass. Then he went on:

'This explains a lot, of course. Sally's conversation with the vicar on Thursday, her telling him that Jimmy was going to have a father.'

'But she was engaged to you!' cried Catherine. 'She accepted you.'

'She never actually said she'd marry me. Sally loved a mystery all right and this one was at my expense. I don't suppose she ever told anyone that she was engaged to me. We all assumed it. She was in love with Ritchie all the time. She knew he was soon coming home. He was pathetically anxious to let me know just how much in love they were. He kept crying and trying to force some of her letters on me. I didn't want to read them. Heaven knows I was hating myself enough without that. God, it was awful! But once I'd started reading I had to go on. He kept pulling them out of that bag he had and pushing them into my hand, the tears running down his face. They were pathetic, sentimental and naïve. But they were real, the emotion was genuine.'

No wonder you're upset then, thought Felix. You never felt a genuine emotion in your life.

Catherine Bowers said reasonably, 'You mustn't blame yourself. None of this would have happened if Sally had told the truth about her marriage. It's asking for trouble to pretend about a thing like that. I suppose he wrote to her through an intermediary.'

'Yes. He wrote through Derek Pullen. The letters were sent in an envelope enclosed in one addressed to Pullen. He handed them over to Sally at pre-arranged meetings.

179

She never told him they were from a husband. I don't know what story she concocted, but it must have been a good one. Pullen was pledged to secrecy and, as far as I know, he never gave her away. Sally knew how to choose her dupes.'

'She liked amusing herself with people,' said Felix. 'They can be dangerous playthings. Obviously one of her dupes thought that the joke had gone far enough. It wasn't you by any chance, was it Maxie?'

The tone was deliberately offensive and Stephen took a quick step towards him. But before he could answer they heard the clang of the front door-bell and the clock on the mantelpiece struck eight.

CHAPTER NINE

1

By common consent they met in the business room. Someone had arranged the chairs in a half circle around the heavy table, someone had filled the water carafe and placed it at Dalgleish's right hand. Sitting alone at the table with Martin behind him, Dalgleish watched his suspects as they came in. Eleanor Maxie was the most composed. She took a chair facing the light and sat, detached and at peace, looking out at the lawns and the far trees. It was as if her ordeal were already over. Stephen Maxie strode in, threw Dalgleish a glance of mingled contempt and defiance, and sat down by his mother. Felix Hearne and Deborah Riscoe came in together but did not look at each other and sat apart. Dalgleish felt that their relationship had subtly altered since the unsuccessful play-acting of the night before. He wondered that Hearne should have lent himself to so palpable a deceit. Looking at the darkening bruise on the girl's neck, only half hidden by the knotted scarf, he wondered more at the force which Hearne had apparently found it necessary to use. Catherine Bowers came in last. She flushed as she saw their eyes on her and scurried to the only vacant chair like an anxious probationer arriving late for a lecture. As Dalgleish opened his dossier he heard the first slow notes of the church bell. The bells had been ringing when he first arrived at Martingale. They had sounded often as a background to his investigation, the mood music of murder. Now they tolled like a funeral bell and he wondered irrelevantly who in the village had died; someone for whom the bells were tolling as they had not tolled for Sally.

He looked up from his papers and began to talk in his calm deep voice.

'One of the most unusual features of this crime was the contrast between the apparent premeditation and the actual execution. All the medical evidence pointed to a crime of impulse. This was not a slow strangulation. There were few of the classical signs of asphyxiation. Considerable force had been used and there was a fracture of the superior cornu of the thyroid at its base. Nevertheless, death was due to vagal inhibition and was very sudden. It may well have taken place even if the strangler had used considerably less force. The picture on the face of it was of a single unpremeditated attack. This is borne out, too, by the use of hands. If a murderer intends to kill by strangulation, it is usually done with a cord, or with a scarf, or stocking, perhaps. This isn't invariable, but you can see the reason for it. Few people can be confident of their ability to kill with the bare hands. There is one person in this room who might feel that confidence, but I don't think he would have used this method. There are some effective ways of killing without a weapon and he would have known them.'

Felix Hearne murmured under his breath, 'But that was in another country and besides, the wench is dead.' If Dalgleish heard the quotation or sensed the slight tensing of muscles as his audience controlled the impulse to look at Hearne he made no sign but went on quietly:

'In contrast to this apparent impulse in the deed we were faced with the evidence of the attempted and partial drugging of the victim which certainly indicated an intention to render the girl insensible. This could have been with the object of getting into her bedroom more easily and without waking her or of murdering her in her sleep. I dismissed the theory of two separate and different attempts on her life in the same night. No one in this room had any reason to like Sally and some of you may even have reason to hate her. But it was straining credulity too far seriously to consider that two people chose the same night to attempt murder.'

'If we did hate her,' said Deborah quietly, 'we weren't the only ones.'

'There was that Pullen boy,' said Catherine. 'You can't tell me that there was nothing between them.' She saw Deborah wince at the solecism and went on belligerently. 'And what about Miss Liddell? It's all over the village how Sally had found out something discreditable about

182

her and was threatening to tell. If she could blackmail one she could blackmail another.'

Stephen Maxie said wearily :

'I can hardly see poor old Liddell climbing up stack-pipes, or sneaking in at the back door, to face Sally alone. She wouldn't have the nerve. And you can't imagine her seriously setting out to kill Sally with her bare hands.'

'She might,' said Catherine, 'if she knew that Sally was drugged.'

'But she couldn't have known,' Deborah pointed out. 'And she couldn't have put that drug in Sally's beaker, either. She and Eppy were leaving the house as Sally took the beaker up to bed. And it was my beaker she took, re-member. Before that they were both in this room with Mummy.'

'She took your beaker in the same way that she copied your dress,' said Catherine. 'But the Sommeil must have been put in it later. No one could want to drug you.'

'It couldn't have been put in later,' said Deborah shortly. 'What chance would there have been? I suppose one of us tiptoed in with Father's bottle of tablets, pre-tended to Sally that it was just a cosy social call, and then waited until she was bending over the baby and popped a tablet or two into her cocoa. It doesn't make sense.'

Dalgleish's quiet voice broke in :

'None of it makes sense if the drugging and the stran-gling are connected. Yet, as I said, it was too great a co-incidence that someone should have decided to strangle Sally Jupp on the same night as someone else set out to poison her. But there could be another explanation. What if this drugging were not an isolated incident? Suppose someone had regularly been doping Sally's evening drink. Someone who knew that only Sally drank cocoa so that the Sommeil could safely be put into the cocoa tin. Some-one who knew where the drug was kept and was experi-enced enough to use the right amount. Someone who wanted Sally discredited and out of the house, and could complain if she consistently overslept. Someone who had probably suffered more from Sally than the rest of the household realized and was glad of any action, however apparently ineffective, which would give her a sense of power over the girl. In a sense, you see, it was a substitute for murder.'

'Martha,' said Catherine involuntarily. The Maxies sat silent. If they had known or guessed, none of them gave a sign. Eleanor Maxie thought with compunction of the woman she had left weeping in the kitchen for her dead master. Martha had stood up at her entrance, her thick coarse-grained hands folded over the apron. She had made no sign when Mrs. Maxie told her. The tears were the more distressing for their silence. When she spoke her voice had been perfectly controlled, although the tears still ran down her face and dripped over the quiet hands. With no fuss and without explanation she had given in her notice. She would like to leave at the end of the week. There was a friend in Herefordshire to whom she could go for a time. Mrs. Maxie had neither argued nor persuaded. That was not her way. But, bending now a courteous and attentive gaze on Dalgleish, her honest mind explored the motives which had prompted her to exclude Martha from the death-bed and interested itself in this revelation that a loyalty that the family had all taken for granted had been more complicated, less acquiescent than any of them had suspected and had at last been strained too far.

Catherine was speaking. She was apparently without apprehension and was following Dalgleish's explanation as if he were expounding an interesting and atypical case history:

'Martha could always get Sommeil of course. The family were appallingly careless over Mr. Maxie's drugs. But why should she want to dope Sally on that particular night? After the scene at dinner Mrs. Maxie had more to worry about than Sally's late rising. It was too late to get rid of her that way. And why did Martha hide the bottle under Deborah's name-peg? I always thought she was devoted to the family.'

'So did the family,' said Deborah dryly.

'She drugged the cocoa again that night because she didn't know about the proposed engagement,' said Dalgleish. 'She wasn't in the dining-room at the time and no one told her. She went to Mr. Maxie's room and took the Sommeil and hid it in a panic because she thought she had killed Sally with the drug. If you think back you will realize that Mrs. Bultitaft was the only member of the household who didn't actually enter Sally's room. While the rest of you stood around the bed her one thought was to hide the bottle. It wasn't a reasonable thing to do but she was beyond behaving reasonably. She ran into the garden with it and hid it in the first soft earth she found. It was meant, I think, to be a temporary hiding-place. That's why she hastily marked it with the nearest peg. It was by chance that it happened to be yours, Mrs. Riscoe. Then she went back to the kitchen, emptied the remaining cocoa powder and the lining paper into the stove, washed out the tin and put it in the dustbin. She was the only person who had the opportunity to do these things. Then Mr. Hearne came into the kitchen to see if Mrs. Bultitaft was all right and to offer his help. This is what Mr. Hearne told me.' Dalgleish turned a page of his dossier and read :

'She seemed stunned and kept repeating that Sally must have killed herself. I pointed out that that was anatomically impossible and that seemed to upset her more. She gave me one curious look . . . and burst into loud sobbing.'

Dalgleish looked up at his audience. 'I think we can take it,' he said, 'that Mrs. Bultitaft's emotion was the reaction of relief. I suspect, too, that before Miss Bowers arrived to feed the child Mr. Hearne had coached Mrs. Bultitaft for the inevitable police questioning. Mrs. Bultitaft tells me that she didn't admit to him or to any of you that she was responsible for drugging Sally. That may be true. It doesn't mean that Mr. Hearne didn't guess. He was quite ready, as he has been throughout the case, to leave well alone if it were likely to mislead the police. Towards the end of this investigation, with the faked attack on Mrs. Riscoe, he took a more positive line in attempting to deceive.'

'That was my idea,' said Deborah quietly. 'I asked him. I made him do it.'

Hearne ignored the interruption and merely said :

'I may have guessed about Martha. But she was perfectly truthful. She didn't tell me and I didn't ask. It wasn't my affair.'

185

'No,' said Dalgleish bitterly. 'It wasn't your affair.' His voice had lost its controlled neutrality and they looked up at him startled by his sudden vehemence.

'That has been your attitude throughout, hasn't it? Don't let's pry into each other's affairs. Don't let's be vulgarly interested. If we must have a murder let it be handled with taste. Even your efforts to hamper the police would have been more effective if you had bothered to find out a little more from each other. Mrs. Riscoe need not have persuaded Mr. Hearne to stage an attack on her while her brother was safely in London if that brother had confided in her that he had an alibi for the time of Sally Jupp's death. Derek Pullen need not have tortured himself wondering whether he ought to shield a murderer if Mr. Stephen Maxie had bothered to explain what he was doing with a ladder in the garden on Saturday night. We finally got the truth from Pullen, but it wasn't easy.'

'Pullen isn't interested in shielding me,' said Stephen indifferently. 'He just couldn't bear not to behave like a little gent! You should have heard him telephoning to explain just how old-school-tie he was going to be. Your secret is safe with me, Maxie, but why not do the decent thing? Damn his insolence!'

'I suppose there's no objection to us knowing what you were doing with a ladder?' inquired Deborah.

'Why should there be? I was bringing it back from outside Bocock's cottage. We used it during the afternoon to retrieve one of the balloons which got caught up in his elm. You know what Bocock is. He would have dragged it up here first thing in the morning and it's too heavy for him. I suppose I was in the mood for a little masochism so I slung it over my shoulder. I wasn't to know that I'd find Pullen lurking about in the old stables. Apparently he made a habit of it. I wasn't to know, either, that Sally would be murdered and that Pullen would use his great mind to put two and two together and assume that I'd used the ladder to climb to her room and kill her. Why climb in anyway? I could have got through the door. And I wasn't even carrying the ladder from the right direction.'

'He probably thought that you were trying to cast suspicion on an outside person,' suggested Deborah. 'Himself, for instance.'

186

Felix's lazy voice broke in :

'It didn't occur to you, Maxie, that the boy might be in genuine distress and indecision?'

Stephen moved uneasily in his chair.

'I didn't lose any sleep over him. He had no right on our property and I told him so. I don't know how long he'd been waiting there but he must have watched me while I put down the ladder. Then he stepped out of the shadows like an avenging fury, and accused me of deceiving Sally. He seems to have curious ideas about class distinctions. Anyone would think I had been exercising *droit de seigneur*. I told him to mind his own business, only less politely, and he lunged at me. I'd had about as much as I could stand by then so I struck out and caught him on the eye, knocking off his spectacles. It was all pretty vulgar and stupid. We were too near the house to be safe so we daren't make much noise. We stood there hissing insults at each other in whispers and grovelling around in the dust to find his glasses. He's pretty blind without them so I thought I'd better see him as far as the corner of Nessingford Road. He took it that I was escorting him off the premises, but his pride would have been hurt either way so it didn't matter much. By the time we came to say good night he had obviously persuaded himself into what he imagined was an appropriate frame of mind. He even wanted to shake hands! I didn't know whether to burst out laughing or to knock him down again. I'm sorry, Deb, but he's that sort of person.'

Eleanor Maxie spoke for the first time :

'It is a pity that you didn't tell us about this earlier. That poor boy should certainly have been spared a great deal of worry.'

They seemed to have forgotten the presence of Dalgleish, but now he spoke :

'Mr. Maxie had a reason for his silence. He realized that it was important for you all that the police should think that a ladder had been available within easy reach of Sally's window. He knew the approximate time of death and he wasn't anxious for the police to know that the ladder hadn't been returned to the old stable before twenty past twelve. With luck we should assume that it had been there all night. For much the same reason he was vague about the time he left Bocock's cottage and lied about the time he got to bed. If Sally was killed at midnight by someone under this roof he was anxious that there should be no lack of suspects. He realized that most crimes are solved by a process of elimination. On the other hand I think he was telling the truth about the time he locked the south door. That was at about twelve thirty-three and we know now that at twelve thirty-three Sally Jupp had been dead for over half an hour. She died before Mr. Maxie left Bocock's cottage and about the same time as Mr. Wilson of the village store got out of bed to shut a creaking window and saw Derek Pullen walking quietly past, head bent, towards Martingale. Pullen was hoping, perhaps, to see Sally and to hear her explanation. But he only reached the cover of the old stables before Mr. Maxie arrived, carrying the ladder. And by then Sally Jupp was dead.'

'So it wasn't Pullen?' said Catherine.

'How could it have been?' said Stephen roughly. 'He certainly hadn't killed her when he spoke to me and he was in no condition to turn back and kill her after I had left him. He could hardly see his way to his own front gate.'

'And if Sally was dead before Stephen got back from visiting Bocock, it couldn't have been him either,' pointed out Catherine. It was, Dalgleish noticed, the first time that any of them had specifically referred to the possible guilt or innocence of a member of the family.

Stephen Maxie said:

'How do you know that she was dead then? She was alive at ten-thirty p.m. and dead by the morning. That's as much as anyone knows.'

'Not really,' replied Dalgleish. 'Two people can put the time of death closer than that. One is the murderer, but there is someone else who can help too.'

2

There was a knock on the door and Martha stood there, capped and aproned, stolid as always. Her hair was strained back beneath her curiously high old-fashioned cap, her ankles bulged above the barred black shoes. If the Maxies were seeing in their mind's eye a desperate woman, clutching to herself that incriminating bottle and homing to her familiar kitchen like a frightened animal they gave no sign. She looked as she had always looked and if she had become a stranger she was less alien than they now were to each other. She gave no explanation of her presence except to announce 'Mr. Proctor for the Inspector'. Then she was gone again and the shadowy figure behind her stepped forward into the light. Proctor was too angry to be disconcerted at being shown thus summarily into a roomful of people obviously occupied with their private concerns. He seemed to notice no one but Dalgleish and advanced towards him belligerently.

'Look here, Inspector, I've got to have protection. It isn't good enough. I've been trying to get you at the station. They wouldn't tell me where you were, if you please, but I wasn't going to be fobbed off with that station sergeant. I thought I'd find you here. Something's got to be done about it.'

Dalgleish considered him in silence for a minute.

'What isn't good enough, Mr. Proctor?' he inquired.

'That young fellow. Sally's husband. He's been round home threatening me. He was drunk if you ask me. It's not my fault if she got herself murdered and I told him so. I won't have him upsetting my wife. And there are the neighbours. You could hear him shouting his insults right down the avenue. My daughter was there, too, it's not nice in front of a child. I'm innocent of this murder as you very well know, and I want protection.'

He looked indeed as if he could have done with protection against more than James Ritchie. He was a scrawny red-faced little man with the look of an angry hen and a trick of jerking his head as he talked. He was neatly but cheaply dressed. The grey raincoat was clean and the trilby hat, held stiffly in his gloved hands, had recently acquired a new band. Catherine said suddenly, 'You were in this house on the day of the murder, weren't you? We saw you on the stairs. You must have been coming from Sally's room.'

Stephen glanced at his mother and said:

'You'd better come in and join the prayer meeting, Mr.

Proctor. Public confessions are said to be good for the soul. Actually you've timed your entrance rather well. You are, I assume, interested in hearing who killed your niece?'

'No!' said Hearne suddenly and violently. 'Don't be a fool, Maxie. Keep him out of it.'

His voice recalled Proctor to a sense of his surroundings. He focused his attention on Felix and seemed to dislike what he saw. 'So I'm not to stay! Suppose I choose to stay. I've a right to know what's going on.' He glared round at the watchful, unwelcoming faces. 'You'd like it to be me, wouldn't you? All of you. Don't think I don't know. You'd like to pin it on me all right if you could. I'd have been in queer street if she'd been poisoned or knocked on the head. Pity one of you couldn't keep your hands off her, wasn't it? But there's one thing you can't pin on me and that's a strangling. And why? That's why!'

He gave a sudden convulsive movement, there was a click and a moment of sheer unbelieveable comedy as his artificial right hand fell with a thud on the desk in front of Dalgleish. They gazed at it fascinated while it lay like some obscene relic, its rubber fingers curved in impotent supplication. Breathing heavily, Proctor hitched a chair beneath himself with a deft twist of his left hand and sat there triumphantly, while Catherine turned her pale eyes on him reproachfully as if he were a difficult patient who had behaved with more than customary petulance.

Dalgleish picked up the hand.

'We knew about this, of course, although I'm glad to say that my own attention was first brought to it less spectacularly. Mr. Proctor lost his right hand in a bombing incident. The ingenious substitute is made of moulded linen and glue. It's light and strong and has three articulated fingers with knuckle joints like a real hand. By flexing his left shoulder and slightly moving his arm away from his body, the wearer can tighten a control cord which runs from the shoulder to the thumb. This opens the thumb against the pressure of a spring. Once the tension on the shoulder is released the spring automatically closes the thumb against the firm fixed index finger. It is, as you can see, a clever contraption, and Mr. Proctor can do a great deal with it. He can get through

190

his work, ride a bicycle and present an almost normal appearance to the world. But there's one thing he can't do, and that is to kill by manual strangulation.'

'He could be left-handed.'

'He could be, Miss Bowers, but he isn't, and the evidence shows that Sally was killed by a strong right-handed grip.' He turned the hand over and pushed it across the table to Proctor.

'This, of course, was the hand which a certain small boy saw opening the trap-door of Bocock's stables. There could only be one person connected with this case who would be wearing leather gloves on a hot summer day and at a garden fête. This was one clue to his identity and there were others. Miss Bowers is quite right. Mr. Proctor was in Martingale that afternoon.'

'What if I was? Sally asked me to come. She was my niece, wasn't she?'

'Oh, come now, Proctor,' said Felix. 'You aren't going to tell us that this was a dutiful social call, that you were just dropping in to inquire after the baby's health! How much was she asking?'

'Thirty pounds,' said Proctor. 'Thirty pounds she was after and much good they would do her now.'

'And being in need of thirty pounds,' went on Felix remorselessly, 'she naturally turned to her next of kin who might be expected to help. It's a touching story.'

Before Proctor could answer Dalgleish broke in :

'She was asking for thirty pounds because she wanted to have some money ready for the return of her husband. It had been arranged that she should go on working and save what she could. Sally meant to keep that bargain to the last pound, baby or no baby. She intended to get this money from her uncle by a not uncommon method. She told him that she was shortly to be married, she didn't say to whom, and that she and her husband would make his treatment of her public unless he bought her silence. She threatened to expose him to his employers and the respectable neighbours of Canningbury. She talked about being done out of her rights. On the other hand, if he chose to pay up, neither she nor her husband would ever see or worry the Proctors again.'

'But that was blackmail,' cried Catherine. 'He should

191

have told her to go ahead and say what she liked. No one would have believed her. She wouldn't have got a penny out of me!' Proctor sat silent. The others seemed to have forgotten his presence. Dalgleish continued.

'I think Mr. Proctor would have been very willing to take your advice, Miss Bowers, if his niece hadn't made use of one particular phrase. She talked about being done out of her rights. She probably meant no more than that a difference was made in the treatment of herself and her cousin, although Mrs. Proctor would deny that this was so. She may have known more than we realize. But for reasons which we needn't discuss here that phrase struck uncomfortably on her uncle's ear. His reaction must have been interesting and Sally was intelligent enough to take the clue. Mr. Proctor is no actor. He tried to find out how much his niece knew and the more he probed the more he gave away. By the time they parted Sally knew that those thirty pounds, and perhaps more, were well within her grasp.'

Proctor's grating voice broke in:

'I said I'd want a receipt from her, mind you. I knew what she was up to. I said I was willing to help her this once as she was getting married and there was bound to be expense. But that would be the end. If she tried it on again I'd go to the police, and I'd have the receipt to prove it.'

'She wouldn't have tried it on again,' said Deborah quietly. The men's eyes swung round to her. 'Not Sally. She was only playing with you, pulling the strings for the fun of watching you dance. If she could get thirty pounds as well as her fun so much the better, but the real attraction was seeing you sweat. But she wouldn't have bothered to go on with it. The entertainment palled after a time. Sally liked to eat her victims fresh.'

'Oh no, no.' Eleanor Maxie opened her hands in a little gesture of protest. 'She wasn't really like that. We never really knew her.' Proctor ignored her and suddenly and surprisingly smiled across at Deborah as if accepting an ally.

'That's true enough. You knew what she was like. I was on a string all right. She had it all worked out. I was to get the thirty pounds that night and bring it to her. She made me follow her into the house and up to her room.

That was bad enough, the sneaking in and out. That's when I met you on the stairs. She showed me the back door and said that she would open it for me at midnight. I was to stay in the trees at the back of the lawn until she switched her bedroom light on and off. That was to be the signal.'

Felix gave a shout of laughter.

'Poor Sally. What an exhibitionist! She had to have drama if it killed her.'

'In the end it did,' said Dalgleish. 'If she hadn't played with people Sally would be alive today.'

'She was in a funny mood that day,' remembered Deborah. 'There was a kind of madness about her. I don't only mean copying my dress or pretending to accept Stephen. She was as full of mischief as a child. I suppose it could have been her kind of happiness.'

'She went to bed happy,' said Stephen. And suddenly they were all quiet, remembering. Somewhere a clock struck sweetly and clearly but there was no other sound except the thin rasp of paper as Dalgleish turned over a page. Outside, rising into coolness and silence, was the staircase up which Sally had carried that last bedtime drink. As they listened it was almost possible to imagine the sound of a soft footfall, the brush of wool against the stairs, the echo of a laugh. Outside in the darkness the edge of the lawn was a faint blur and the desk light reflected above it like a row of Chinese lanterns hung in the scented night. Was there the suspicion of a white dress floating between them, a swirl of hair? Somewhere above them was the nursery, empty now, white and aseptic as a morgue. Could any of them face that staircase and open that nursery door without the fear that the bed might not be empty? Deborah shivered and spoke for them all. 'Please,' she said. 'Please tell us what happened!'

Dalgleish lifted his eyes and looked at her. Then the deep level voice went on.

3

'I think the killer went to Miss Jupp's room driven by an uncontrollable impulse to find out exactly what the girl

193

felt, what she intended, the extent of the danger from her. Perhaps there was some idea of pleading with her — although I don't think that is very likely. It is more probable that the intention was to try to arrange some kind of a bargain. The visitor went to Sally's room and either walked in or knocked and was let in. It was a person, you see, from whom nothing was feared. Sally would be undressed and in bed. She must have been sleepy but she had only taken a little of the cocoa and was not drugged, only too tired to be bothered with finesse or rational argument. She didn't trouble to get up from her bed nor to put on her dressing-gown. You may think, in view of what we have learned about her character, that she would have done so had her visitor been a man. But that is hardly the kind of evidence which is worth very much.

'We don't know yet what happened between Sally and her visitor. We only know that, when the visitor left and closed the door, Sally was dead. If we assume that this was an unpremeditated killing we can make a guess at what happened. We know now that Sally was married, was in love with her husband, was waiting for him to come to fetch her, was even expecting him daily. We can guess from her attitude to Derek Pullen and from the careful way in which she kept her secret, that she enjoyed the feeling of power that this hidden knowledge gave her. Pullen has said, "She liked things to be sweet." A woman I interviewed for whom Sally had worked said, "She was a secretive little thing. She was with me for three years and I knew no more about her at the end of them than when she first came." Sally Jupp kept the news of her marriage secret under very difficult circumstances. Her behaviour wasn't reasonable. Her husband was overseas and doing well. The firm would hardly have sent him home. The firm need not even have known. If Sally had told the truth someone could have been found to help her. I think she kept her secret partly because she wanted to prove her loyalty and trustworthiness and partly because she was the kind of person to whom secrecy made its appeal. It gave her an opportunity of hurting her uncle and aunt for whom she had no affection, and it provided her with considerable entertainment. It also gave her a free home for seven months. Her husband has told me, 'Sally always did say that the un-married mothers had the best of it.' I don't suppose any-one here agrees with that, but Sally Ritchie obviously believed that we live in a society which salves its con-science more by helping the interestingly unfortunate than the dull deserving and was in the position to put her theory to the test. I think she enjoyed herself at St. Mary's Refuge. I think she sustained herself by the know-ledge that she was different from the others. I imagine that she relished in advance the look on Miss Liddell's face when she knew the truth and the fun that she would have mimicking the inmates of St. Mary's to her husband. You know the sort of thing. "Let Sal tell you about the time she was an unmarried mother." I think, too, that she enjoyed the feeling of power which her hidden know-ledge gave her. She enjoyed watching the consternation of the Maxies at a danger which only she knew had no reality.'

Deborah moved uncomfortably in her chair.

'You seem to know a great deal about her. If she knew the engagement had no reality why did she consent to it? She would have saved everyone a great deal of trouble by telling Stephen the truth.'

Dalgleish looked across at her.

'She would have saved her own life. But was it in character for her to tell? There was not much longer to wait. Her husband would be flying home, perhaps in the next day or two. Dr. Maxie's proposal was merely one additional complication, adding its own stimulus of ex-citement and amusement to the total situation. Remem-ber, she never overtly accepted the proposal. No, I would have expected her to act as she did. She obviously disliked Mrs. Riscoe and was becoming more audacious in show-ing it as the time for her husband's return drew nearer. This proposal offered new chances of private amusement. I think that, when her visitor came to her, she was lying back on her bed in sleepy, happy, amused confidence, feeling perhaps that she held the Maxie family, the whole situation, the world itself in the hollow of her hand. Not one of the dozens of people I have interviewed has described her as kind. I don't think she was kind to her visitor. She underestimated the force of the anger and desperation which were confronting her. Perhaps she laughed. And when she did that the strong fingers closed around her throat.'

There was a silence. Felix Hearne broke it by saying roughly :

'You've mistaken your profession, Inspector. That dramatic histrionic was worthy of a larger audience.'

'Don't be a fool, Hearne.' Stephen Maxie lifted a face drained of colour and etched with weariness. 'Can't you see that he's satisfied enough with the reaction we're providing.' He turned to Dalgleish with a sudden spurt of anger. 'Whose hands?' he demanded. 'Why go on with this farce? Whose hands?'

Dalgleish ignored him.

'Our killer goes to the door and turns out the light. This is to be the moment of escape. And then, perhaps, there comes a doubt. It may be the need to make certain just once more that Sally Jupp is dead. It may be that the child turns in his sleep and there is the natural and human wish not to leave him crying and alone with his dead mother. It may be the more selfish concern that his cries will awaken the household before the killer can make good his escape. Whatever the reason, the light is momentarily switched on again. On and then off. Waiting at the edge of the lawn and in the shelter of the trees Sydney Proctor sees what he thinks is the awaited signal. He has no watch. He must depend on the flashing light. He makes his way along the edge of the lawn towards the back door still keeping in the shadow of the trees and the shrubs.'

As Dalgleish paused his audience looked towards Proctor. He was more self-possessed now and seemed, indeed, to have lost both his earlier nervousness and his defensive truculence. He took up the story simply and calmly as if the recollection of that dreadful night and the intense and concentrated interest of his audience had released him from self-consciousness and guilt. Now that he was beyond noisy self-justification they found him easier to tolerate. Like them he had been in some sense a victim of Sally. Listening, they shared the desperation and fear which had driven him forward to her door.

'I thought I must have missed the first flash. She'd said two flashes so I waited for a bit and watched. Then I thought I'd better take a chance. There wasn't any sense in messing about. I'd come so far and I might as well go on with it. She'd see that I did, anyway. It hadn't been easy to raise the thirty quid. I'd got what I could from my Post Office account, but that was only ten. I hadn't much at home, only what I'd put by for the instalments on the telly. I took that and pawned my watch at a shop in Canningbury. The chap could see I was pretty desperate I suppose, and didn't give me what it was worth. Still, I had enough to keep her quiet. I'd written out a receipt for her to sign, too. I wasn't taking any chances with her after that scene in the stables. I thought I'd just hand over the cash, make her sign the receipt and get off home. If she tried any more funny business I could threaten to charge her with blackmail. The receipt would be useful if it came to that, but I didn't think it would. She just wanted the money and afterwards she'd leave me in peace. Well, there wouldn't be much sense in trying it on again, would there? I can't raise money to order and Sally knew that well enough. She was no fool was our Sally.

'The heavy outside door was open just as she said. I had my torch and it was easy to find the stairs and get up to her room. She'd shown me the way that afternoon. It was a piece of cake. The house was dead quiet. You'd have thought it was empty. Sally's door was shut and there was no light showing through the keyhole or under the door. That struck me as queer. I wondered whether to knock, but I wasn't keen on making a sound. The whole place was so quiet it was eerie. In the end I opened the door and called to her quietly. She didn't answer. I shone the light of the torch across the room and on to the bed. She was lying there. At first I thought she was asleep and — well, it was like a reprieve. I wondered whether I ought to leave the cash on her pillow and then I thought, "Why the hell should I?" She had asked me to come. It was up to her to stay awake. Besides, I wanted to get out of the house. I don't know when I first realized that she wasn't asleep. I went up to the bed. It was then that I knew that she was dead. Funny how you can't mistake it. I knew that she wasn't ill or unconscious. Sally was dead. One eye was closed but the other was half

197

open. It seemed to be looking at me, so I put out my left hand and drew down the lid. I don't know what made me touch her. Damn silly thing to do really. It was just that I had to close that staring eye. The sheet was folded down under her chin just as if someone had made her comfortable. I drew it down and then I saw the bruise on her neck. Until then I don't think the word "murder" had come into my mind. When it did, well I suppose I lost my head. I ought to have known that it was a right-handed job and that no one could suspect me, but you don't think like that when you're frightened. I still held my torch and I was shaking so that it made little circles of light round her head. I couldn't hold it steady. I was trying to think straight, wondering what to do. Then it came over me that she was dead and I was in her room and with the money on me. You could see what people would think. I knew I'd got to get away. I don't remember reaching the door but I was too late. I could hear footsteps coming along the passage. They were only faint. I suppose I wouldn't have heard them in the ordinary way. But I was keyed up so that I could hear my own heart beating. In a second I drew the bolt across the door and leaned back against it, holding my breath. It was a woman on the other side of the door. She knocked very quietly and called out, "Sally. Are you asleep, Sally?" She called quite softly. I don't see how she expected to be heard. Perhaps she didn't really care. I've thought about it a good deal since but, at the time, I didn't wait to see what she would do. She might have knocked louder and set the kid bawling or she might have realized that something was wrong and fetched the family. I had to get away. Luckily I keep myself fit and heights don't worry me. Not that there was much to it. I got out of the side window, the one sheltered by the trees, and the stack-pipe was handy enough. I couldn't hurt my hands and my soft cycling shoes gave me a grip. I fell the last few feet and turned my ankle, but I didn't feel it at the time. I ran into the shelter of the trees before I looked back. Sally's room was still in darkness and I began to feel safe.

'I'd hidden my cycle in the hedge at the side of the lane and I was glad to see it again, I can tell you. It wasn't until I got on that I realized about my foot. I couldn't grasp the pedal with it. Still, I got on all right. I was beginning to think out a plan, too. I had to have an alibi. When I got to Finchworthy I staged my accident. It wasn't difficult. It's a quiet road and a high wall runs on the left of it. I drove the cycle hard against it until the front wheel buckled. Then I slashed the front tyre with my pocket-knife. I didn't need to worry about myself. I looked the part all right. My ankle was swelling by now and I felt sick. It must have started raining some time in the night because I was wet and cold, although I don't remember the rain. It took some doing to drag myself and the bike into Canningbury and it was well after one before I got home. I had to be pretty quiet so I left the bike in the front garden and let myself in. It was important not to wake Mrs. Proctor before I had a chance to alter the two downstairs clocks. We haven't a clock or watch in the bedroom. I used to wind the gold one every night and keep it by the bed. If I could only get in without waking the wife I reckoned I should be all right. I thought I was going to be unlucky. She must have been awake and listening for the door because she came to the top of the stairs and called out. I'd had about as much as I could take by then, so I shouted at her to get back to bed and I'd be up. She did what she was told – she usually does – but I knew she'd be down before long. Still, it gave me my chance. By the time she'd got on her dressing-gown and come pussy-footing down I'd got the clocks put back to midnight. She fussed about getting me a cup of tea. I was in a sweat to get her back into bed before any of the town clocks struck two. It was the sort of thing she might notice. Anyway, I did get her back upstairs eventually and she went off to sleep quickly enough. It was different with me, I can tell you. My God, I never want to live through another night like that! You can say what you like about us and the way we treated Sally. She didn't do so badly out of us to my way of thinking. But if she felt hard done by, well, the little bitch got her own back that night.'

He spat the shocking word at them and then, in the silence, muttered something which might have been an apology and covered his face with that grotesque right hand. No one spoke for a moment and then Catherine said :

'You didn't come to the inquest, did you? We wonder-ed about that at the time, but there was some talk that you were ill. Was that because you were afraid of being recognized? But you must have known by then how Sally died and that no one could possibly suspect you.'

Uunder the stress of emotion Proctor had told his story with unselfconscious fluency. Now the need for self-justification reasserted itself and brought a return of his former truculence.

'Why should I go? I wasn't in a fit state for it anyway. I knew how she had died all right. The police told us that when they sent someone round on Sunday morning. He didn't take long before he was asking when I'd last seen her, but I had my story ready. I suppose you all think that I ought to have told them what I knew. Well, I didn't! Sally had caused enough trouble while she was alive and she wasn't going to add to it now she was dead if I could help it. I didn't see why my private affairs should have to come out in court. It isn't easy to explain these things. People might get the wrong ideas.'

'Worse still, they might understand only too well,' said Felix dryly.

Proctor's thin face flushed. Getting to his feet he deliberately turned his back on Felix and spoke to Eleanor Maxie.

'If you'll excuse me now I'll be on my way. I didn't mean to intrude. It was just that I had to see the inspec-tor. I'm sure I hope this all turns out satisfactorily, but you don't want me here.'

'He talks as if we're about to give birth,' thought Stephen. The wish to assert an independence of Dalgleish and to show that at least one of the family still con-sidered himself a free agent made him ask :

'Can I drive you home? The last bus went at eight.'

Proctor made a gesture of refusal but did not look at him.

'No. No thank you. I have my bicycle outside. They've made a good job of it, all things considered. Please don't bother to see me out.'

He stood there, his gloved hands hanging loosely, an unlikeable and pathetic figure but not without dignity.

'At least,' thought Felix. 'He has the grace to know when he's not wanted.' Suddenly, and with a stiff little gesture, Proctor held out his left hand to Eleanor Maxie and she took it.

Stephen went with him to the door. While he was away no one spoke. Felix felt the heightening of tension and his nostrils twitched at the remembered smell of fear. They must know now. They had been told everything except the actual name. But how far were they letting themselves recognize the truth? From under lowered eyelids he watched them. Deborah was curiously tranquil as if the end of lying and deceit had brought their own peace. He did not believe that Deborah knew what was coming. Eleanor Maxie's face was grey, but the folded hands lay relaxed in her lap. He could almost believe that her thoughts were elsewhere. Catherine Bowers sat stiffly, her lips pursed as if in disapproval. Earlier Felix had thought that she was enjoying herself. Now he was not so sure. He noticed with sardonic satisfaction the clenching of her hands, the nervous twitching at the corners of her eyes.

Suddenly Stephen was back with them and Felix spoke. 'Hasn't this gone on long enough? We've heard the evidence. That back door was opened until Maxie locked it at twelve-thirty-three a.m. Some time before then someone got in and killed Sally. The police haven't found out who and they aren't likely to find out. It could have been anyone. I suggest that we none of us say anything more.' He looked round at them. The warning was unmistakable. Dalgleish said mildly:

'You are suggesting that a perfect stranger entered the house, made no attempt to steal, went unerringly to Miss Jupp's room and strangled her while, with no attempt at raising the alarm, she lay back obligingly on the bed?'

'She could have invited him to come, whoever he was,' said Catherine.

Dalgleish turned to her.

'But she was expecting Proctor. We can't imagine that she wanted to make a party of that little transaction. And whom would she invite? We have checked on everyone who knew her.'

'For God's sake stop discussing it,' cried Felix. 'Can't

you see that's what he wants you to do! There's no proof!'

'Isn't there?' said Dalgleish softly. 'I wonder.'

'We know who didn't do it, anyway,' said Catherine. 'It wasn't Stephen or Derek Pullen because they've got alibis and it wasn't Mr. Proctor because of his hand. Sally couldn't have been killed by her uncle.'

'No,' said Dalgleish. 'Nor by Martha Bultitaft who didn't know how the girl had died until Mr. Hearne told her. Nor by you, Miss Bowers, who knocked at her door and tried to speak to her after she was dead. Nor by Mrs. Riscoe, whose finger-nails would inevitably have left scratches. No one can grow nails that length overnight and the murderer didn't wear gloves. Nor by Mr. Hearne, whatever he might like me to think. Mr. Hearne didn't know which room Sally slept in. He had to ask Mr. Maxie where he should carry the ladder.'

'Only a fool would have shown that he knew. I could have pretended.'

'Only you weren't pretending,' said Stephen roughly. 'You can keep your bloody patronage to yourself. You were the last person to want Sally dead. Once Sally was installed here Deborah might have married you. Believe me, you wouldn't have got her on any other terms. She'll never marry you now and you know it.'

Eleanor Maxie looked up and said quietly:

'I went to her room to talk to her. It seemed that the marriage might not be so bad a thing if she were really fond of my son. I wanted to find out what she felt. I was tired and I should have waited till the morning. She was lying there on her bed and singing to herself. It would have been all right if she hadn't done two things. She laughed at me. And she told me, Stephen, that she was going to have your child. It was so very quick. One second she was alive and laughing. The next she was a dead thing in my hands.'

'Then it was you!' said Catherine in a whisper. 'It was you.'

'Of course,' said Eleanor Maxie gently. 'Think it out for yourself. Who else could it have been?'

The Maxies thought that going to prison must be rather like going to hospital, except that it was even more involuntary. But were abnormal and rather frightening experiences to which the victim reacted with a clinical detachment and the onlookers with a determined cheerfulness which was intended to create confidence without giving the suspicion of callousness. Eleanor Maxie, accompanied by a calm and tactful woman police sergeant, went to enjoy the comfort of a last bath in her own house. She had insisted on this and, as with the final preparations for hospital, no one liked to point out that bathing was the first procedure inflicted on admission. Or was there, perhaps, a difference between prisoners in custody and those convicted? Felix might have known but no one cared to ask. The police car driver waited in the background, watchful and unobtrusive as an ambulance attendant. There were the last instructions, the messages for friends, the telephone calls and the hurried packing. Mr. Hinks arrived from the vicarage, breathless and unsurprised, steeling himself to give advice and comfort but looking so desperately in need of them himself that Felix took him firmly by the arm and walked with him back to the vicarage. From a window Deborah watched them talking together as they passed out of sight and wondered briefly what they were saying. As she was mounting the stairs to her mother Dalgleish was telephoning from the hall. Their eyes met and held. For a second she thought he was going to speak, but his head bent again to the receiver and she passed on her way, recognizing suddenly and without surprise that, had things been different, here was the man to whom she would have instinctively turned for reassurance and advice.

Stephen, left alone, recognized his misery for what it was, an overmastering pain which had nothing in common with the dissatisfaction and ennui which he had previously thought of as unhappiness. He had taken two drinks but realized in time that drinking wasn't helping. What he needed was someone to minister to his misery and assure him of its essential unfairness. He went in search of Catherine.

He found her kneeling before a small case in his mother's room wrapping jars and bottles in tissue paper. When she looked up at him he saw that she had been crying. He was shocked and irritated. There was no room in the house for a lesser grief. Catherine had never mastered the art of crying appealingly. Perhaps that was one reason why she had learnt early to be stoical in grief as in other things. Stephen decided to ignore this intrusion on his own misery.

'Cathy,' he said. 'Why on earth did she confess? Hearne was perfectly right. They would never have proved it if she'd only kept quiet.'

He had only called her Cathy once before and then, too, he had wanted something from her. Even in the moment of physical love it had struck her as an affectation. She looked up at him. 'You don't know her very well, do you? She was only waiting for your father to die before she confessed. She didn't want to leave him and she promised him that he wouldn't be sent away. That was the only reason why she kept silent. She told Mr. Hinks about Sally when she walked back to the vicarage with him earlier tonight.'

'But she sat so calmly through all the disclosures!'

'I suppose she wanted to know just what happened. None of you told her anything. I think she worried most thinking that it was you who had visited Sally and locked the door.'

'I know. She tried to ask me. I thought she was asking me if I was the murderer. They'll have to reduce the charge. It wasn't premeditated after all. Why doesn't Jephson hurry and come? We've telephoned for him.'

Catherine was sorting a few books she had taken from the bedside table, considering whether to pack them. Stephen went on:

'They'll send her to prison either way. Mother in prison! Cathy, I don't think I can bear it!'

And Catherine, who had grown to like and respect Eleanor Maxie very much, was not sure that she could bear it either and lost her patience.

'You can't bear it! I like that! You don't have to bear it. She does. And it's you that put her there, remember.'

Catherine, once started, found it hard to stop and her irritation found a more personal expression.

'And there's another thing, Stephen. I don't know what you feel about us . . . about me if you like. I don't want to talk about this again so I'm just saying now that it's all over. Oh, for heaven's sake get your feet out of that tissue paper! I'm trying to pack.'

She was crying in earnest now like an animal or a child. The words were thickened so that he could only just hear them.

'I was in love with you, but not any more. I don't know what you expect now, but it doesn't matter. It's all off.'

And Stephen, who had never for one moment intended that it should be on, looked down on the blotched face, the swollen protuberant eyes and felt, irrationally, a spasm of chagrin and regret.

5

One month after Eleanor Maxie had been found guilty on the lesser charge of manslaughter Dalgleish, on one of his rare off-duty days, drove through Chadfleet on his way back to London from the Essex estuary where he had laid up his 30-foot sailing-boat. It was not much out of his way, but he did not choose to analyse too precisely the motives which had prompted him to these three additional miles of winding, tree-shadowed roads. He passed the Pullens' cottage. There was a light in the front room and the plaster Alsatian dog stood darkly outlined against the curtains. And now came St. Mary's Refuge. The house looked empty with only a lone pram at the front door steps to hint at the life inside. The village itself was deserted, somnolent in its tea-time five o'clock calm. As he was passing Wilson's General Stores the front door blinds were being drawn and the last customer was leaving. It was Deborah Riscoe. There was a heavy-looking shopping-basket on her arm and he stopped the car instinctively. There was no time for indecision or awkwardness and he had taken the basket from her and she had slid into the seat beside him before it had struck him to wonder at his boldness or her compliance. Stealing a quick glance at her calm uplifted profile, he saw that the look of strain had gone. She had lost none of her beauty but there was a serenity about her which reminded him of her mother.

As the car turned into the drive of Martingale he hesitated but she gave an almost imperceptible shake of the head and he drove on. The beeches were golden now but the twilight was draining them of colour. The first fallen leaves crackled into dust beneath the tyres. The house came into view as he had first seen it, but greyer now and slightly sinister in the fading light. In the hall Deborah slipped off her leather jacket and unwound her scarf.

'Thank you. I was glad of that. Stephen has the car in town this week and Wilson's can only deliver on Wednesdays. I'm always running out of things I've forgotten. Would you like a drink, or tea or something?' She gave him a quick mocking smile. 'You aren't on duty now. Or are you?'

'No,' he said. 'I'm not on duty now. Just indulging myself.'

She did not ask for an explanation and he followed her into the drawing-room. It was dustier than he remembered, and somehow more bare but his trained eye saw that there was no real change, only the naked look of a room from which the small personal change of living has been tidied away.

As if she guessed what he was thinking, she said:

'There's only me here most of the time. Martha has left and I've replaced her by a couple of dailies from the new town. At least, they call themselves dailies but I can never be sure they'll turn up. It adds spice to our relationship. Stephen is home most week-ends, of course, and that helps. There will be plenty of time for a good clean-up before Mummy comes home. It's mostly paper work at present, Daddy's will and death duties and lawyers fussing.'

'Ought you to be here alone?' asked Dalgleish.

'Oh, I don't mind. One of the family has to stay. Sir Reynold did offer me one of his dogs but they're a little too bite-happy for me. Besides, they aren't trained to exorcise ghosts.'

Dalgleish took the drink she handed him and asked after Catherine Bowers. She seemed the safest person to mention. He had little interest in Stephen Maxie and too much interest in Felix Hearne. To ask after the child was to evoke that golden-haired wraith whose shadow was already between them.

'I see Catherine sometimes. Jimmy is still at St Mary's for the present and Catherine comes down with his father quite often to take him out. She and James Ritchie will get married, I think.'

'That's rather sudden, isn't it?'

She laughed.

'Oh, I don't think Ritchie knows it yet. It will be rather a good thing really. She loves the child, really cares about him, and I think Ritchie will be lucky. I don't think there's anyone else to tell you about. Mummy's very well really and not too unhappy. Felix Hearne is in Canada. My brother is at hospital most of the time and terribly busy. Everyone's been very kind though, he says.'

'They would be,' thought Dalgleish. His mother was serving her sentence and his sister was coping unaided with death duties, housework and the hostility or – and she would hate this worse – the sympathy of the village. But Stephen Maxie was back at hospital with everyone being very kind. Something of what he felt must have shown in his face for she said quickly :

'I'm glad he's busy. It was worse for him than for me.'

They sat together in silence for a little time. Despite their apparent easy companionship Dalgleish was morbidly sensitive to every word. He longed to say something of comfort or reassurance but rejected each of the half-formulated sentences before they reached his lips. 'I'm sorry I had to do it.' Only he wasn't sorry and she was intelligent and honest enough to know it. He had never yet apologized for his job and wouldn't insult her by pretending to now. 'I know you must dislike me for what I had to do.' Mawkish, sentimental, insincere and with an arrogant presumption that she could feel about him one way or the other. They walked to the door in silence and she stood to watch him out of sight. As he turned his head and saw the lonely figure, outlined momentarily against the light from the hall, he knew with sudden and heart-lifting certainty that they would meet again. And when that happened the right words would be found.